CADENCES
How Far Do You Want To Go?

Linda M. Mutty

For Kathy and Jason
and
For Mom and Dad

2016

"How far do you want to go?" The question tossed back over her right shoulder.

"As far as you want, I guess. I'm okay." The response barely escaped Pete's lips. He knew it didn't matter what he said. Not really.

"Okay. Another couple of miles then. To the junction."

All he heard was "couple of miles". The rest scattered somewhere.

Almost two months ago when they began planning the hike, energy levels were at hundred percent. Anticipation of an amazing adventure away from the craziness of their lives, propelled them through the following weeks until the first day of September when they boarded a flight to Portland. From the airport, a bus took them to the Cascade Locks on The Columbia Gorge where they began their hike south on the Pacific Crest Trail through the remote wilderness of the Oregon Cascades and then into the Sierras; their destination, Yosemite National Park. Two months on the trail seemed daunting to him, at first, but Kit reminded him of their combined wilderness experiences and skills. No excuses for not going. What better companions could they have than each other? Hard to argue with her there. Pete wished he had, though.

*

August heat trapped between two mountain ranges became one with the poisonous atmospheric mass that lay heavily upon everything and everyone. Pete slugged his way through his day at work, slugged his way home, only to collapse on the couch while a small fan forced stagnant air to move around in his small apartment. It was at moments like this that he couldn't imagine what had possessed his grandparents to move to this valley in the first place. When was that? He didn't have the energy to be precise in his mental calculations. Probably in the early 1950s? What did they call it? Not Silicon Valley. Something softer. More familiar. A place? Santa Clara Valley. Yes. Fruit bowl? Something to do with fruit. The heat played with his thinking so that it didn't really matter what it was called. Expended energy he couldn't afford right now.

His parents were both born and bred in this valley, as was he. Their memories of the place were foreign to him. He tried to imagine what it must have been like as they recalled orchards for as far as the eye could see, sleepy little towns within the vast valley at the end of the San Francisco Bay that had not yet blended into one another with nothing to set them apart as they once were. Narrow two-lane roads that ribboned their way through the pitch-black darkness-no illumination other than the moon and stars. In slow moving cars, dodging Jack Rabbits whose aim it was to reach the other side unscathed. Each road leading the traveler to a known destination so that the palpable darkness on some nights was nothing to fear. The fragrances of the orchards in full bloom. The stench of drying fruit laid out on wooden racks under the warming sun. A sun that shone through an unpoisoned atmosphere. Ranch and farm lands that nestled up to the boundaries of new homes, like his grandparents', whose back fence was the only obstacle preventing the horses who grazed just on the other side from entering their backyard. Their source the great bay, multiple dry creek beds that wove their ways through the valley's terrain in the summer months, enticed "hobos" with the welcoming shade and privacy of overhanging oak trees while children, forbidden by their parents to play in the creek beds disobeyed those commands in search of treasures, sunning blue belly lizards, and of the world of their own imagination. In the winter months, the storms flooded the narrow beds while churning up debris and mud so that the water was angry and dangerous. All were forbidden by common sense to even try crossing a wooden footbridge when the water slammed into the bridges' sides. Neighborhoods whose unspoken mandates were practiced daily; civility, respect for elders, responsibility, patriotism, kindness, compassion, and caring. In and out of each home, not just your own. Then, the word neighbor had a different connotation than now. Pete understood that plainly as he attempted another mental task, that of identifying his immediate neighbors on either side of him and below him. No idea who they were, much less what they looked like. Occupants. He decided that the descriptor should be occupant. Of a dwelling. Not home, house. Not even close.

Years ago, after their deaths, Lucas and Tilly Murphy's home had been raised, the land paved over, to make way for modern concrete blocks of buildings. Good thing his grandparents weren't around to see that, he thought. A sudden longing overwhelmed him to visit his parents' home, James and Barbara Murphy, which used to be a ten-minute drive but now at least thirty to forty-five minutes, depending, on traffic. Not worth the effort or gas. Besides, they weren't there anymore. Hadn't been for sixteen years, each leaving this world within a week of the other. Parentless at fourteen, his mother's sister, Emily Aimes, Auntie Emee, single and available, adopted him and lived with Pete in his childhood home until selling it when Pete went off to college. Assuming the role of his parents, Emily was the one to reveal to Pete that his father was adopted at birth. Attempting to ease the blow, she followed this news by letting him know how special they were in God's eyes that both he and his father had been saved.

His adoptive grandparents and parents left this life with a gift basket of amazing memories, ones that they had tried to share with him but because they were not his, hard to recall and easier to forget. He would never be able to gather and store memories as meaningful as they must have been to them. Ones that, one day, he could share with his children. The world just wasn't the same. Never mind that he had never had a meaningful relationship that would even begin to lead to romance, marriage, and a baby carriage or two. He might live in the present day where there was no need for the first two, but he was a throwback to different times, to his parents' and their parents' way. And possibly to that of his real grandparents? Perhaps, he thought, that was why he could conceive of no other approach. And he wasn't willing to anyway.

A hunger pain shut down any further meanderings. He hadn't eaten anything since breakfast, if he could call it that. A bruised Washington Delicious that he found at the back of the refrigerator. He hadn't bothered to eat around the bruised flesh. An apple is an apple. All good. Why hadn't he eaten more? And why hadn't he eaten lunch? Too hot. Too stupid. The group had invited him. Not convincingly but had made the effort to include him. No. He wasn't hungry. Needed to work through. Get it off his plate. No pun intended. But thanks.

The same empty refrigerator as this morning. Why even bother looking? Make an effort. Get off this couch, wash your face, and get some food. Plenty of fast food chains to choose from. Not going to starve. A thought flashed and was gone instantly. Something about planning ahead-grocery shopping?

*

He followed Kit, keeping a comfortable distance from her and from any dust she kicked up. Two miles was nothing. Not compared to almost two hundred and forty miles they had already hiked. For some reason, though, he was ready to drop his pack calling it a day sooner than he knew she would agree to. They had put in fifteen to twenty miles a day for the last twelve days. With a little more than three quarters of the way still to go, at this rate they would complete the trek within the two months, as planned. Surprised by his sudden fatigue, he wondered if this was all he had in him. That another six weeks was not in the books for him. He had no doubt that she was good to go. She had proven that by keeping an even pace well ahead of him even over the roughest terrain. It was almost as though she was enjoying rubbing in the fact that her physical prowess far outweighed his. She was unforgiving, he decided. Had she even once asked if he was doing okay? He couldn't recall it if she had. Forced march. That was what this was becoming. Trying to prove something to someone, he realized. She was proving nothing to him. Well, not completely true; she was proving to be a bitch in the wilderness, and he had no place to hide.

The junction was in sight. The wooden sign post would give them options. Go west. Turn around and go north. Continue south if you dare. At least that was how he would interpret them. Never mind the trail names. Who was going to remember them anyway? Just head in the right direction.

"Okay. Looks like we head up Goat Head Ridge. Another five miles and then we'll camp." She adjusted her pack by leaning forward and pulling on the shoulder straps. Unholstering her water bottle from a side pocket of her pack, she drank sparingly and then holstered it again. "You ready?" Another tossed over the shoulder communication.

"Hold on, Kit. I need a break. As a matter of fact, I want to call it a day." There. He said it. Her back to him, he could only guess her facial expression. Definitely not attractive.

"Seriously?" A long pause before she turned to face him.

"Five more miles before the sun sets is nothing. We've set up camp in the dark before. Are you worried or something?"

"Not worried. Just exhausted and please don't ask me why? I just am." He was exhausted, he realized, as soon as he said it and not just physically. He had been in a mental disagreement with her all day. Negative thoughts consuming him. "Let's head up a mile or so and camp just off the trail somewhere. I really need to, Kit." No whining, no pleading. Just stating the simple fact. Take it or leave it. For the sake of compromise, he thought.

"Okay. If that's what it takes to get us somewhere other than here, let's do it." She turned abruptly and headed up the trail. He lost sight of her as she marched around a bend. For that, he was momentarily thankful.

He had met her a year ago. Turned around and walked right into her in a crowded sporting goods store. Polite apologies and reassurances of "no problem" were quickly exchanged. Didn't see her again until standing in line at the checkout. She stood behind him and the only reason he knew this was that she had leaned forward enough so that her words were audible in the din of the store's noises. "Watch out. No sudden turns. I'm right behind you. Fair warning."

A year later, those words suddenly came to mind. As he pushed his body to move forward, it occurred to him that this was just one more sign and that he should have paid better attention to the spirits that surrounded him. They had screamed at him at the time, he was sure, but the second moment of contact with her drowned them out. For each bootstep he took now, a sign appeared to him from the dust cloud of his own making. The clarity was stunning. Stunning enough that he stopped moving forward so that he could catch his breath, so suffocating were his thoughts. No, not his thoughts but her. Kit was suffocating him. He no longer knew who he was anymore. It was all about her. Her desires. Her needs. Her demands. Dammit! No! Enough distance was between them in just the short time that she had turned the bend. Not to mention twelve months' worth taking its silent toll.

The decision came easily and, surprisingly, without guilt. He sighed heavily as he made an about-face, readjusting his pack as if that was going to make a difference in the exhaustion that was quickly overtaking him, and took a step forward, then another, until he had comfortably distanced himself from the last twelve months of his life and from the person who had consumed him. Not once did he look back. Not once did he hear her voice calling his name. At the junction, again, he headed west choosing not to backtrack. Three hundred miles from home either way. Maybe less. He should check his topo. The thought brushed by. He needed to find a place to camp before too long. Then he would take stock of his situation.

*

"You been on the trail long?"

Suddenly self-conscious about his appearance and odor, Pete took the question the wrong way. "Sorry." He moved his body closer to the door while opening the window.

"No man! Close the window! Got the air on."

"Sorry." Pete shut the window but stayed against the door.

"No worries. I didn't mean anything about your condition, if that's what you thought. No man. Just wondering how long you were up there." The driver's tone was relaxed and friendly.

"Oh. Yeah. Well, started the first of September. What's today's date?" He couldn't think clearly enough even though he knew it somewhere in his brain.

"September 21. So, you've been out for almost three weeks."

Pete was surprised by the simple calculation. Three weeks? It seemed like forever.

"Yeah. I guess so." He had lost track of time. His solo hike back to the nearest highway had taken only a week? Maybe because he was solo, free of the mental weight that had slowed him down?

"So you finished your trek?"

Pete realized that this guy assumed that he had been hiking by himself. '*Your* trek'. '…how long *you* were up there'.

"Ah…yeah." No need to go into detail with this stranger. The lift was appreciated, and small talk would stay just that…small talk.

"Well, good for you, man. I mean, for doing it. I always thought that if my life had taken a different path, I would spend it outside, away from the crazies, you know? Get real and just commune with mother nature. I don't need much. Not really. Even now, working full time driving these highways day after day. Seeing what could have been from the inside of this cab." His voice dropped off, almost like he had fallen asleep. Pete took a quick glance at him to make sure that wasn't the case. "Name's Eric, by the way." He released his right hand from the steering wheel, reaching over to Pete.

"Pete. Good to meet you, Eric. And thanks again for stopping." The firm handshake between the two men was reassuring to him. He suddenly felt on solid footing again. And free.

The miles accumulated as the semi carrying the two men wound its way south on Interstate 5. The mountain passes soon gave way to rolling foothills and then to flatlands of ranches and open space that appeared to go on forever. The 505 cut off was less than a mile away when Eric finally spoke again.

"There's a rest stop up here. Going to stop for a while. How far did you want to go?" He looked straight ahead when he spoke.

"How far are you going?" Pete hadn't thought it through but if he could get into the Bay Area from here, he could easily get home on his own.

"Expected to be in LA by tomorrow afternoon. Straight down 5." This time, Eric momentarily turned to Pete.

"Oh. Okay. Thought, maybe you were heading to the Bay Area. No problem. I can hitch from the rest stop. 505 is just up the road. Catch someone heading west. Appreciate the lift this far."

His eyes now on the road again, Eric was smiling. "You'll get a lift up here. No problem. Man, if I wasn't doing my thing right now, I'd say to hell with it all and take you myself. You from the Bay Area?"

"Yeah. Born and raised. So were my parents." He felt pride in saying this. "You? Where are you from?"

"Born there but not from there. Raised up north. We passed by it. Shasta City. A far cry from what you know as home."

"Man, I'll say." Pete had stopped in Shasta City only twice before, each time to gas up. He had considered other stops like Redding or maybe Anderson but had always passed them up. Something drew him to Shasta. Kind of like Eric's firm shake,

Shasta City was grounding for him.

"So, you've seen some changes?" Sarcasm accompanied the question.

"Yeah, sure, but not like my parents saw. The valley isn't anywhere like it was when they were kids. The stuff they told me about it…well, it's hard to believe. You know, the city of San Jose has even set aside a farm house and the land surrounding it as a kind of museum so that kids can see what it was like in San Jose not that long ago. I mean, I can't believe it. But, hey, I guess that's the way everything's going nowadays."

"Don't get me started." Eric tightened his grip on the steering wheel and visibly sat taller in his seat, staring straight ahead. "Everything is moving too fast. Nobody is thinking stuff through. Just tear down, build, tear down, build. Crazy, just crazy." He looked at his side view mirrors and turned on the signal. "Man, oh man…."

Pulling into the rest stop, Pete was anxious. The hours passed with this stranger had been a relief and he only now realized it. He wished he could say something meaningful to Eric, something that would show his appreciation. Not just for the ride but for saving him. Less said the better, he thought.

"You hungry?" Eric, leaning forward a bit and shutting down his machine, tossed the question back over his shoulder. Disturbingly familiar, Pete thought.

"Yeah but it's okay. I can wait."

"Wait for what? I've got extra in the cab. Don't mind sharing with you, if you don't. Besides, who knows when you'll get your next ride."

He was hungry. Just hadn't focused on it. The last time he ate? Early this morning on the trail. "Sure, then. Thanks."

*

Shasta City Eric pulled out of the rest stop an hour later leaving Pete fed and rested. Pete thanked him for his kindness and wished him well. The next time he was in Shasta City, look him up, Eric offered. Gave Pete his cell number and address. Peter felt the ground shifting again as the rig vanished into traffic.

He hadn't given Kit a thought since he made his decision at the trail junction. And he still didn't feel any guilt for leaving her alone up there. He tried. Just because if something happened to her, he would have to feel some guilt, wouldn't he? Did he have a good enough reason to have left her like that? The authorities wouldn't think so. What about her parents? There would be plenty of blame thrown his way by them both. Neither one liked him to begin with and to find out that he had abandoned their daughter in the wilds? Might as well finish digging his grave now.

He began digging it only two weeks after he met Kit. She insisted that he meet her parents. Just a quick introduction over a cup of coffee at some place he didn't know. No strings attached. No commitments. Just an introduction. He had wondered, at the time, about her motives but brushed his concerns aside. She hardly knew him. He hadn't even considered the hike at that point. Just a nice hook-up, as he saw it. What harm could it do?

Plenty, he found out. Kit conveniently neglected to mention to him that she hadn't seen her parents in years. That she had completely cut them off from her life. That her intent in introducing Pete to them was meant to hurt them. A tease at reconciliation. Only to end with Kit vehemently landing the final blow. They would never see her or her boyfriend again. She and Pete would never have them in their lives. Just wanted them to know what they were missing. Her mother in tears and her father speechless, Kit dragged Pete, confounded, out of the coffee shop.

Had his common sense kicked in, he would have parted

ways with her. He wanted no part of a family trauma, and he didn't want to be used or to be deceived. But Kit convinced him that she was the victim in all of this. She asked his forgiveness and he gave it. The love they made that night had been the best of his life.

For a moment, as he sat on the curb with his thumb out pointing south, he entertained the idea of going back. Maybe not on the trail but alerting a park ranger that she was alone. That he couldn't keep up with her (basically true) and that he had to turn back without letting her know. No need to offer more than that. But how was he going to explain that it took him almost a full week to alert anyone? In a comfortable rig's cab with a nice enough stranger chalking up the miles south without having to lift a finger? He couldn't call someone? Suspicious behavior for sure.

Then again, what if she couldn't care less about what happened to him? Maybe she was jumping for joy out there realizing that the baggage was gone. She was free of him. He was a big boy. He'd turn tail and cut short the trek. The more he tried to read her mind, the better he felt. Wasn't she planning on making the trek by herself to begin with? Going back to the random meeting in the sports store. That was why she was there, to buy supplies for her hike. He just happened to stumble upon her and somehow worked his way into her solo plan. True, he had worked his way into her life a bit more than that in a year's time and she into his. But not with any kind of permanency. More like a hook-up for the sex and, sometimes, the company. She could take him or leave him, he knew, and had known it since day one. Even though she had used him to get back at her parents, he had to hand it to her. She was her own person, confident and directed. She knew where she was going. Maybe that's what attracted him to her because, if he was honest with himself, he was the exact opposite. She appeared to like him, to want to be with him. Temporarily, he guessed. Opposites attract. He heard that. But there isn't a follow-up line about how long.

She was going to be fine, he concluded. Probably never see her again after this, but that was okay. If he did run into her again? Apologies, niceties in the face of whatever she threw at him. Then separate ways. But he would need to get back to her place before she did so that he could get his stuff out of there. Not much to retrieve but the junk meant something to him.

The car passed him and then slowed down pulling over to the curb. Pete, lost in his thoughts about the next phase of his life, was unaware of the idling vehicle until the driver hit the horn. Arm still extended, he turned and seeing the next lift, pushed himself up from the curb, grabbed at his pack and awkwardly made his way to the waiting car. The passenger window was lowered, and Pete bent down to see the driver.

"Where're you headed?" yelled the elderly woman behind the wheel. She looked perturbed like she wanted to get going. "Well?" Purple knit palms played a rhythm on her steering wheel that only she could hear.

"Thanks for stopping. Heading to the Bay Area by 505." For some reason, he found himself yelling right back at her.

"505? That cutoff, right?" She did not wait for his confirmation. "Boring as hell but cuts off some time. Okay. Get in." Still thumping a gloved rhythm.

"So, you are going that way?" Pete wasn't sure he was about to make a smart move one way or the other. He had heard of crazies up here, especially the trollers who made the stretch of Interstate 5 both north and south, their predatory highway. Besides, based on the vintage of the car, easily 60s or 70s model sedan, he silently questioned its dependability. "I mean, to 505 and onto 80 West?"

"Sure, if that's where you want to go." Now she turned away from him and stared straight ahead. "Come on. Get in. Wasting precious time and gas." The rhythm stopped, and Pete could see that she had tightened her grip on the wheel.

"That's okay. I'm going to wait here. I don't want to put you out. Thanks anyway."

He wasn't getting in the car, period. Just a feeling but he remembered how stupid he had been about not paying attention to 'signs' before.

"Suit yourself. Too bad for you." She resumed her palm

thumping. "You headed to the Bay Area. Me, I'm headed there too, to San Jose. But suit yourself." She hadn't bothered to look at him when she said this, but he thought he saw a sliver of a smile.

"Really. To San Jose?" His dilemma confronted him like a two by four coming down on his head.

"You're wasting my time. Get in or get out of the way." This time, she turned and looked directly at him, oversized sunglasses sliding down her nose.

"Okay. Sure. Thanks." He was conscious of his hand clutching the door handle and awkwardly trying to get in.

"Throw that in the back. No room up here. Careful of those boxes." Her head jerked in the direction of his backpack and then the back seat.

"Yeah, of course."

Staring out of the front window, Pete took a minute to gather himself. He was sitting in a car with a bench seat, something he'd only seen in movies, with a perfect stranger who was odd from the get-go, heading south, he hoped, towards 505 then west to 80 and home. That was the plan. That was what was discussed. Now all he could do was pray that she didn't head straight south on 5 and quickly make an exit to head back north to some remote cabin in the Sierra foothills somewhere off the beaten trail and he never to be heard from again. He glanced at the door lock. It was unlocked. Easy escape if he had to.

He guessed her to be at least in her late eighties. The faded purple crocheted hat on her head appeared to be almost as old, and he figured it had never seen the inside of a washing machine. Framing one side of her weathered face, the only side he was privy to, were wisps of the whitest hair he had ever seen. Almost translucent as the late afternoon sun shone through the windshield.

Her profile did not allow him to see her face straight on, so he was left wondering what her eyes looked like. He remembered his grandfather's eyes when he was ninety. A milky-white film invaded both eyes, so Pete was never sure if his grandfather saw him or anything clearly. Hopefully, this woman who temporarily held his fate in her gloved hands, had eyes as clear as a mountain stream.

"Thanks for stopping for me." Pete said, breaking the deathly quiet between them.

"Well, if you had hemmed and hawed any longer, you wouldn't be sittin' here with me. I can't keep wasting time. Don't have enough of it to be careless with it." She kept her eyes on the road but her grasp on the steering wheel had relaxed. "Where're you going in the Bay Area?"

"San Jose." He waited for her to respond, sure that she would with some delight. She didn't say a word. Just nodded her head and then tightened her grasp once again.

Passing the sign for 505, Pete sat up a bit straighter and leaned forward. Pointing to the cutoff he said, "So, will you be taking it? The cutoff? It's coming right up."

"What do you take me for? Of course. Didn't I tell you I would? You got to listen better. I hate it, but I hate wasting time more."

Of all the times he had driven this cutoff, none had been as long as this time seemed to be. Not a word spoken between them until the sign for 80 West-San Francisco appeared. He would breathe again once she had merged into traffic heading home.

"Hold on to something! I'm not all that good at merging and playing in this traffic." Her words hung in the air, a warning and a threat that brought him to full attention.

My god! Was this how it was going to end? If she had said something earlier, he would have offered to take the wheel. To make matters worse, they were hitting the evening rush hour traffic that stretched for miles at nearly a standstill in most places. He was aware that she was rolling down her window. Shoving her arm out as far as she could while waving her purple hand at drivers coming along side, she didn't wait but accelerated right in front of them. Not once, not twice, not three times but four times she pulled this antic and successfully found her way to the HOV lane. He tried to recover his normal breathing and realized how tense he had been for the last few minutes.

"Okay. Get ready to pay your way. Sit up straight so everyone can see we got two people in this car. Not like the cheaters."

*

Kit knew what he was going to do even before he did. And judging by the distance she had gained on him, she knew that she was right. She was finally alone. She had called his name only twice; once about five hundred feet up the trail waiting only a minute for a reply, and again a few more feet along, but this time she kept moving. She could probably gage accurately how far down the trail he was by now. Mistake number one-hooking up with him. Mistake number two-planning this trek together. Mistake number three-hanging in with him for as long as she had up here. What a loser! Good riddance but travel safe.

Kit realized that she would have to pick up the pace if she was going to camp before it got too dark. Not one to miss a beat, she mentally began a checklist of her pack's content. With each step taken, she checked off the essentials she had made sure were in her pack, not his, just in case. Other than a second set of hands and his physical strength, which she questioned, nothing was missing that would prevent her from surviving to the end of the trek. True, her food supply wouldn't be as plentiful. He had insisted on carrying half of it, but she could make due. What he didn't know was that she had thrown in extra for herself anyway. Not the first time for her where a trek had gone south. Bad memories but lessons learned.

She, like Pete, had grown up in San Jose. Her parents were still alive and well. Enjoying early retirements from the tech industry, each had healthy benefits packages and had made plenty while employed to enjoy the rest of their lives comfortably. She was grateful for this because it meant that she would never have to be responsible for them. Not like some of her older friends whose parent or parents were struggling financially to survive in the valley. Added to this, their health, in some cases, was failing them. She had spent enough hours listening to her friends whine on and on about how hard it was to suddenly be the parent. Especially when you had kids of your own. Something that they didn't wish on their worst enemy. Not the kids but having parents who were suddenly kids in need.

As an only child, Kit never lacked for anything. Her parents were strict and disciplined with her so that she didn't consider herself spoiled. Others thought so but she ignored their assessment of her. She paid her dues and now, at twenty-eight, had no parental attachment or responsibility. One of her roommates once asked her exactly how she paid her dues during a heated argument about paying her fair share for the food and rent of a small two- bedroom apartment on First St. off campus. Kit refused to live in a dorm as her parents wanted, at least for the first year. Shaking her with their ultimatum that support would be there for a dorm but not for living anywhere else, Kit amplified the situation with them by refusing to speak to them ever again after letting them know in no uncertain terms that she would do it all on her own. No thanks to them. And she had.

With no communication between parents and child for the last ten years, Kit earned her BA in Recreation and found work in a printing shop that almost paid the rent. She supplemented her income by taking groups on trail hikes, easy ones, at first, until she felt confident enough in her skills to charge good money for longer treks, overnighters or longer. It wasn't long before the printing shop was history. She made enough to have her own apartment, to run treks whenever she chose, and charge the earth, just because people were rich enough and stupid enough to pay her. The best part of it was that she was away from the valley more than she was in it, a blessing, if she considered good fortune to be such. In her mind, more like luck and well deserved.

Pete had not been a customer. One of the few excursions she had taken with someone who meant something more to her than a paycheck. She liked him, at first. He was nerdy but had a great sense of humor. He liked her which was more important. Difficult to get along with, as described by many of her past and present acquaintances, Pete had never mention this about her. Instead, he went along to get along, she figured. And that worked out just fine for her.

He stayed at her apartment most nights of the week, only taking breaks when he needed. This didn't bother her either. The time alone was welcomed, and she began to count on his absences. And when he was there, the sweetness of their companionship was what they both needed. She always knew, however, that the whole thing with Pete was temporary. No way could she see herself with him permanently. Such a baby, really.

He told her about his family, including his grandparents, what he could remember about them. She remembered feigning interest in the topic as he carried on about them. He definitely had issues when it came to his parental attachment, she remembered thinking, until he revealed to her that they died, one right after the other. No sympathy aroused but more surprise on her part. She marveled at how someone her age could have dead parents. The finality of this thought stopped her in her tracks but not for long. What it meant to her was that it was one less complication in her life. Meeting his parents. No need to worry about that.

*

Not until they were across the Benicia Bridge was the silence broken. She was the first to speak, waking Pete from one of those half-sleeps that only a long car ride can produce.

"What part of San Jose you say you're from?"

Startled by the unfamiliar voice while trying to comprehend his whereabouts, he pushed himself up in the seat, wiping the thread of drool from his chin. Passing on his right was familiar terrain. He became depressed at the thought of the long drive south on Interstate 680. The sun would be setting very soon, he figured, and he was still miles away from the apartment. "What?"

"I said, where are you from in San Jose?" Her smoker's voice filled the car. She didn't turn to him but focused on the traffic all around her.

It suddenly dawned on him that if they were here then he had survived her manic maneuvers on 80. He couldn't remember falling asleep, but he must have been out for a couple of hours, at least. A little gift from God, he mused. "From the west side. You know Bollinger Road, Old Highway 9? Out in that direction." He was about to add that she could drop him off anywhere at this point. He could get home from here, but she responded quickly.

"I'll be damned. Are you telling me true? I don't remember the last time someone called the old highway by its rightful name. Bet your parents remember it a whole lot differently than you do." Her voice dropped off. He could tell that she was elsewhere.

"Yeah, they did. My grandparents had their version too. Sure would have liked to see it in the fifties. I mean before it started changing."

He felt her woolen hand on his knee before he realized that she had reached over to him.

"You just be sure that you keep your family's memories in safe storage. Nothing can change them on you." She patted his knee a couple of times and then returned to her two-handed grip of the wheel.

Something about her. He couldn't place it. Couldn't come up with the correct description. He didn't know her from Adam. Didn't even know her name. Was repelled by her antics and elderliness. Would be grateful for the ride, of course, but couldn't wait to open the door and wave goodbye. But whatever this nondescript feeling was, he couldn't shake it. He wanted to keep talking to her. About what? He wasn't sure. Logic would tell him, he thought, that he was associating her with his grandparents, maybe even his parents. Not by her immediate characteristics that he had been introduced to on this part of his journey, but by something much deeper and possibly, not retrievable. Never meant to be, he concluded.

"Sure. I've got my memories locked up right up here." He pointed to the side of his head. She didn't bother to look over at him but nodded her head almost imperceptibly. He saw it, though, and suddenly felt in sync with her.

"So, like I said, you can drop me anywhere you need to. I'm good from here on out."

She did not respond immediately keeping her eyes on the road.

"I'll take you where you need to go." This time, she turned briefly, to acknowledge him. "By the way, name's Hellenia. You?"

Had she read his mind? "Pete. Good to meet you, Hellenia and thanks for the lift."

"Hell! You can call me Hell. I've got no problem with that. All my friends call me Hell."

He watched a fractured grin fall into place on her aged face.

"Well, Hell. Hell, yes, that's great. So, if you are serious about taking me all the way, you could drop me at Bollinger Road and 9. You know where the old nursery used to be up there on the corner? You could drop me there. I'm practically at my front door." Not exactly true but a few blocks to walk was a piece of cake, he thought, if he compared it to the trek he had only just escaped from.

"Bought my whole garden there. That was a long time ago. Great family they were. You know that they were interned during the war? Just ripped right up from their home and land, a young couple with babies in tow, and dumped up there until the government decided they were no longer a threat. A threat! Makes my stomach turn just to think about it."

He remembered, now, his grandparents telling him about the Japanese couple that lived down the street and how they as kids and their whole family had been interned as well. None of it made a whole lot of sense to him at the time. In high school, there was no mention of this happening in the textbooks. It wasn't until college when he found his way into an American History (1850-1950) course that he confronted a history of his country that was foreign to him. He wished he had paid better attention to his parents and had asked questions.

"Yeah. I agree." He wasn't sure that was the best response to her comment, but it was the truth.

"Okay. I'll get you to the top of Bollinger, if that's what you want."

Conversation over. It threw him for a minute. "Yup. That would be great. Thanks, Hell." A hard word to use in this capacity, he thought.

The rest of the drive fell back into silence as if the well had prematurely run dry for them both. He suspected, that if he probed, she would open like a book. He knew he had living history right next to him in a confined space for at least another couple of hours. Something was nudging him to take advantage of the opportunity. Something else was warning him to be prudent and to ride the silence out.

The corner was dark. The street light was out in front of the abandoned nursery, and the only illumination came from her headlights. As she backed out and turned onto the main road, he caught sight of the nursery's faded sign. "BONSAI NURSERY". He watched Hell drive away as he stood in the darkness of a familiar place.

*

In all the years that she had been hiking on her own for days on end, she never concerned herself with the "what-ifs?". Others had. Repeatedly. She stopped telling her friends when she was going off on her own. Taking a group was one thing. No possible way to keep it quiet with all the paperwork and legalese that had to be translated to layman's terms and then filled out correctly. But planning a hike with no one else involved was escapism at its best. She had been doing it for so long that preparation was almost robotic. Her pack was always supplied with the necessities even while leaning against the wall of her bedroom between trips. Updating supplies was part of her planning. The only real effort she needed to make was to familiarize herself with topo maps. Her clothes were neatly rolled and stored in the pack, never in her chest of drawers, which only contained the bare necessities for city living.

If her relationship with her parents had not imploded, her lifestyle would be a different story. She knew that they would be breathing down her neck, constantly concerned for her well-being, her mother finding any opportunity to remind Kit of what a difficult birth she had had to endure. That was why Kit was so special to them. Trying their hardest to set her up with available sons of their friends. Hammering her with all their questions about how she chose to run her life and suggestions as to how to do it better. The right way. When those suggestions became ultimatums, her decision to cut her parents from her life was an easy one.

The solo hikes had provided plenty of time for her to question the decisions she had made so far in her life. Some of them took no time at all to mull over while others, like her parents, would not leave her alone. As hard as she tried to convince herself that she knew better, that she knew what she was doing and that she was far better off on her own than being subjected to their control, the questions were always there with each step she took on the trail. And with each step forward, she tried to focus on the path in front of her, around how many more bends, how many more ascents, how many breathtaking views waiting for her to take in, and how many more miles to find her way to the end of the trail, her way out.

She woke early, something that she liked to do on the trail. The best time was just before sunrise. A spirit world time when the anticipation of a new dawn filled her with reverence for her existence and all who silently accompanied her; when her nocturnal spirit companions found their way home before the daylight blinded them; when only a few animals stirred around her, unseen but seeing every move she made. She lay in her bag, eyes half shut. The insulation of her cocoon kept her warm through the September nights when the temperature could drop dramatically from the late summer daytime heat. And right now, just before sunrise when the cold still lingered, she stayed buried beneath the warmth of the material surrounding her.

She let very little of anything grow on her, especially people. Kit thought of herself as spontaneous and she lived for moments of discovery. Anything to keep life interesting. So, when she turned her head to see if Pete was awake yet, an unsettling reality struck her hard. The past twelve hours or so since she had last seen him played out in front of her like a fast-forwarded video. How could she forget that she was on her own again? Had he managed to attach himself to her more than she thought? Yes. Had she allowed him to do so? Yes. What other reasons could there be for her thinking that he was sleeping in his bag right next to her? Twelve hours ago she was glad to be rid of him. She'd gone through the mental calisthenics to justify moving on without him, all the advantages that came with that decision. And as far as she could remember, sleep came easily with no regrets or concerns for her former companion. And that was the answer. She had not weakened nor become submissive. She figured it out just in time before turning her head to see the dawn's glow beginning over the eastern ridges in the distance. A blessed sleep that can drag the conscience into numbness and a palpable darkness that temporarily erases the experiences of the waking hours. A fleeting gift that the conscience jealously grabs back for safe keeping and further use. Simple explanation.

Fully awake now and satisfied with her explanation, she sat up, pulling the bag's warmth up and around her shoulders while she burrowed the rest of her body further into the bag. The lingering night shadows of the sky quickly disappeared as the sun popped up above the purple ridge. She was always surprised by sunrises, how quickly they happened, just like sunsets. If you turned away even for a moment, you could miss them. The mark of time, one more time.

As she headed out, she gave no thought to altering her plans. Finishing the hike was her goal. She was looking forward to putting the miles behind her and adding her accomplishment to her way-to-go-girl list. She and Pete had met some interesting people on the trail, each with a story or two to share, if either party was interested to stop long enough. Generally, it was expected of strangers who were all sharing the experience of the PCT to take the time to connect. As she recalled these moments that they had shared, it dawned on her that Pete did most of the talking. He was a natural that way. Like a chameleon, his character adapted quickly to each encounter. She realized that it was purposefully done to put the stranger at ease. She had to give him that much. She knew that any future encounters on her part would not be so natural. Her guard would remain up just because. Because she was female. She hated going to that bottom line but there it was. No matter how experienced she was out here, there was no accounting for the other guy's intentions. At least, she realized, Pete had been a friendly buffer.

*

As he unlocked his apartment door, glad to be back in familiar territory, a thought came to him. "Parental attachment." And he dismissed it immediately. Familiar territory had been a forced choice when he left home. Choosing to go to college nearby was because of money. His Aunt Emily helped him when she could, but he never depended on it. His parents had put some aside for him but not enough. Student loan debt was incentive enough to finish in four years, get a job, and start the payback. Yes, it was convenient to be close to his aunt, but he never felt guilty if he said no to a dinner invitation from her. She said that she understood. Maybe next week? His response that it was a good possibility-just would have to see how things were going-always satisfied her, it seemed. He regretted, now, that he hadn't said yes more often. He missed his aunt. Her death, like his parents, came too soon, but unlike his parents, hers was expected. She lived long enough to cry at his college graduation. In a very short time, her brave battle with cancer ended. Surprised by a sudden longing to see his aunt, he closed the door behind him, repeatedly blinking to prevent any tears falling.

The place stank. Not just a stale stink but a nauseating stink. Something had died in his apartment. All he wanted to do was kick off his boots, leave his clothes in a pile by the door, and take a good long shower. But the stink prevented him from doing anything before he found its source. He had not had a decent wash since the last opportunity on the trail-a makeshift shower and toilets. And it had to be quick. The water supply was limited, and he wasn't the only one waiting to use it. Thankful that a fellow PCer had built it at some point for everyone's use, he longed to stay under the cool water indefinitely. Enough of a wash to get the first layer of dirt and sweat off his skin, he had exited the stall nodding to a young girl who waited her turn.

Opening the sliding window in the living room, he knew the first place to look. But the contents of the fridge were intact. And the stink wasn't as strong in the kitchen, he discovered, as he moved through the apartment. About to enter the bathroom, barely enough space to move around in, he stopped short and threw his hand over his nose and mouth. His gag reflex was attempting to function, but he controlled it enough to focus on the disaster in front of him. Both the toilet and the shower stall had backed up and the overflow, he estimated weeks old, covered the floor and had just stopped short at the threshold. A mixture of solid and liquid waste, hair, and god-only-knows-what, some of it seemingly in a state of petrification while the rest of it unwilling to do so, repelled him as he did a quick about face, grabbed his cell from his pack, and ran out of the apartment.

*

She had nowhere to go. Not anymore. Not in this place. But she headed down Bollinger Road as if she did. As if she knew exactly where she was going and needed to be. Catching a glimpse in the rearview mirror of her young travel companion, standing alone in the dark, she wondered if he really did have anywhere to go or was all his talk just bull. Most likely, he just wanted out. Away from the old bat. Not the first time. He was just too polite to tell her to her face.

What used to be a country road, pitch black during the dark of the moon and barely drivable even in a full moon, so full of aged wagon ruts and scattered debris left by winter storms or, worse, the creek overflows that flooded the area, Lawrence Station Road, now an expressway, loomed in front of Hellenia. She would need to decide quickly in which direction she would go. North or South? Heading north would take her back to the known. Heading south-well, it was just too late, she decided. Thirty or forty years ago? Absolutely. Not now. And she knew all this even though she allowed herself the freedom to decide.

She would head back to where she just came from. "Them mountains," she told anyone who asked. "Been in them mountains better part of my life. Intend to end my life in them mountains. Intend to be buried in them mountains." However, she never revealed where her life began.

*

Of course, he had to leave a message. Where was a landlord when you needed one? An absent one at that. The best he could do now was call one of his buddies and crash at his place until he heard back from the guy. The problem was that he had left his pack in the apartment. All his IDs, clothes not contaminated with the stink, and any toiletries were in the bag. He wasn't about to take anything out of the apartment if the stink had set in to everything, and he was sure it had. A quick grab and he would be out of there.

Pete waited for Zeke in front of the apartment complex. He knew that he couldn't smell the place from this far away, but he figured what he was still smelling was either on his clothes, caught in his nasal cavity, or indelibly imprinted in his brain for the rest of his life. Maybe it was all three. He tried to imagine the smell of wood smoke from a campfire, or the strong whiffs of sunbaked sage along the trail. And he almost got there. But the visual invaded his thinking and then the stink. Maybe this was Karma. What goes around comes around. You left her up there and this is what you get. He hadn't thought about Kit since his lift with Eric. Completely gone from his thoughts. Until just now.

"Hey, man."

He didn't hear Zeke pull up and Pete jumped in surprise. "Damn! What the…?"

"You called me, remember? Where's your head?"

"Yeah. Yeah. Thanks." Pete got in beside Zeke. "Sorry about the stink."

"What stink? Oh, you mean your lack of hygiene for the last month? Don't smell a thing." Zeke leaned in and then away from Pete. "No, wait. Is that crap I detect?"

"Seriously. You do smell it!"

"Seriously, dude. No. I don't. Just pulling your chain. Relax. Let's get out of here."

*

The second-best time of day on the trail was the early morning, before ten, when her body was rested, fed, and fresh. All her senses were working at full capacity and the world and all its wonders gifted her with a positive outlook. This morning was no different. She had spent some time before heading out checking maps and making calculations. Reassured that her food supply was sufficient to see her through, she figured that she would be done and off the trail in just over a month now, barring any unforeseen issues. Now on her own, she could easily make good mileage even through parts of the trail that were described as difficult. She didn't doubt herself in any way. What she couldn't account for was out of her control. She would deal with whatever came her way. No problem.

She had made the decision to start the Pacific Crest Trail in Oregon and finish it in California. A substantial trek of 1,213 miles from start to finish. Beginning at the Cascade Locks on the Columbia Gorge, her plan was to finish in Tuolumne Meadows and relax in Yosemite for a few days before heading back to the Bay Area. The whole endeavor would take two months if all went well. Starting in September, she figured she'd avoid the summer trekkers while also avoiding any early winter storms. She knew that returning at the end of October might be a bit iffy, but she would be prepared for the worst. She wasn't a novice at this. Twenty miles a day was doable-what she would have to do to get to Tuolumne before November-but if, for any serious reason, she could always cut it short and get off the trail before then.

There were moments, she confessed to herself one evening while prepping dinner, that she missed the company of a human being. The occasional wildlife that appeared fell into the bird category, for the most part. Depending on terrain, very little else confronted her, especially at the higher altitudes. Not that she didn't love the birds of prey that played on the thermals high above her or the song birds that she could never see but whose songs accompanied her along the trail. There were times that she shared the trail with other hikers, momentarily stopping to chat about starting points and destinations. Sometimes, a warning about a bear siting further along or the reassurance that the next station was not that far. And then she would be alone again. But she knew that she would have these moments of loneliness even before starting the journey. It was just a matter of psyching herself out of the negative and back to the positive, which she had no trouble doing.

She made the progress that she intended and at the end of two weeks by herself her confidence kicked into high gear. She felt great. No physical issues to deal with. No emotional baggage to weigh down her thoughts as she put one foot in front of the other. Just a clear head and a well-trained body to depend on. Not taking anything for granted, she had done due diligence in preparation for the trip right across the board. So, she thought, it was no wonder she was on top of the world.

She had crossed paths with another solo hiker three days ago. He seemed okay outwardly, but in their brief conversation Kit picked up on his mental state. Things he said alerted her. He wasn't a threat to her by any means, but she figured he was a threat to himself. He swore a lot about the difficulty of the trail, the unwillingness of most of the folks he met along the way to offer him any help when it was obvious to him that he needed it. Kit asked what kind of help he needed. And then a laugh sprang forth that sent shivers down her spine. Just as suddenly, he stopped laughing and looked at her like he had never seen her before, then letting her know that he really didn't need help. Just pulling a stranger's chain. "You know," he said, "a social experiment." When he continued the conversation by asking her name and where she was headed, the alarm bells were deafening. She gave false responses to both questions, then wished him well and left him standing in the middle of the trail. Not daring to look back, her sense of hearing was working overtime while she strained to hear footsteps behind her. Nothing, as she put the miles between them.

*

Driving his rig through the LA traffic was a thing of great skill. He developed a thick crust when it came to car drivers, in general. Eric forgave them for their errant road behaviors. He knew they had no idea what his world up here was like. The brotherhood that he belonged to was the elite when it came to control behind the wheel. He was proud to be a trucker. Thirty-five years pushing the miles behind him, and for the most part, loving every minute of it.

Times like right now as he crawled along the interstate not making any time, he wondered what else he could be doing with his life. Not getting any younger and finding himself reflecting on what he had left was becoming a frequent mental exercise and not a positive one. Sure, he had money saved, had a pension, would be on social security in two years, and owned a small house up in Shasta City, but what then? All he really knew was trucking. And he met lots of folks over the years, some nice, some not so nice but no one he couldn't handle. Folks in Shasta were great, and he knew just about everyone, including the returning tourists who found themselves drawn to the place but could never put into words why.

Then his thoughts became punishing. He could have done something different, like his sister had done. He could have found a job that let him see the world, something that he figured was out of his reach now. But he would have liked to travel. Someone said to him once that they envied him because he was independent, seeing the sites, all the while working in a dependable job. He laughed at those observations. Not that they weren't true but that they were and therein lay the irony. Great job if you don't mind stopping every trip at the same truck stops, small talking with the same waitresses year after year who were just as stuck as he was, racking up the same miles on the same highways, delivering the shipments to the same warehouses or docks year after year, heading back the way you came because your next pick-up was waiting for you and if you didn't get there on time, you lost it, meaning you lost money and credibility, and then resting your head in your own bed for a couple of days before it started all over. When he got into these funks, he had to see them through because he knew he could. Situations like the one right now, all around him - at 7:30 pm, when folks should have been home a couple hours ago, having dinner with their families, getting the kids ready for bed, and then winding down themselves before it all began again- were the trigger.

Eric's attitude, in the end, was positive because, frankly, what else was there? And so he sat, picking up radio calls from other truckers around him, giving them a "hey" while overlooking the roofs of cars below him, patiently holding on until he and everyone else reached their destinations.

*

"So, you don't mind me staying here for a while?" Pete watched Zeke pull out extra bedding from the hall closet.

Tossing it at Pete, he said, "Dude, only if you get in the shower right now and take care of business, man. Not joking."

Zeke had been Pete's best friend since their freshman year in high school. He was the exact opposite of Pete. Zany, out there with his sense of humor, and definitely not shy when it came to the opposite sex. Almost embarrassing at times. But Pete liked to think that he picked up a lot from Zeke about dealing with females. High school had been a training ground, and the best teacher he ever had had been Zeke.

The double dates came first and when Zeke felt that Pete could handle it, they went separate ways. "You're on your own, dude," when Pete resisted the new strategy the first time. And he had taken this girl out, just the two of them, on a safe date. Dinner and a movie and a dictated curfew by her father put the fear of god into Pete so that he made sure he delivered her home thirty minutes before the deadline. No kiss, just a timid hug to officially end the evening before handing her over to her waiting father. Never dated her again. He never really could say why.

Plenty of girls followed the first right through college but no one was special. Not in the way that some of his other friends experienced. He could tell that they were on to the final stage of courtship leading to marriage well before they were twenty-five. Burdened with a kid or two, a mortgage, and a job they had to keep but hated, their lives were done for, as far as Pete was concerned.

Zeke felt the same way. The two of them had hung in there, single and happily independent. Neither one would admit to the other that lately thoughts about approaching their third decade in less than a year hounded them. And now Pete found himself, at twenty-nine, dependent on his best friend's goodwill and couch to get him through. Well, not exactly true. He had the wherewithal to get a hotel room while waiting for his apartment to be repaired. As a matter of fact, he hadn't needed to call Zeke at all, but he did. And it felt okay and he knew Zeke felt okay too. It was just the way things were between them but they both knew that this would change someday.

*

Once out of the valley, she breathed a sigh of relief. Familiar territory lay in front of her for miles heading north. She liked driving at night. Never did have any trouble like a person her age should have. The darkness that surrounded her felt comfortable and protective. Nothing out there that could harm her, not if she just kept driving. And even then, Hellenia mused, who in their right mind would take advantage of her in any way seeing that her old age would scare them off pretty darn quick.

She stopped for gas, ate her meals, and took care of her business at the same truck stop every time. People knew her there and watched out for her, checking in with friendly conversation but always asking her if she was doing okay. Did she need anything? How was her baby holding up? (referring to her 1966 Valiant) And Hellenia would always tell them that she was just fine and so was her baby but appreciated their concern. It was never spoken about but all who knew her knew that she was homeless. Her car's content, carefully arranged to fit in the trunk with a few items neatly boxed on the back seat, would give no indication to the casual passerby that this was someone's dwelling. She had her pride. Besides, it was nobody's business but her own.

Her destination going north never changed either. She had, at one time, considered crossing the border into Oregon, maybe landing in some rural town where she could be left alone, but nothing came of it. At that point in her life, she figured that she was too old to start over. Living in her car gave her all the privacy and independence she wanted and every time she pulled into Shasta City, making her way down the familiar main street until she turned off into a dirt alley that ran between a group of WWII era type housing, did she stop her car. She was home for the time being. Even here, between backyards where life went on all around her, she was left alone. No one minded a harmless old woman spending a few nights in the alley. The important thing was that they knew she was there and she knew they knew. Just short of what neighborhoods were supposed to be.

On the road, if fatigue overcame her, she'd pull off into a rest stop. Parking under a light, even in the middle of the day, she covered her windshield with a sun protector, secured towels in the driver and passenger's side windows, and quickly fell asleep. And always, for some reason she never understood, she would jerk awake as if someone sitting next to her had poked her in the ribs. The duration of her sleep was less than fifteen minutes, usually. But she found that it was enough to revive her so that she could drive on until she reached the truck stop. When she thought about her current life, her routine so firmly in place, she chuckled aloud that she was like a little baby on a good nap schedule. And maybe she was. Full circle and all.

*

The good sleep came in the alley. Surrounded by life but separated from it and alone, she felt secure. Sleep came quickly and soundly and, without fail, her internal clock nudged her from sleep, still in the darkness well before dawn. Lying across the front seat, she remained in her most recent sleeping position, taking inventory of her aging body, a checklist, making sure everything seemed operable. Only after this mental exercise did Hell push herself up, slowly swinging her legs down below the steering wheel while grabbing the back of the seat for balance. And then she would just sit. No predictable amount of time but time enough to let her night catch up with her.

Before removing the window coverings, she sat in the driver's seat, staring straight ahead. She could easily be taken for dead, if folks could see in, but they didn't, and she wasn't. She was remembering her dreams. Well, one very long dream that caught hold of her just as she closed her eyes for the night and stayed with her until she opened them in the early morning. It wasn't the same dream each night because her story was full of events that led her to this alley. She knew she couldn't live long enough to dream her lifetime. But maybe that was what she was trying to do; trying to relive it one more time before she couldn't. And for some reason she could never figure out, this place, this land, this active volcano that loomed over Shasta City, was allowing her to try. She felt it in her bones as strongly as she felt the arthritis that had set into her joints. And that's why she always headed north but never crossed the border, and always found her way to the alley whose earth grounded her, secured her, and confounded her.

Sometimes, her dreaming was consumed by her life now. Other times, night after night, she would dream about the ranch, deeply in the past. Not as often would she be visited by Joe, her late husband. And almost a dream-afterthought would her children appear. On the nights when her dreaming carried her back to her parents' ranch, she slept peacefully. The images were clear and palpable, welcoming her back to a time in her life when she was truly happy. She floated through her dream-state feeling the warm earth under her bare feet as she chased the chickens around the coop. The old California oaks that spotted their land, some cut down by her father to make room for the ranch's needs, shaded her in the hottest part of the afternoon as she lay beneath them, separating herself from the rest of the world.

When she turned eight, her father said she was old enough to ride alone. Her favorite pony, Brindle, took her on long rides through the country as she straddled his bare back holding onto his rust-colored mane. In her dream, she rode him for miles and miles, feeling his body's sweat mingling as one with her own damp bare legs, his smell and that of the dust kicked up by his pounding hooves. In the spring, if her dream settled there, the scent of wild flowers, acacia, and sun-roasted sage dominated her senses. The velvet green of the surrounding east hills after a wet winter loomed in the distance. And the valley was filled with the sweet scents of a variety of blooming fruit trees in orchards that seemed to go on forever. In her dreaming, she sometimes floated above the sea of pink, white, and red flowers that thickened the tree branches like a blanket; at other times, she dreamt that she was walking on this same fragile sea for miles, never tiring.

Her dreams never allowed her to go back to infancy, to the day she was born. She wondered if anyone's did. Her waking memories of her birth were formed by her mother's brief description to Hellenia when she was only six as she wondered aloud how human babies came into this world. She knew about the animals on the ranch but never made the connection between their birthing and her mother's. "You was pushed out by me and none too soon. Never had such pain as you coming into this world." That was all her mother said about the process and that was all Hellenia knew about babies being born. It wasn't until her mother started showing with Hellenia's little brother that she began to ask more questions.

Now twelve, not yet a woman but knowing she would be some day, her need to know outweighed simple curiosity. Not because her mother wanted her to but out of necessity, Hellenia attended to her mother when she gave birth to her second child. Her father's absence was unexplained. As the years went by, Hellenia's mother never did have a conversation with her daughter about why her father's absence stretched on and even as her brother grew to be a young man, their father's whereabouts and name were never mentioned again. Her brother "never had a father", he would tell anyone who asked, and Hellenia would never correct him.

And when the ranch dreaming came, her father's two appearances were always the same. One of those, the last time she saw him, stooped over a fence post trying to unwind and cut away the rusted barbwire that had snagged one of the colts, was reoccurring and troubling. The colt's cries from the pain and needing his mother while her father's harsh words filled the air as he struggled to free the frightened, wounded animal were crystal clear in tone and intensity as she dreamt. Just as the gentleness of his gestures and voice were once the colt was free, not letting it run directly back to its mother but speaking soothing words to it as he carefully ran his hands over its body, down its legs, while reassuring both the colt and himself that no harm was done to it, and then nuzzling his forehead against the colt's and whispering something to it that only they both could hear. Then freeing it, her father, pushing himself up from the disturbed ground and wiping his sweating face with the rag from his back pocket, smiled, a smile that appeared rarely and never because of her or for her, and that lingered as he watched the baby find its way back to safety.

The second appearance was always hazy, yet Hellenia knew this dream well and did not welcome it. The yelling began slowly building in intensity, and she could never see who was yelling. But she knew the voices, that of her mother and father. And with this dream's visit, she would struggle with its content. Was it real or did she fantasize it? Someone else's distant memory that somehow found its way into her subconscious? Interfering with her memories? Her grasp on reality? And always, in her dream, settling with what she knew to be the truth all along. The moment that her young world shattered. Nothing was the same after. And then her father couldn't be found in any of her dreaming. Only her mother and infant brother appeared, if she looked hard enough.

Every night as she settled herself on the front seat, she silently welcomed the dreams to come. If she could have, she would have forbidden the bad ones' arrivals, but nothing in her life had been in her control. She knew that, and it hadn't taken her eighty-nine years to figure out that truth stayed with you as far as you were going to go.

*

The thought shook him right out of his sleep. He lay on his back on Zeke's couch staring at the ceiling in the darkness. Zeke hadn't asked him about Kit and Pete hadn't even thought of mentioning her or their situation to Zeke. Weird. Zeke knew the plans. Pete had made sure to fill him in before they left so someone would know their whereabouts. Zeke had even agreed to pick them up in Yosemite at the end of the two months. This didn't make any sense. Tempted to wake him, he decided against it. In the morning, he would bring it up. And as he tried to settle back into sleep, he remembered one more thing that he needed to do. Get over to her apartment first thing. Sleep snuck farther away from him as he mentally walked through her place trying to remember what he had there that was his. Not much but he wanted it out of there and back in his own place.

Now fully awake, checking his phone to find that it was only 4 a.m., he sat up as a string of whispered profanity momentarily relieved his frustration. He didn't have a place to go back to! Not for a while, he guessed. The landlord hadn't called back by the time he and Zeke called it a day last night and there were no messages on his phone. How long he could depend on Zeke's good graces was questionable. Not one to take advantage of anyone, especially his best friend, he would have to get things moving fast. He didn't care about the early hour as he called the landlord's number again. His call went to voicemail, and this time he made sure that his frustration was evident to the guy. No threats but so close.

Over coffee and leftover burritos from the night before, Pete waited to see if Zeke was going to say anything about Kit. Nothing. Unable to contain himself any longer, he put down his burrito and looked directly at Zeke who was still eating and texting at the same time.

"Dude, aren't you wondering about me and Kit?" He waited for Zeke to look up. "Dude?"

Zeke finished a mouthful of burrito, sent his text, and looked up at Pete.

"What, man? I figured if you had something to tell me, you would. Not my business, dude."

Simple and direct. That's what he liked about Zeke. He took life in stride and never let any of it get to him. At least, that's the way it looked to Pete.

"Can I tell you? I mean it's all kind of weird, me getting picked up early and all. Not to mention, there's no Kit with me." Pete tried to sense his friend's willingness to further the conversation.

"Okay. I get it. You and Kit called it quits somewhere along the way. I could have predicted that before you two even left." Zeke looked down at his phone again. "Right?"

"Right." What more was there to say? Totally unnecessary with this guy. Should have known he'd figured it out. A wave of relief swept over Pete until he remembered what he needed to do first thing this morning. "So, I was wondering if you wouldn't mind giving me a lift to her apartment? Need to get my stuff out of there."

"That's cool. When you want to go?" Still multi-tasking, Zeke shot a quick glance Pete's way and then back to his texting.

"When you're ready. No real rush, I guess. Just want to close the book on this one." Pete realized that this was the first time he had verbalized aloud his decision. And he still felt good about it.

"Give me five and I'll meet you at my car." With that, Zeke slid off the chair that he had half straddled to begin with, thumbs still at work, and headed into the bathroom.

Not much, Pete realized, as he gathered his belongings. What was his he threw into two boxes. The best part was that nothing stank; not his stuff and not her stuff. Everything in her apartment smelled like Kit. Fresh, nothing overwhelmingly sweet or artificial. Just fresh.

Zeke waited in his car. He didn't offer to help probably because he knew that Pete's belongings didn't amount to much. At least not over here. Pete's apartment was another matter. Going over there was like stepping into the past. Zeke figured that Pete kept every memento from his high school days, all his stuffies from his childhood, and every book he had read since he first learned how. Pete's place reminded him of his grandparent's place with all the framed photos everywhere. Zeke would never tell Pete that, though. He knew that they meant everything to Pete, especially the ones of his parents. Pete had told him about what happened to them, and it took Zeke a long time to shake off that information. Something no kid should have to go through.

"Okay. Can you pop the trunk?"

Deep in thought, he didn't see Pete until he heard his voice. "Dude! You surprised me. Don't creep up on people like that. Dude!" Zeke popped the trunk still feeling his heart pumping overtime.

"Sorry, man. Thought you saw me." Pete walked to the back of the car and found room for his belongings. Not the neatest of guys, Pete thought, as he tried to take a quick inventory of the trunk's content. "Everything but the kitchen sink," his mother used to say. And maybe that's in there as well, he mused.

"Where to?" Zeke, in what was becoming his normal pose, still texting to who knew who, asked without looking up.

"When do you need to be at work?" He hadn't considered, until just now, that it was a Tuesday and Zeke had a job.

"Taking the day to be your servant." This time he did look directly at Pete and grinned, the grin that Pete remembered from high school when Zeke would concoct a "day off" from school for the two of them. And Pete would go along with it because Zeke made it sound so right.

"Are you sure? I can manage on my own. Got to take care of business with this damn landlord." Still no replies appeared as he checked his phone.

"Sure. Anyway, two heads are better than one. How can I help with this jerk? You want me to text him? Put the fear of God in him?"

Pete, knowing full well that Zeke would do just that and compounding what was probably going to be a problem no matter which way he attacked it, replied, "No, no. Dude, it's my problem. My solution. How about we just hang? Wherever you want. You know I owe you, dude."

"You up for the beach? Get a little surf and turf and…who knows?"

"Man, could do with sand between my toes for a change." As he spoke, Pete recalled the unforgiving boulders, dirt, and dust of the trail and how his feet at the end of each day, screamed for their release from the sweaty confines of his leather boots. "I'm in."

"That's my unhappy camper. Okay, ladies. Get ready 'cause Pete and Zeke are about to change your day." Pete turned to Zeke, exchanging a high five to seal the deal, temporarily forgetting that his stinking apartment still stank.

*

A group of three hikers heading north warned her of two impassable places on the trail heading south. They described to her a freak wind storm that blew up with no warning and whose intensity wreaked havoc with some of the weaker trees. They still couldn't believe their luck. They survived it unscathed other than still being completely shaken by the strength of Mother Nature. The trail was blocked by at least two massive trunks that they encountered. They had no idea what damage lay further south. They assured her that she could probably find a way around them or climb over them. However, it took the three of them to work as a team to maneuver the height and breadth of the trunks. No way to crawl under them, they assured her. They asked her if she had any climbing equipment with her, rope or something to get her over them. She assured the concerned group that she would be fine. Had equipment and knew how to use it. Wishing each other good luck and safe travels, Kit didn't wait for them to turn from her and head up the trail. Turning her back to them first, she shot one arm up above her head and gave them a half-hearted wave.

She began her fifth week in great spirits. Still feeling good, no physical complaints and having overcome a moment or two of loneliness, she faced the next leg with optimism and anticipation. But that changed instantly after her encounter with the hiking trio. And as she put one foot in front of the other, she made a working plan for surmounting the waiting obstacles and whatever else lay in her way. She would walk the length of the fallen trees until she found a space to crawl under. There was always a space to crawl under. Obviously, between the three hikers, their experience added up to little more than zero, she mused.

What she hadn't considered surprised her. With all her experiences as a solo hiker, it shouldn't have but it did, and the intensity of the thought stopped her in her tracks.

Was she doubting herself? Not sure that she could finish this? The trunks and whatever else loomed in front of her were not the problem. It was that she was even having these thoughts. They hadn't hit her until the trio. Solo hikers were one thing, on the same level as she was, but the three of them seemed to be in such a good place even after their harrowing experience. Maybe, having someone to reassure you was not such a bad thing, Kit thought. But this realization was drowned out by her combative and assured sense of self. She relied on herself for everything and had survived just fine. A weak moment, she realized, that she almost succumbed to. No. She was on her own; her choice, her adventure, her accomplishment.

The first trunk was larger than she imagined. Had she taken the time to study the trees on either side of the trail, she would not have been so surprised. The girth of many of them, the old stands, was at least twenty-five feet. As she stood next to the fallen trunk, she stepped on tip-toes to see over it. The force of its collision with the earth created a trench in which it lay and some of the displaced earth and debris clung to the bark's rough surface while much of the soil formed mounded walls along the trunk, much like crib bumpers she once saw in her friend's baby nursery. She tried to see the top of the tree, how tall it had been when standing, but the devastation it caused to other trees and anything else in its way as it crashed to the earth, prevented her. And turning, she was taken aback at how close the exposed root bed was to the trail.

For just a moment, the immensity of the devastation before her and the tree's proximity to the trail, made her uneasy. She had no control here. None. Ahead of her, more trees still standing but for how long? If the storm had not already knocked them over, how many were weakened enough to fall right in front of her, or worse, on her? Another weak and illogical moment and she shook off these thoughts.

Once on the other side of the fallen giant, having gone around it at its shortest length close to the root bed, she continued down the trail. Figuring out the best way to overcome the next one, Kit felt a surge of energy, an adrenalin rush. She was in control again but now, as she moved forward, she was more aware of the trees that stood on either side of her. The second trunk was even larger than the first. When the giant ripped its way out of the earth it called home for at least a few hundred years, she guessed, it created a massive debris field that extended well beyond its root bed. This time, it would not be as easy an accomplishment.

The only pressing issue she was having with all of this was that it was eating away at her daylight. And not knowing how many more she was going to encounter, she contemplated an earlier camp time than she wanted. She figured, when all was said and done, that she would lose at least a couple of hours. But her better sense told her to move on. Get out of this area before something happens. She did not welcome the idea of spending the night in such an unstable section of the trail. Hike on until she came to some clearing. Checking her topo map again, she was relieved to see that not far, maybe ten or so miles ahead, was another check point.

Other than a few smaller trees blocking or partially blocking the trail between the monster trunks and the check point, she made good time but still arrived after dark. It did not matter. She was just grateful to be clear of the last miles and to settle in for the night. Even better, she was the only one in the area, as far as she could tell. But she heard them before she could make them out, coming north. A young girl, probably around 18 or 19 and what appeared to be a boyfriend about the same age. Which, she decided, explained why they weren't practicing any trail etiquette. They seemed surprised to see her hunched over her small cooking stove, the only light illuminating the immediate area coming from her lamp.

"Woah! Hey there!" the boyfriend announced. "Sorry about the noise. Didn't expect to run into anyone here." He turned to the girlfriend who vigorously nodded her head.

"No problem," Kit lied. She did not look up or acknowledge them further.

"Well, okay. Do you mind us bunking down here? We'll find a spot farther away." The boyfriend's laugh was awkward and forced. "You know, privacy."

The girlfriend laughed, obviously embarrassed.

"No problem." Kit still focused on the warming soup. "But keep it down, if you don't mind. Been a long day."

"We'll try but no guarantees." Again, the awkward laugh. "No, seriously, understood."

As the two moved away from Kit, their hushed whispering and stifled giggles angered her. "Idiots," she thought.

The boyfriend stayed true to his word apart from some unintelligible heated words that escaped into the night. Kit heard them but in a half sleep as she soon drifted into the sleep of the dead.

*

Pete knew that Zeke was a good friend but didn't realize how good until, one night over a pizza and a couple of beers, Zeke brought up the subject of Pete's apartment.

"Hey, we should toast each other." Zeke raised his beer glass. "To…to hanging in there with you and you hanging in there with me for two weeks now." His expression was unreadable, so Pete wasn't sure what to make of the toast.

"Sure. Two weeks together. Why can't the whole world get along like we can?" Better to make light of whatever was behind his best friend's thinking. But Pete knew. "Look, Zeke. I understand, man. The landlord said at least a month, if not longer. And, frankly, I'm not sure I would move back in there anyway. I need to find my own place. You, me…we need our separate space. No problem."

Zeke said nothing as he took the last swallow of his beer. Placing his glass down, he reached for another piece of pizza.

Pete did the same. "I'll pay you, of course, for rent. You know I appreciate everything."

"Yeah, sure. That's fine." Zeke's words were distorted as he spoke through a mouthful of pizza dough. Swallowing, he grabbed his empty glass. "You want one more?"

"Sure. Thanks." Pete watched him as he headed toward the bar. Trying to figure out what was up with him, Pete thought about the past two weeks. Had they gotten along the way he implied? Or had he crossed some line with Zeke without knowing it and just made things worse as time went on? That wasn't the way Zeke operated, though. Up front and blunt. He would have made a point of telling Pete if that was the case. But something was up and the only way to get it out of Zeke was to play it the way Zeke would if the shoe was on the other foot.

Pete waited for Zeke to get comfortable again. Full glasses and plenty of pizza left between the two of them, Zeke reached for another piece without saying a word. Like he had shut Pete off completely.

"Okay. What's bothering you?"

Zeke, for a moment, stopped chewing and looked up at Pete. "Dude, since you asked, I'll tell you."

"Great. I wish you would." Nothing looked good to Pete right now, not the pizza and definitely not the beer.

"Did you ever stop to think that maybe I like having you stay at my place? Yeah, of course, helping with the rent would be great and the food. But that's nothing compared to the company." Zeke looked down while he spoke avoiding eye contact, something so out of character for him that Pete had to try to focus on his friend's words instead of his demeanor. "You and me, dude. We're best friends. Always have been. What are friends for if they can't be there for each other?"

What the hell was going on? Pete couldn't comprehend what Zeke was talking about because this wasn't the Zeke he knew, or he thought he knew. Since when did the maudlin become one of his character traits?

"Are you trying to tell me that you don't care how long I hang at your place?"

Zeke slowly looked up and his eyes met Pete's. "Yeah, that's what I'm saying." He took a sip of beer. "What I'm really saying is that you can stay with me forever."

Whatever noise filled the restaurant was instantly silenced as Pete digested Zeke's meaning. And as suddenly as the silence had fallen all around Pete, Zeke's words blared at him again and again for what seemed an eternity. Zeke even disappeared from Pete's perception as he struggled with the obvious truth about his best friend. A truth that had been hidden from him until now.

"Are you okay?" Zeke's voice, soft and full of concern, penetrated Pete's mental turmoil.

Pete couldn't look at Zeke, not until he gained control, could speak rationally, while trying to preserve Zeke's dignity, not to mention his own.

"Look," Zeke's voice even gentler than before, "the last thing I want to happen is for you to walk away. But if you have to, then do it. Judging by your face, you are blown away." Pete didn't detect Zeke's attempt to lighten the moment.

"Okay, okay. First of all, I'm not going to walk away, Ezekiel."

When was the last time he had called him by his proper name? He couldn't deny that a crevasse had instantly been created in their relationship whether he wanted it to happen or not. He had never felt so far away from his friend as he did now. Pete struggled to form his thoughts before speaking.

"We are best friends, and that should count for something. I'm just having trouble understanding why you never said anything before?" He consciously lowered his voice so that Zeke had to lean further across the table. "Being gay is no big deal nowadays. Zeke, you should have said something." Too late to take them back, his words visibly stung Zeke, placing the blame on him, something Pete he had no intention of doing. But there it was. His coping mechanism had backfired on him, and he could do nothing but watch his friend shut down on him.

Zeke sat back avoiding eye contact. Grabbing the half empty glass, he guzzled the remaining beer and with glass in hand said, "I'm getting another." Pete watched as Zeke walked to the end of the bar, hardly stopping to leave his empty on the counter and then continue out the door.

Pete remained at the table unable to leave. Deep in thought, he lost track of time.

"Can I get you or your friend anything else?" Her voice broke through his confounded thoughts.

"Uh, no. No thanks. Just the check." Pulling out his phone, he checked the time astonished to see that he had been alone for almost thirty minutes. It seemed only moments ago when Zeke left.

"No problem. Figured that's what you were waiting for. Here you go. Thanks for coming in."

Once outside, he tried phoning Zeke but kept getting his voicemail. No responses from his texts either. Trying to make it as clear as he could in his final text to Zeke, Pete let him know that his decision not to go back to Zeke's tonight was an easy one to make. He figured that they both needed some time to assimilate what Zeke's revelation meant to each of them and to their friendship. He would be in touch. Reading the text numerous times before sending it, Pete assured himself that Zeke wouldn't misinterpret his words. He hadn't had the gift of time before when he shut his friend down so thoughtlessly, so cruelly, and, for all he knew, maybe permanently. He had fallen into the crevasse and until he could hear Zeke tell him that he was forgiven, and everything was going to be just fine, would Pete be able to start the ascent out of one of the deepest holes he had ever fallen into.

*

David Eagan sat across from his wife, Jean, at breakfast just as they had done for the last thirty-five years. However, since their retirements, the neck-breaking pace of this meal that once started their individually frenetic work days, had slowed dramatically. So much so that two hours could pass without a care as they leisurely read through the daily newspapers, three to be exact. When one or the other made the move to get up, it signaled that this section of their long day was finished. On to something else. What that would be would not be determined immediately as neither one of them wanted the responsibility of planning the day further. If they were truthful with each other, they would realize that life held no interest for them like it used to. And they both longed for some excitement, some surprise that would get their juices flowing again, but neither one told the other, afraid that this revelation would separate them further causing one party to feel less than while the revealing party suffered frustration silently. And so, the hours passed each day, sometimes with a diversion, most of the days not. And the routine that they so passively accepted as their reality remained in place.

When their daughter was born, they had been married almost five years and their careers were well on the path to security and further advancements in the tech field. The baby was not planned but both David and Jean were thrilled to welcome her. They could afford a baby and Jean's forced time off from work. Once the baby was old enough, Jean placed her in the new daycare program at work, a blessing for parents, and Catherine thrived. Had there been any grandparents in the picture, they would have been called upon to help with the baby. David's father passed two years ago, unexpectedly, from a heart attack. His mother was still alive but never recovered from losing her husband. She quickly slipped into mental illness and was institutionalized. Jean purposely kept her parents' existence a secret never revealing to Catherine, when she became old enough to ask, anything about her grandparents. Catherine was told that she didn't have any and when she was old enough to understand the concept, that they were dead.

An only child, she became the center of her parents' world and, over time, her mother's unhealthy need to control her daughter resulted in Catherine's decision to separate herself from her parents. If her father had just once stood up to her mother and supported Catherine, then she could forgive him for supporting his wife's every decision concerning their daughter. But he never did, and it was clear to Catherine how much she really mattered to either one of them. When she turned eighteen, she made her move out of the house, leaving her parents angry, hurt and spiteful. She didn't care. She wanted to survive on her own and completely cut off from them.

For nine years, no communication or contact of any kind between Catherine and her parents occurred. But just days before her twentieth-eighth birthday, a month before meeting Pete, she came face to face with them in a crowded mall. If their eyes had not met simultaneously, they could have avoided one another. Perhaps because blood is thicker than water, neither party retreated but stood frozen as the masses brushed by them. Seeing her mother's stunned expression, Catherine instantly initiated the first move, a self-defense maneuver, and moved towards them. Her focus remained on her mother. She saw her father only peripherally.

"Hello. It's been a long time. You look well." Catherine heard her forced pleasantry voiced aloud but felt strangely disconnected from the body that produced it. She waited for a response.

Her mother turned to her husband, grabbing his arm for support, and keeping it there as she stared at Catherine. It occurred to Catherine that she should walk away, not waiting for her mother to engage in what would be a limited, polite interchange. Her mother had too much pride to make a scene.

"Catherine?" Her mother's mouth remained slightly opened after she spoke her little girl's name.

"Yes. Have I changed that much?" She watched as her mother turned toward her husband, silently communicating with him. Her mother did not turn back around but kept her eyes on her husband's confused expression.

"Catherine, we knew this day might come." He paused, glancing at his wife. Her eyes were sharply focused on his. His words, barely intelligible in the din of the busy passage way, were controlled. "We want you to know that you will always be welcomed in our home, your home. The past is the past." He meant every word but as he felt his wife's body stiffen against his own, he knew that he had crossed his wife. That he had knowingly contradicted her silence gave him the strength he had not felt in years He did not anticipate his daughter's response.

Catherine felt nothing. And she wasn't about to pretend that the reunion her parents had expected on "this day" would obliterate the past. A tearful moment full of hugs and kisses was someone else's longing, not hers. That this brief communication had taken place at all only strengthened her resolve never to cross the threshold of her parents' home again.

"The invitation is appreciated but not accepted. You two take care." She walked past them, keeping a good distance, as she made her way upstream through the oncoming shoppers. It never occurred to her that her father had finally stood his ground against his wife.

David felt the weight and rigidity of his wife on his arm lighten as they watched their child disappear. He wanted to follow her, to talk with her, to ensure that she was all right. But he knew he wouldn't. There was no point. Almost ten years had passed, and he had grown used to the idea that he no longer had a daughter. That he could never hope to walk her down the aisle. That his dream of becoming a grandpa was not to be. That, in the end, she would not be there to say goodbye when his life ended.

Catherine sat in her car, unable to let go of her anger towards her mother. Her thoughts swirled as she kept coming back to her father's shallow words and her mother's intentional silence. She knew that she had always been willful and a challenge which was why her mother overstepped the boundaries in controlling her daughter. Catherine was sure that her mother did not understand to this day how much Catherine owed to her. Had her mother not been who she was with Catherine, Catherine would never have learned to fight back so vehemently, so determined never to let her parents win. And the result? The ultimate backlash of a well-intentioned kind of love that severely scarred their daughter's well-being and outlook on life and towards the people she had yet to meet.

The shock of seeing Catherine did not subside as David and Jean drove home. Neither said a word. And once in the house, they went their separate ways keeping busy and avoiding one another at all costs. They each knew that if they let their guard down in front of the other, the ensuing volleys of blame, angry words, hurtful accusations would fill their evening and lapse into the following days. So deeply infected by the event that had taken place in their home ten years ago, and, just today, a husband's betrayal of the agreement he and his wife had made that their child was no longer welcomed in their home, neither had sought consolation from the other. Instead, the open wound festered and sickened them and their marriage. But they had stayed together for appearances' sake, had told lie after lie to both themselves and their friends about their wonderful daughter whose career kept her so busy that coming home for a visit had not been possible. Maybe this year, they would lie.

*

She dug out the mole skin from one of the smaller pockets of her back pack. Detecting the soreness on her heal growing steadily during the morning, Kit figured it was Murphy's Law. With only one week left until she reached Tuolumne Meadows, having racked up over a thousand miles wearing the same boots day in and day out, only to have to resort to babying a sore heel for the last hundred or so miles? Unbelievable, she thought. But she knew that she was fortunate to travel this far and the only complaint a sore heel. No, not fortunate, she corrected her thinking. Good preparation on her part and her skill saved her. Nothing more.

The late October weather held no surprises. She was prepared to deal with Mother Nature one way or the other. A few welcomed early light rainfalls were a change of pace from the cold nights and sunbaked days. The earth's dampened soil released puffs of steam along the trail as the sun warmed it. A musky scent filled her nostrils as she labored the ascents, breathing heavily and evenly. The earth beneath her was slippery in some places so that her focus on staying upright became intense, tiring her prematurely. But once she reached the end of each ascent, she stopped for a moment, leaning over while stretching out her back, hands on her knees, as she caught her breath. The downhill was more harrowing as the weight of her pack worked against her pushing her forward before she was ready to take the next step. Concentration on staying upright took more out of her than any ascent, but she knew that this would be the case. She took her time maneuvering over small rock outcroppings and exposed roots that crisscrossed the trail before her. And she loved every minute of it. She felt completely alive, every part of her body working in sync; alert and responsive. This, to her, was what it was all about. This was what she would do for as long as she could. This was what it meant to be alive.

*

His freight was headed for a dock in Long Beach. He would have made his delivery in time but the three separate accidents between him and the Long Beach dock, a matter of sixty miles, which translated into an extra three hours of travel, prevented him and everyone else from getting to their destinations on time. He learned the hard way not to let frustration take over. He played tunes that he could sing to, had his soda and a bag of pretzels at the ready, and slowly rolled along trying to keep some distance from the car in front of him, never succeeding as some idiot trying to get ahead, always filled the gap. Unwilling to cuss the driver out, Eric did the opposite. He laughed quietly as he contemplated the progress he was making. One step forward, three steps back. That was just the way it was in these conditions because not everyone played by the same road rules. Another tune, a swig of soda, and gnawing on pretzel sticks, he passed the time while time passed him and there was nothing he could do about it.

Pulling into the dock or the warehouse always felt like a satisfying climax. Not one to dwell on the sexual connotation of this experience, he couldn't help but briefly make the connection each time. And the fatigue that hit him hard he likened to the few minutes of love words he would whisper to his entangled partner just before he rolled over and slipped into the best sleeps of his life.

Turning over his freight, signing off on goods received, he would climb back into his cab and give himself a minute, if he was able, to just sit before leaving the dock one more time. He never told anyone this because they would think he was crazy, but he knew what he heard each time. In the silence of the cab, he sat and waited, tuning everything else out. Leaning back with his head against the headrest, eye lids slowly lowering until he saw nothing, he heard it. The deep sigh of relief, of freedom from a burden so carefully taken care of and now someone else's responsibility, escaped from within the metal framework of his truck, through the fabric that softened the cab's interior, seeped from the air vents and the speakers, and swirled around Eric as if commiserating with him, once again, about the long haul. If Eric allowed his thinking to go one more step toward what most would interpret as lunacy, he had no problem in declaring that his only true friend who completely understood him was his truck.

He reached Shasta City two days later after leaving the LA area. Spending the first night in his cab at a rest stop somewhere between LA and San Luis Obispo, he splurged and spent the second night in Monterey at a motel that catered to truckers. Treating himself to a fish dinner on the wharf followed by a walk along the recreation trail, the thought crossed his mind, as it did any time he spent time here, that maybe he should reconsider living so far north. The sea and the salty air, the climate, and the people all were welcoming and comfortable. Considering the next day's travel, the Central Coast was nearer to most of his destination runs. Just about forty-five minutes east of here, one of the largest truck depots existed in Salinas. It made sense every time he mulled it over. But once back in the truck, heading east to Interstate 5, his seaside meanderings dissipated the farther he traveled until he began to feel the tug of Shasta City bringing him closer to it with every mile that passed. By the time he exited the highway and dropped into town having taken in the beauty of the mountains all around him and having paid silent respect to the volcano that loomed over the town, he knew he was home. There was nowhere else he wanted to be.

As he passed one of the alleyways just off the main street, he took a quick glance. Then he checked the time, realizing that it was only four, too early in the afternoon for the old Valiant to be parked for the night.

*

The number of people on the trail picked up the closer she came to Tuolumne. A rude awakening, she thought, that the last seven weeks on this trek was so close to being over. True, she could still go for a day or two not seeing another human, but it didn't compare to a whole week or more being completely alone as she had experienced. She knew she would need time to adjust to being back in the "civilized" world, and the irony of that thought made her laugh out loud. Then an overwhelming sadness and depression quickly followed, consuming her thinking as though deeply mourning a great loss. She was forced to stop, hunching over, alone on the trail, and uncontrollably weeping until she could weep no longer.

Still hunched over, gasping for breath, as she struggled to regain her composure, she sensed that she was not alone. She quickly straightened up, wiping her face on her shirt sleeves while trying to focus on the invisible presence she knew was close by. Her first thought was that of an animal somewhere just off the trail. Had it been watching her all this time? Watching with curiosity the weakened human's breakdown? Watching and knowing it had the upper hand, the advantage if it chose to take it? Her imagination was running rampant. Fool, she admonished herself. Focus. Focus. Breathe...Breathe. Focus. She heard nothing but her own heavy mouth breathing. Forcing her lips to close and moving the air through her nose instead, she felt a shortness of breath, a tightness in her chest that would not subside. Giving in to her discomfort, she opened her mouth again and kept it open as she filled her lungs repeatedly. No longer concentrating on another's presence, she listened to her own rebellious body and fought off what she knew to be panic. Of what, she couldn't identify. No, not true. She always knew its cause. At this moment, so close to the completion of her dream hike, her body silently screamed, "Enough! I'm not going any farther with you. Not until you admit how messed up your life is."

She was not mistaken about a presence close by. Deep in

her own mental turmoil, she was unaware of their approach and was startled as they came up behind her.

"Hey there! I remember you." The male voice was vaguely familiar to her as she forced herself to turn around while controlling her sanity. "Remember us?" He was pointing to his female hiking partner.

"Are you okay?" The female's concerned voice penetrated farther than her companion's and, for a moment, Kit felt more tears well up. "You're not okay, are you? Can we help you out?" She moved closer to Kit.

Her own words formed sluggishly in her mind, and she concentrated on voicing them without allowing herself to weep in front of these two strangers. "I am...okay. Thanks."

"Well, you don't look okay, not like when we saw you the last time. You sure you're okay?" He moved closer to Kit, standing beside his companion.

Seeing them side by side, she remembered. Her frustration with their presence, the two lovebirds, the nervous giggles, and the suppressed, angry words in the night. And here they were showing concern for her. "I am." She guarded her words so as not to reveal her momentary weakness. "Good to see you both again," she lied. "I thought you were heading north?" She couldn't remember if they had told her this or that she just assumed it.

The male laughed loudly. "It's a whole lot farther than we thought." He turned to the female. "She made me do it." Laughing again, he reached out and playfully shoved the female's shoulder, knocking her off balance.

Regaining her footing, she turned to him, one hand raised as if to reciprocate, a flash of anger crossing her face, then dropped her hand to her side. "Yeah, sure. I made him do it." She looked directly at Kit, her words coated with innuendo that only females could interpret.

The pair made her uncomfortable and now, it appeared, that they were all heading in the same direction. "So, you are heading back? How far?" She could feel her strength renewing as she regained some control while plotting her next move.

The two simultaneously shrugged their shoulders reminding her of *Alice in Wonderland*'s strange twins, Tweedle-Dum and Tweedle-Dee. "Appears that way, doesn't it?" The female fell into a stream of giggling as her companion spoke. "I mean, hey man, we're no fools. That trail just keeps going north right up to Canada. Did you know that? Way too far. We don't have enough weed to get us there." Looking at his companion, he joined her with laughter that crushed and deafened her giggles.

Kit didn't care if they heard her or not as she spoke through their laughter. "Keep safe, then," she said, as she turned away from them, forcing her legs to move her as fast and as far away from them as she could go. As she placed one foot in front of the other, quickly distancing herself from them, their combined hysterics diminished in intensity until she could hear nothing but one lone song bird somewhere high in the fragrant pines that surrounded her.

The unease of this latest encounter did not diminish, however. As Kit moved on, she tried to shake off the weirdness of the couple by excusing their behavior because of whatever they were on. Certainly not just weed. She only tried smoking it once and regretted it ever since. Keeping her body pure was her mission, but she slipped one time because a weakness got the best of her. Peer pressure. She joined in and hated herself for it afterwards. Never forgave herself. It disgusted her. She had no tolerance for anyone who depended on the highs to have a good time. And what she witnessed of those highs, always disturbed her. Their behavior was no longer who they really were, and she was never sure of their next move. She lost them until they came down. And even when they were down, she couldn't trust them because they never stayed down. She hated it. All of them. Most of all, herself for being so weak.

"Hippie shit!" she said out loud. "Stupid Hippie shit!" She felt better hearing her words spoken aloud and not that of her internal meanderings. But wary that she might not be alone on this section of trail with its blind corners, she thought better of carrying on her one-way rant. Tightening her lips and lowering her voice to a whisper, her words even surprised her. "Hope they laugh themselves over the edge."

*

Pete had purposely excluded two people from his life recently. Both were unfinished business which he would have to face eventually. He hadn't considered, however, until just now, their connection to one another which was, he realized, of his own doing. As he checked his phone, the date, November 2, caught his eye. No sooner did it sink in that this was their pick-up date, did he remember that Zeke agreed to be their ride out of Yosemite. He never got back to Zeke since that night in the pizza parlor. Weeks ago now. As each week passed, it got harder for Pete to call him just because so much time had passed. He figured that Zeke hadn't called him maybe for the same reason.

And then there was Kit. He had no idea what Kit might be expecting. She probably figured that Zeke and he had gotten together since he returned, and that Zeke knew that she was up there on her own. But Pete wondered if she was worried about getting back since his departure from their plan. He should call her. But what would he tell her? He considered that Zeke, being the good guy that he is, was already heading up to get her because he kept his word. He needed to call Zeke, just to be sure. But he couldn't. He wasn't ready. Anyway, knowing Kit, she probably had altered the plan already. Probably on the road with some other hook-up she made. She could take care of herself.

He sat on the edge of his bed, his dilemma paralyzing him. How could he have made such a mess of things? He didn't feel that badly about Kit because he knew that she didn't need him for any reason. But Zeke was a different story. They were like brothers, and he knew that you weren't supposed to abandoned family, even if they were forced to abandon you. He knew what his weaknesses were, but he didn't know how to overcome the ones that counted. He learned to compensate in the workplace-easy to pretend to be someone, something you're not when you know that it's not permanent. But because of his inability…no, his fear of nurturing a strong friendship, the work it takes, the permanency once committed, and the inevitable loss that eventually everyone must face, Pete continued to obstruct his will power with negative thoughts producing no positive results. Well, not entirely true. The only consistent result for him was just not to care. To go on about his business not worrying about it. Consequently, time passes. Still sitting on the edge of his bed, he mentally started calculating how much time had gone by since he last saw Kit, since he last saw his best friend. Over seven weeks since he turned his back on her. And a bit less since he watched Zeke walk away from him. None of this was going to go away. He knew this.

Zeke did not pick up the call. Pete left no message the first time. On his second call, he left a short message asking about the planned pick-up and to let him know one way or the other. Then he texted the same message.

The return text was almost immediate. "On my way. No word from her. Sticking with plan."

Pete reread the text over and over. What he was looking for, what he hoped would be more from Zeke was not there. What Zeke did message did not bother Pete, about Kit not making any contact. Zeke understood the situation enough to know that Kit might not want anything to do with either one of them. It was Zeke's decision to take off not knowing the outcome.

Pete was left with nothing satisfying. Nothing that he could grasp as a lifeline to a friendship that he was trying to cling to, half-heartedly, he admitted to himself. He deserved whatever came his way from either one of them. He just wasn't ready, and he began to think that he never would be.

*

The figures kept appearing. The first time, they were nothing more than wisps of vapor loosely moving in and out of human form. No one identifiable. No gender. No faces. Only separate shapes that suddenly loomed large and then, just as suddenly, retreated to mere specks. The second time, when these wisps appeared, she thought she heard them speak but could not understand them. Their forms still unidentifiable. The third time, a few weeks later, they appeared one last time. This time, they were no longer separate but entangled. The energy that Hellenia felt disturbed her so that, in her deepest sleep, she reached both hands out, trying to disentangle them. But she could not reach them no matter how hard she tried. She cried out in her sleep, a desperate attempt to draw their attention to her, a wail that shook her from her dreaming as the entangled grouping vanished into darkness.

Hellenia felt her heart beating overtime. Her eyes opened suddenly to the darkness surrounding her and she shut them immediately, willing that her dreaming continue. But nothing came to her as she lay on her back between the front doors of the Valiant.

*

Zeke had plenty of time to think about what he was doing. He was keeping his word. He was going to be there to fulfill his part of the plan. It was the right thing to do. That was the answer to "why" he was doing it. But he also considered the possibility that she might not want him there. Probably why he hadn't heard from her yet. And it appeared, based on his text, that she hadn't contacted Pete either. She had plenty of time to get ahold of either one of them. She would have been off the trail for at least a few days, resting up at the lodge. But what the hell? If she wasn't there, she wasn't there. The drive up was just what he needed to be on his own and to hear his own thoughts. Maybe even be inspired to find some peace despite himself. Maybe, if she wasn't there, he would stay a few days in Yosemite. Everything will work out, he thought.

The plan was to meet at the lodge. Just call when he arrived. As he pulled in, he felt good. He had made it. No problems along the way. Here, where he was supposed to be. Fulfilling the agreement. The nagging thought that only one half of the pair would appear, the half that he had no strong connection to, not like he had with Pete, played with his positive outlook. He was upset with himself after he said a silent prayer hoping that she wouldn't show up. That she might already be gone. Figured out her own pathway without having to confront either one of them. Good for her, if she had, he thought. Good for him as well.

She wasn't picking up. He tried several times leaving voicemails, each time a bit more anxious sounding. Texting produced no responses either. After an hour of hanging by the car, thinking that she might walk right up to him on her way back from a swim or walk, he decided to go to the registration desk to see if she had checked out. She hadn't checked in, he was told. Had made reservations three months ago for a three-day stay for two adults beginning three days ago but was considered a no show. No, the hotel clerk hadn't heard from her. Could he be of service in any other way?

Zeke sunk into the cushion of a lobby chair. He needed to sort this one out. His first thought was to contact Pete, but he hesitated. He didn't want to get into anything with him. He just wanted an answer. Did she call him? He knew, though, that it wouldn't be that clean. Did she decide to stay on the trail longer or perhaps have some delay that prevented her from arriving on time? Maybe she injured herself, slowing her down. But Zeke knew the protocol well enough to understand that if she was injured, someone along the trail would come to her aide and, if bad enough, get her off the trail for medical help. He figured she would have someone alert him or Pete. He wasn't sure what to do next.

"Excuse me, sir?" The hotel clerk was standing in front of him. "If you are concerned about Miss Eagan's whereabouts, you should probably contact the rangers. Was she on the PCT? On any of the park's trails? They might be able to assist you." He waited for Zeke's response.

"Oh. Sure. Yeah. Yeah, she was. That's a good idea. Thanks."

The clerk nodded, turned toward the desk and then turned back. "Hope you two make contact. Good luck."

Reality was starting to take hold. National Park Rangers about to be involved with what he thought was going to be a simple pickup? And what could he tell them. He knew nothing about the actual trek. He knew where they started and when, and he knew where they were to end it and when. That was it. How could he expect them to track her whereabouts? Pete said that by the time they reached Tuolumne Meadows, they would have walked a little over twelve hundred miles. That was a lot of trail to cover. He didn't even have a photo of her. Didn't know her middle name, couldn't remember her address. Really didn't know anything about her other than what Pete had told him. And that amounted to just about nothing. He was being forced into a corner. He would have to call Pete. Have him talk to the rangers. There was nothing else he could do.

Pete picked up on the second ring, startling Zeke out of his thinking that maybe he was making a mountain out of a mole hill.

"Zeke? Hey, what's up, man?" Pete worked hard to control his emotions, stunned to see Zeke's number come up.

"Yeah, hey. Listen, dude." Zeke did the same. "It's Kit. She didn't show up."

"You up there already?" Stupid question but he had to say something.

"Yeah. Supposed to pick you two up today. Remember? She never checked in."

Pete could detect the stress in Zeke's voice. The guy was worried. "Listen. Don't sweat it. She's probably still up there on her own timetable. Probably forgot she even had plans on the backend." He knew that none of that was true. Not for Kit. Miss Organized, USA. "Sorry you made the trip, man, for nothing."

"Yeah, I thought of that. But I can't just leave without knowing what's up. What if she comes off the trail three days later than planned and I missed her?"

Pete detected a hint of a whine in Zeke's voice and tried to ignore it. "Well, if she does, whose fault is it? You were there when you said you'd be. You haven't heard anything?"

"No. And I've tried. Nothing. Now I'm told to check in with the rangers here in the park. But I don't know what I can tell them. You should be the one talking to them. Not me."

There it was. The blame was starting. Ignoring it, Pete attempted to calm him down. "Okay. I'll be happy to talk with them but do me a favor. Take some time to breathe and step back from it for a minute before you make that move. Consider this. If she comes off the trail any time after you leave, she's got both of our numbers. If she really wants us there or, now that I think about it, you there, then she'll make the call. She's a big girl and doesn't need either one of us. Right?"

"Right. But what about the hotel reservation? Wouldn't she have contacted them if she had changed her mind?"

"Maybe, but I don't think her cell would work out there. And maybe she just didn't think it important enough. I don't know, Zeke, but I am pretty damn sure that we've got nothing to worry about. If you're going to feel better by involving park rangers, then go ahead. Have them call me. No problem. Can't hurt, I guess."

"Okay. Then that's what I am going to do. I just can't leave without someone knowing. You know what I mean?"

Pete hated that expression, as if Zeke was speaking a foreign language. Of course, he knew what he meant. "Yeah, no, I get it. Are you heading back after?"

"Not sure. Guess it depends on what happens next. Maybe you should be up here instead of me?" Another ding.

"Well, depending, maybe I should." He took a deep breath. "Listen, Zeke. About what happened…I want…"

"Talk later, dude. Expect a call." Zeke shoved his phone into his pant pocket and made his way over to the visitor center. "I'm taking it from here but only this far", he mumbled under his breath as he entered the meadow. "You better damn well get your skinny ass up here, pronto."

*

He had three days off before his next run. As much as he wanted to, sleeping in was not an option. His body ran like a finely tuned Swiss watch when it came to his sleep cycle. Rise at 4:30 a.m. sharp and lights out by 10:00 p.m. Day in and day out. When he awoke in his bed the first morning home, he took a minute to adjust to his surroundings. Stretching his limbs out was a luxury in this bed compared to the cab's bed. But he never lay there long, and he never veered from his morning routine, no matter where he was. His coffee brewed, he made sure that he caught up on the news before heading out the door or switching on the truck's ignition. The need to stay connected was important to Eric.

What information he didn't get, he could always depend on the locals to fill him in at the coffee shop, where he had his breakfast. And he always took their renditions on the national and local news with the understanding that the truth lay somewhere in between, if at all. But this part of his morning at home always humored him, and he took the hearsays, the politically colored phrasings, exaggerations, embellishments, and the positively untruths in stride. He decided that it was his morning mental exercise, deciphering truth from fiction. Above all else, he loved these people, truth tellers or not.

Walking down Main Street to breakfast, his own coffee mug in hand, he took his time. Taking in the town, building by building. Stopping to admire a garden in full bloom, a new paint job on an old place, sharing friendly greetings with others out starting their day, noting the uneven sidewalk that he would try to remember to report to Stan at city hall. There was always something new to see, if you paid attention to your surroundings, Eric would always mention to a passerby. And they would wholeheartedly agree with him.

Passing by the alley, he was surprised to see the old car still there. Any other time, it would be gone by now. He figured whoever lived in it always got an even earlier start on their day than he did. The window coverings had not been removed. No sign of life. The thought crossed his mind that he should check on the occupant. But he decided against it. Probably better to let it be. If it was still there when he returned from breakfast, he would let Willy know. He had known Willy since they were little boys. A vague memory now, he remembered Willy and his mom coming over to welcome them to Shasta just after Eric, his sister, mom and Benny arrived in town. He was one of Eric's first friends here and had done well for himself. Police Chief William Burns but everyone who knew him back then still called him Willy.

As expected, the news swirled around him, sources from the booths, tables, and from the counter. Affirmations or denials of this brand of news was a sure thing as he watched either May or Elsie approach him to take his order, even though they knew it already. They made sure that he heard it all, then threw in their two cents, and always ended it with, "You know how it is around here, honey." Eric played his part, as expected, and nodded his head in agreement, forcing a laugh that he continued until either May or Elsie went back behind the counter.

Left to eat his breakfast in peace, he savored the home cooking in front of him. He had heard that food was a strong part of a person's psyche that began its imprinting from almost day one. He figured that his mother must have made some pretty good breakfasts when he was a kid because breakfast was his favorite meal of the day. But he could never recall any one particular breakfast food. It was just the total sum that she put in front of him for the first few years of his life. Taking that first bite of pancakes always brought him back to the old homestead. A term not used anymore, he knew, but for some reason, he had always referred to it this way. Another successful imprinting whose source he couldn't begin to identify with any accuracy. He guessed it came from his mother. Maybe his father but he could never remember his father, not his voice, what he looked like, nothing about him came to mind.

"See you didn't like your meal, mister." Elsie held a pot of coffee in her right hand and the check in her left. "You're a growing boy. You need to clean your plate." She paused. "More coffee?" She was already pouring before Eric could even nod his head.

"You know, you folks gotta figure out how to cook. You gonna run a business, you gotta know what you're doing." He handed her his empty plate that had been wiped clean of any evidence of a hot breakfast.

She laid down the check and took the dish from him. Exaggerating her examination of the dish, top and bottom, she shook her head slowly. "No need to wash this plate, now, is there? Looks like you did it for us."

"Yes, ma'am. And I'll do it again tomorrow morning, God willing." He gave her one of his warm smiles that endeared him to the ladies.

"We look forward to it, Eric. Nice to have you back in town for a few days. You have yourself a real good day now. See you tomorrow."

As he watched her walk away, he knew why this place, assured of his return, always waited for him at the end of a run. He was meant to be here and to be with people who understood this. There were plenty of strangers who came and went, but people like him with roots in this place, were always welcomed home no matter how far away they wanted to go or for how long.

*

She felt the heat of her body rising under the old grey blanket that had kept her comfortably warm throughout the chill of the night. Now it was a burden on her, and she grabbed at it, wrestling it to the floor of car. Free of its weight, she felt no relief. As she became fully conscious, she raised her hands to her face and covered her eyes from the brightness that filled the car. Even with the coverings still in place, the light penetrated the interior. Alarmed, Hellenia slowly maneuvered her body to a sitting position and assessed the situation. It had to be later than she normally awakened. Not bothering to let her body adjust to waking as she normally did, she removed the coverings and confirmed that, indeed, the light was different-the sun too high in the sky for the start of her day. She rolled down the driver's window to cool down the interior only to find that the October heat was worse outside than in.

She could wait no longer. Never mind that she was out of sorts by this unexpected change in her routine. She couldn't afford to stay here, in this alley, any longer. She couldn't afford anyone taking notice of her. She couldn't afford being seen.

Instead of backing out on to Main Street, as she always did in the darkness well before sunrise, she pulled straight forward out of the alley having crossed two neighborhood streets that ran parallel to the main road. She made a sharp left onto the third street and followed that out to the freeway entrance, all the while hunched down as far as she dared so as not to be seen while trying not to run into something or someone.

Heading south on Interstate 5, she tried to relax. She knew that it would only be a matter of time before her safe place in Shasta City would no longer be safe. She knew that, once recognized, her world would shatter. She had depended for so long on the protection of the mountain, resting each time she returned, in its immense shadow. Its energy sustained her and filled her with peace. She had no other way to describe it.

As she drove south once again, she could not think about

the day in front of her; the places she would stop, how far she would go this time, the stranger whom she would find in the front seat of her car with her. Her thoughts kept coming back to this morning. Waking up late, staying later than she had ever risked doing before. Then she recalled part of a dream. One that only came to her a few times and one that she could make no sense of. It was an ugly dream, an unwelcomed one. It lingered with her somewhere in her subconscious and nagged at her in the daylight. She could do nothing about it, though. She didn't understand it, but it had prevented her from leaving early this morning, so fatigued was she from the experience, and it caused her to come this close to revealing truths that she could never afford to reveal, even to herself.

*

As he approached the alley way, Eric slowed his pace. Fully prepared to turn around and report the car, he was surprised to see it gone. His thinking over breakfast led him to surmise that since it was still there, out of character, it might still be there when he returned. He further conjectured, even though he didn't like to think about things like this, that, upon Willy's inspection of the car, a body would be located somewhere within. Any further ruminations on his amateur detective's part were interrupted by Elsie's friendly banter. As he picked up his pace again, still a gentle saunter, he headed home. And he wondered where home would be for the old white car tonight.

1948

Pregnant with her second child, her first just turning one when she knew but did not tell Joe right away, Hellenia worried. Fresh on her mind was her little boy, a sickly infant who needed every moment of her attention. And Joe had made it clear that he was sick and tired of being neglected by his wife, all for a sickly kid who probably would amount to nothing, especially when it came to helping him out on the ranch. Joe was no help.

To Hellenia, he was trying to prove that he could handle the ranch just as her father had. When her parents died, she inherited the place. And when she met Joe, he was eager to marry her, move in, and make the ranch his own. He was always out working the land and when he came home for supper, he was just too tired to do anything but eat and sleep.

She vowed that she would never get pregnant again. She blamed Joe for this second baby. Not to his face, though. And when she did tell him, he turned his back on her, slammed the door behind him, and didn't come home for three days. He never apologized, never recognized her pregnancy in any way other than to comment on how fat she was getting, and he constantly complained that he didn't know how he was supposed to feed another kid.

So Hellenia continued to worry and to suffer this second pregnancy by herself. Her little boy, still sickly, was not bedridden as much as in his first year of life. And as the time grew near for her to give birth, she prayed that this baby would be healthy from the start. She would be able to nurse it for a whole year, not like her little boy who refused to take her breast. She had suffered his rejection of her, had cried so many tears that she thought she had none left to shed.

But her tears flowed freely after she pushed one last time, trying to control her breathing, so that she could hear her baby's first cries. And when her little girl made her presence known to the world, Hellenia wept harder. With her daughter in her arms, she wept for her safe delivery, for the health of her little boy, for her absent husband who made it clear that he wanted no part of her problem, and certainly no part in helping to bring another kid into their world, and finally for herself because she could see no way out of this life without destroying those whom she loved.

It was a Sunday, a beautiful mid-September golden afternoon, almost a year to the day of her daughter's birth. Hellenia finished nursing, bundled her daughter and lay her on the bed. She put on her light coat, and slung her bag over her shoulder, already filled only with the necessities for her children and picked up her baby, lodging her on her hip. She found her little boy playing quietly in the front room and, kissing him softly on the top of his head, helped him put on his jacket. She said nothing to him as she took him by the hand. He grabbed a wooden horse that lay among his toys, and Hellenia smiled at him, giving him silent permission to take it with him.

"I'm going into town for a bit. Be back in a few hours. In time to make supper."

Joe didn't look up from the local paper he had been reading, didn't say a word. She thought she heard a grunt and that was enough for her to know that he had heard her.

"Gas in the truck?"

Another grunt.

She never set foot on the ranch in San Jose again. The place was sold after Joe died, about three years after Hellenia deserted him. He was too young to take his own life, but that's what he did.

The new owners, despite the previous tragedy that had taken place on the property, were eager to save the ranch. Their efforts to farm the land led them to planting an apricot orchard that, in time, provided a good standard of living for their family. They bought up the property on both sides of them as the elderly owners died or moved and expanded the orchard so that their children would inherit the riches of their parents' endeavors. And two of the three sons stayed on, brought up their families in the beautiful valley, and thrived on the rich fertile soil of their father's making. Only part of the original farm house still stood, purposely preserved as a relic of a very different time. The sons' children wanted nothing to do with the orchard and, in time, the pressure and temptations of riches struck a death knell for the trees, the land, and old structures. Every single acre was churned up and paved over. And the office buildings in the industrial park were now occupied by a generation who had no clue and who couldn't care less, that a suffering wife, an unhappy husband, and their two children had once tried to live their lives on this land.

Seventy years later, as the old white Valiant passed the sterile office buildings, it slowed down just enough before entering the expressway, so that the driver might remember and apologize, one more time.

2016

Kit did not show up. Zeke had decided to stay in Yosemite with the hope that she would appear at some point, a few days, maybe a week later than planned. The rangers spoke with Pete, got the information they needed, but they weren't going to start a search and possible rescue until a week had passed. Understandable, Zeke admitted when he was also told, but worrisome. Pete never did come up thinking that he had done all that he could do after speaking with the ranger. He had made sure to describe Kit as an experienced hiker with an independent streak. He let the ranger know about his departure from the hike and a bit of what led up to it. He told the ranger that he was confident that she was fine and would come off the trail when she was good and ready. The ranger had hoped that that would be the happy result. They would be checking with hikers on the trail in the area who might have crossed paths with her. The ranger told Pete that if they began a search, he would be informed.

Zeke called Pete, letting him know that he was heading back. Couldn't afford any more time off work. Would Pete consider coming up now? Now that an official search was in place for Kit? Listening to the voicemail, Pete struggled with his feelings. Should he be there? And if he did go, what could he do? The rangers knew their business and didn't need him in the way. And if he stayed here, he would need to face Zeke. Kit had made sure of that. If that hadn't happened, then this wouldn't happen, and we wouldn't be where we are now. Domino effect. This thought played over and over as he tried to think clearly. He was blaming Kit, he realized, for everything. And he felt okay with that.

He decided that he would confront Zeke so that at least one part of his life made better sense. He could handle it. He just wasn't sure that Zeke could. But he was determined that their history together as best friends was important enough to preserve, even if the dynamics of the friendship had shifted. He texted Zeke, asking him to call.

It crossed Pete's mind that maybe he should contact Kit's parents. Knowing their daughter's history with them, they would probably give him the cold shoulder. Probably wouldn't even remember him. His one and only time with them had been brief and uncomfortable. Kit never mentioned it again. And he knew better never to bring them up. But it bothered him that he was the last to see her and that fact alone should be enough for him to have the decency to let them know. He didn't know anything, really, yet, but he thought that he should give them the option of worrying about her or not. Their decision, not his.

Jean Eagan answered and responded to Pete's phone call as he suspected she would. Not remembering who he was or ever having met him, she politely let him speak. When Pete was finished, she thanked him for calling. Nothing else. Not one word of concern, not one question. Not even the utterance of her daughter's name. She hung up on Pete before he could say good-bye.

1948

In those days, a woman with two babies in tow and no husband in the picture, was shunned by most. Without knowing why the woman was in this position, assumptions were quickly made, none complimentary. Little sympathy was given to her and even less was the desire to learn the truth. But one person would not ignore Hellenia's little family and because of his kindness, Hellenia and her babies were given temporary protection and shelter. He wanted nothing from her other than she accept his kindness. Hellenia did and stayed with him for a month until he decided, one day, that he was moving north. Up to the mountains to a place called Shasta City. She and the children were welcome to travel with him, if they wanted to. Maybe she could have the fresh start that she longed for. He assured her that, once there, they could go their separate ways. That is, once she was ready to do so. He still knew some folks up there, and he was sure that they could give her work and a place to call home for herself and the babies. No questions asked.

Hellenia did not hesitate to say yes to his offer. She had had no contact with Joe ever since setting foot off the ranch. She had no intention of doing so ever again. And he had not sought after her and the babies. All the more reason why the decision to go north was an easy one to make. However, some part of her still loved the man and he was the father of her babies. In a weakened moment, she wrote a short letter letting him know she was leaving town for good, never saying where she was headed, but that she and the babies were all right. She wished him good luck and signed her name, *Hell*.

In the moonless jet black, darkness of the country road, the car slowly pulled up to the rural mailbox. The engine idled as Hellenia reached out of the passenger window, opened the box, and dropped her letter into it. Closing the lid, she tried to focus on the outline of the farmhouse through the darkness one last time. Rolling the window up, she turned to her babies in the backseat, finding some comfort in their quiet, slumber breathing as they lay together under warm blankets. She turned back and looking straight ahead, she nodded to the driver who slowly pulled away from a life that Hellenia had decided would go no farther.

Joe, awake in the early hours of the morning, unable to sleep once again, heard the car pull away. He lay there, alone, in their bed staring at the darkened ceiling, trying to remember what his babies' faces looked like, but saw nothing, his vision blinded by the tears he refused to let fall.

2016

Zeke arrived back at the apartment to find Pete sitting on the front step. He wasn't surprised to see Pete, knowing that the unfinished business of Pete's own making had to be resolved eventually. He remembered Pete trying to bring it up, but he had shut him down. Not the best timing, Zeke thought, as he pulled into the driveway leading back to the parking stalls. He had driven straight through from Yosemite with only one stop for gas. Now, hungry, hot and tired, he tried to control his emotions as he considered the best way to handle Pete.

He had plenty of time to think things through as he headed west to the Bay Area. But he never did come up with an answer. The question? Now that he was out, did he want to remain friends with Pete? No. Better question. Could a friendship exist between them, now that everything had changed? He felt that he knew Pete well enough to know that Pete would never be able to sustain any form of friendship, even if he said he could. He would be doing it only to protect Zeke's feelings and he didn't want any of that. The real question? Would Pete ever accept what Zeke really wanted? The answer was clear. No, he wouldn't. He couldn't. The years had passed while Zeke fell deeper and deeper in love with Pete. And Zeke hoped that, one day, when the time was right, he would reveal his hidden truth to the only person he cared about, and that Pete would open his arms to him and never let him go. Now, what he had so many times imagined would take place was nothing more than the ugly reality that his charade was over, leaving him lost and broken. As he walked back to the front of the building, he decided that he wanted no part of a conversation whose purpose was to mend the unmendable, to alter the unalterable.

"Pete." Zeke acknowledged him as he watched Pete approach.

"You made good time." Pete held out his hand, but Zeke didn't shake it.

"Yeah, drove straight through," Zeke said as he headed toward the stairs. He was about to add that he was tired, not to mention hungry, but he knew to avoid any suggestion of heading out for a meal.

"Okay. I guess this might not be the best time to talk." He raised his voice a little as Zeke walked past him.

Stopping half way up the staircase, he turned to Pete. The words Zeke wished he could say filled his head, but he heard himself speak others.

"It's never going to be the best time to talk. Quit thinking about yourself and maybe worry about your girlfriend, for a change. Have a nice life."

He turned and each step he took to the second-floor landing felt like quicksand under his feet. He prayed that he could reach his door, unlock it, and slip inside without hearing Pete's plea for him to turn around. But he heard nothing and as he closed the door behind him, he moved to the living room window. Pulling the curtain open only far enough for him to peek out onto the lawn below, where Pete had been standing, an audible heave escaped his body, followed by sobs, as his knees buckled, collapsing his body to the floor.

1948

Benny and Savannah Hopkins knew of Hellenia and Joe Terner as neighboring ranchers in the Santa Clara Valley. With a few miles between them, the two couples only saw each other in town, at a grange meeting, or over a meal in one or the other's home and not very often. Sometimes, when Joe was mending fences or checking on crops, he saw Benny doing the same and, from a distance, raised a hand in greeting. Neither man made the effort to start a conversation as there was too much work to be done. Besides, that was women's business. But, like all good country folks, they all knew that if they ever needed anything, they were there for each other. Hellenia knew that but had never acted on it until now.

The last time she and Joe saw Benny was at Savannah's funeral, almost four months ago to the day. She and Joe and the babies were present as his young wife was laid in the ground. A bad heart failed her one morning, just shy of her twenty-first birthday. Benny found her behind the house, her lifeless body entwined in the damp laundry she was hanging out to dry. How long she had been there, he couldn't say. Childless, Benny stood alone, surrounded by a few town folks with whom he did ranching business. He was only twenty-five, the same age as Hellenia. Weeks after the funeral, folks were still talking about Benny's tragic loss while some were scheming as to how their spinster daughters could meet him, get married, and make some grandbabies. But Benny wanted no part of it. He heard the rumors when in town and began avoiding the trip until he could no longer, with supplies running low.

At first, Benny had a difficult time trying to understand what Hellenia was revealing to him about her marriage to Joe. He didn't hear much of anything she was saying, so stunned was he that she and her children were standing in his living room without her husband accompanying them. Any sound she produced was drowned out by his own mental calisthenics silently firing questions at her about Joe's whereabouts. He was so dumbfounded that when she stopped speaking, the silence grew unbearable between them. Her baby daughter startled him, her sudden cries breaking through the silence. Hellenia, not asking and unable to wait for Benny's response, moved past him and sat on the couch with her little boy who hung on tightly to his mother's skirt. Unbuttoning her blouse, she gently shifted her daughter in her arms to receive her breast. Benny turned away, uncomfortable about such a natural act. He and Savannah had wanted children. They had dreamed together of raising their family on the ranch and, maybe someday, one of their children would take over. None of that was to be.

His initial reaction had been to dismiss Hellenia's situation and to convince her to go back to Joe. He admitted that he didn't know anything about a marriage with children, but he guessed that things changed between a husband and wife, somehow. Even so, it was her duty to stay by her husband and not to take his children away from him. Benny did not know Hellenia very well and certainly not the mother who sat before him nursing her child. Any communication between them had always been filtered through Savannah, "women talk", he called it. He saved his words for Joe.

As the September afternoon began to fade and an early chill crept into the house, Benny stoked the fire whose warmth began to fill the room. Relaxed now, having adjusted to the fact that an unaccompanied married woman and her babies sat within an arm's reach from him, he became a willing participant in a conversation that played on his sympathies. He didn't realize it at the time, but his concern for Hellenia and her children grew out of his own loss. His offer to let them stay with him was a dangerous one and he knew it. But he also knew that he would not throw them out of his home with nowhere to go. And when time passed, his offer to take Hellenia and her children north to Shasta City with him did not seem unusual to either one of them. She agreed to go. She came to depend on Benny's companionship. He assuaged his loss. It never occurred to either one of them to ask themselves how far they wanted to go.

2016

Pete sat in his car replaying what just took place. The more he tried to make sense of his friend's tongue lashing, the more confused he became. What did he do wrong? What did he say that would result in Zeke's anger? His refusal to head back to Yosemite? What he said in the restaurant to Zeke when he opened up to him? He was clearly upset with Pete then. Something about Kit? He couldn't unravel the strings of thought that tangled any clarity in his thinking. And then it hit him. He hurt. His whole body ached with hurt. He had somehow lost his best friend. This thought overwhelmed him and the hurt deepened. He sat back in the seat, forcing his head against the headrest while clutching the steering wheel with both hands in a vice grip, struggling to hold onto reality. His chest suddenly convulsed as if trying to catch his breath. He was taken by surprise as his body, no longer in his control, released an almost primordial cry which opened the flood gates. Not a young man's weeping, stifled by embarrassment, but the weeping of a soul who was suffering yet one more loss in its young life.

He had no idea how long he sat there. The fatigue that followed alerted him and brought him back to the present moment. Wiping his face with the sleeves of his shirt, his focus returned. He needed to leave, to get home, to find the familiar again, the known.

A block from his apartment, he was forced to pull the car over and park. Her face appeared as sharp and articulated as if she were standing right in front of him. Without expression, without emotion, without substance. It slowly blurred as Zeke's angry face surfaced from Kit's. And Zeke's did the same giving way to an older, indistinguishable face, male or female he could not identify, and that face did the same so that an even older, ashen crumpled face appeared no more distinguishable than the previous but with a familiarity that demanded to be recognized. But Pete could not. Any recognition was blocked from him. This imagined image was produced by his own confusion, he was sure, and to be disturbed by it was wasted energy.

It suddenly became crystal clear. He needed to be there. His decision to go to Yosemite was firm. It didn't matter to him who or what brought him to this determination and by accepting this, the turmoil most recently experienced dissipated so that the path was clear for him, and he realized that he now knew how far he had to go.

*

    The couple approached the ranger as they descended the final switchback just a few miles from the entrance into Tuolumne Meadows and the final trail head. They weren't surprised by the officer's presence because they were so close to the park now, but they felt uneasy, quickly glancing at each other as if to communicate an understanding.

    The ranger was young, probably no more than his late twenties, but carried himself with the authority of a seasoned park ranger. Weighed down, it seemed, by pounds of leather paraphernalia encircling his waist, including a firearm, he moved up the trail with surprising ease.

    "Good morning!" The officer placed his hands on his waist belt as if to balance himself.

    "Morning," the male responded. His companion said nothing.

    "Coming off the trail here?"

    "Yup."

    "Are you both doing okay? You're just about there." The officer's smile reminded the female of a track coach she had in high school. The smile that said good job, but you can do better, so do it.

    "Yup. Sure. We're doing great. Like you said, we're almost there. Thank God!"

    "You both been on the trail for long? I ran into a guy who just finished his tenth PCT hike coming from Washington and ending here." The officer appeared to be impressed. "His eleventh will be from Canada to Baja next year. Pretty impressive."

    The couple remained silent.

    "So, sorry. How long have you been hiking?"

    "Well, kinda lost sense of time, officer," the male responded, "but we started at the trail head maybe two months ago?" He looked at his companion for affirmation. She nodded in agreement. "Didn't go as far as we planned."

    "Oh? Why not?" The officer shifted his stance, keeping

both hands in place on the belt. "What was your destination?"

The couple simultaneously looked at each other as if searching for an agreed upon response. The female took a step forward.

"It's my fault." She could feel her companion's eyes searing through her body. "I'm just not as strong as I thought I was. He was really good about slowing things down for me," she glanced quickly over her shoulder at her companion, "but I still couldn't make it, so we made the decision to turn back and here we are." As she spoke, her comfort level rose. "I mean, we didn't head into this cold. We worked up to it. Daily hikes with full packs around our neighborhood. People thought we were nuts until we told them what we were conditioning for. Then they were really impressed, weren't they, honey?" Turning to her companion, she did not wait for his response but plunged ahead. "We were too, if truth be told. I never imagined I would try something like this, not until I met...him." She caught herself in time. No names, not unless forced to reveal, she remembered him saying again and again. "So, here we are." She knew that she had said too much of nothing, really, but enough of nothing to be suspect. Idiot, she thought. Stepping back, she stood next to her companion sensing his anger towards her.

"What did you say was your destination and where did you turn around?" He knew she hadn't said.

"Where were we headed, honey? I've forgotten already." She couldn't hide the nervous laugh that accompanied her question.

"We were supposed to go as far as Burney Falls. Where we decided to turn back, I can't say. Somewhere, maybe just after passing Lassen? Something like that. We didn't get very far."

"Sorry that you couldn't complete what you set out to do. The trail is going nowhere so you can give it another try sometime in the future, right?

"Right," the male responded. "So, I guess we might as well keep going seeing as we're this close to the end. You have a good day, officer." He started to move forward but the officer did not give way, blocking the path.

"One more thing. Sorry to keep you. We have a report of a missing hiker. I'm checking with everyone I encounter on the trail as to whether they may have seen her. A young woman, late twenties, five feet nine, about a hundred twenty pounds, long brown hair, blue eyes, goes by the name of Kit but real name is Catherine…Eagan" He flipped the page of his notepad and continued reading. "Hiking alone, carrying a North Face pack, last seen wearing brown shorts, blue shirt with a red bandana tied around her throat. Let's see…oh yeah. Been on the trail starting at Cascade Locks in Oregon and was supposed to end here, in the meadow. She had a companion but split somewhere around the Shasta/Lassen area. Been on the trail since September first and now is overdue by two weeks." He flipped through more pages. "That's what we have. Have you seen her?"

The female knew not to speak but grew nervous as her companion hadn't immediately responded. She dared not even look at him.

"Wow. That's too bad," he finally said, and she breathed a bit easier. "We haven't seen that many folks out here. There was a guy we shared a meal with somewhere, but I can't tell you where. And there was a couple, older folks. We talked with them but not for long. But we didn't see this woman at all. Like I said, not many people out there."

"Ma'am, what about you?" The officer couldn't put his finger on what he was feeling but he sensed that he couldn't just end it here. "Would you have seen anyone who fits this description?"

"No. We've been together the whole time, well maybe potty breaks, but anyone he's seen I've seen. Maybe she passed us up when we set camp early or something. We didn't like hiking too late in the day. Or maybe we didn't make it far enough to even cross paths." She knew she should stop. "Anyway, that's kinda scary, her not turning up and all. I'm just grateful to see you and that trail head up ahead. Can't finish this adventure any-time too soon for me. Some hot bath somewhere close by has my name on it, that I can tell you."

"Well then, if that's all you have for me, you better head

on down before the hot bath gets cold." He didn't crack a smile when he said this. "Oh, one more thing. Sorry. Need to see some form of identification and your permits. Routine in a situation like this one."

Her companion responded. "Sure, of course. Hope she is found soon. Sorry we couldn't be more helpful, officer." He dropped his pack and dug into one of the side pockets. His companion did the same. Overly eager to end this encounter, they both shot their hands forward with the requested information.

The officer examined each permit and ID methodically, running his index finger under every word of the printed material. He looked up at the male and back down again at the photo and then up once more. He did the same for the female. Stanley Wendwork and Bethany Travis. He held the IDs up as if seeking a better light and continued to examine them. Finally, he gave the materials back to the couple. "Thank you. All seems to be in order. So, if anything comes to mind, I want you to report it to the rangers in the valley. Understood? Even the smallest detail could help. Okay?"

Her companion responded, "Will do, officer."

Closing his notepad and shoving it into his shirt pocket, he adjusted his waist belt, resting his hand on the gun's grip. "Safe travels and better luck next time." He stood to the side of the trail and let them pass. Once out of his sight, he took his notepad out of his pocket and took several descriptive notes of his impressions. The Body Cam captured everything else he needed.

1948-1950

Benny was right. Hellenia and her children were welcomed by the small community of mountain people with no questions asked. The assumption on their collective part was that the couple was husband and wife and was blessed by two beautiful children. Neither Benny nor Hellenia led them to believe otherwise. It was not part of any plan to deceive on their part. It just happened, a seamless and harmless weave into the community's fabric. Benny's acquaintances who knew him when he was a boy growing up in Shasta City and who had known his parents, now resting in peace, kidded with him one night at a community dinner, that they hadn't been invited to the wedding. Benny made light of it, joking that their mountain mules would buck at the notion of heading to the flatlands. They agreed that he had a point and that was the end of any wedding talk. Minding their own business, they didn't pry into Hellenia's background other than to ask if she had been born in the Santa Clara Valley and had she ever been to the mountains before. Confirming that she had been born there but had not been this far north in her life, everyone seemed perfectly satisfied, and the conversation turned to catching Benny up on all that had taken place in Shasta City since his family left for the valley seeking work a little over thirteen years ago when Benny was twelve.

The couple and the children lived in a small house on the northern edge of the town. The base of the volcano was within an easy stroll, and Hellenia made it a habit to take her children on this walk every day. Her growing fascination with Mt. Shasta led her to the general store more often than necessary. Harold, who owned the store, was a grandfather and a great grandfather. And he was also a living source of information for anyone who had the time to give him. His father had been a geologist and his grandfather an archeologist. From them, he knew enough about the local landscape and its history to educate Hellenia about the soil under her feet.

Harold had gone to college but had made a shameful mistake, and his family, demanding that he make things right, had had a terrible time accepting what he had done. The young lady, who had been his wife for sixty-one years and who passed on just the year before Hellenia and Benny arrived, became pregnant when they were both eighteen and both in their first year of college. Unable to continue with his education, he was forced to find work to support his young wife and soon to be born child. He never went back and neither did she. If you asked Harold if he had any regrets about how his life had turned out so far, he would say absolutely none. Well, one regret. That his Betty left without him. Not that he wanted to rush anything, but at his age, seventy-nine, soon to be eighty, she wasn't that far ahead of him, he would add with a chuckle. He was sure that he would catch up with her one of these days. His humor was never lost on Hellenia who proved to be the perfect audience for Harold.

Perhaps she reminded him of one of his daughters who all had left Shasta years ago for the big city where they raised their own families. Where they were so busy with their lives that a trip north to visit never seemed to work out. And, although Hellenia's memories of her own father were few, perhaps Harold reminded her of the gentle man who had freed colts that had wandered too far from their mothers. In any case, the two made a connection and fed each other's soul under the shadow of the mountain they called home.

In the year that followed their arrival to Shasta City, Benny did not pressure Hellenia to consummate the façade they had created and maintained. It was not easy for him as he grew beyond fondness for her and her children, out of respect for her situation, to a longing for more. He suspected that she had no desires for him. Nothing she said or did in the quiet of the evenings after the children were asleep and before he and Hellenia went to their separate sleeping areas gave him any indication that she might also be longing for more. He told himself that he could bide his time, that if it was meant to be it would happen. The last thing he wanted to do was ruin what they had established together. Judging by Hellenia's state of well-being, it appeared that she did not want that either. Caught between a rock and a hard place, he was unable to move forward or backwards in the relationship.

She felt it inside her before she confirmed it. She knew that her next period would not appear nor would any of them for at least another ten months. And when the date came and went with no signs of her menstrual cycle continuing uninterrupted, an uncanny calm settled within her. The baby growing inside of her did not immediately affect her. She felt no connection to it other than a growing resentment that it would demand of her system more than she was willing to give. But she knew she had no choice. Ending the pregnancy was not an option. Seeing it through was the consequence of her weakened, foolish state only weeks ago when Benny and she lay together for the first time. She contemplated such a union but never gave Benny any hints that this was the case. Too much to protect and maintain. Besides, she didn't love him. She respected him and was grateful for all that he had done for her small family, but nothing more. However, she longed for someone's touch again. To be caressed and loved. And because of this longing on both of their parts, the inevitable took place.

Soon her dreams were filled with Joe. Never of Benny. She woke in a soaking sweat feeling exhausted and confused. What she could remember of these dreams disturbed her, but she kept them to herself. And her waking hours were consumed with making plans. The one thing she understood clearly was that she would not tell Benny about the pregnancy. She could not do that to him. She could not pretend that she loved him, that this baby, his baby, would make her love him. He deserved to be loved again. Then her thoughts would hear Joe's complaints about another mouth to feed, would remember his angry exits and extended absences from her all because he wouldn't accept the consequences of their actions together. And what assurance did she have that Benny might not react the same way? How could she really know without revealing to him her secret? She wasn't willing to take the chance.

And when she thought she had made the decision to move forward, her two children who Benny treated as his own, plagued her thinking with their imagined protests. They wanted to stay. They wanted their mother to stay. They wanted Benny to be their father.

She had done this before. All too familiar. Much too easy. Having put her young son and daughter to bed, lingering with them longer than usual after they fell asleep, she bent down and kissed each one's cheek while breathing in their childhood scent one last time. As she rose from the bed, she felt something under her foot in the darkness of the room. Reaching down, she picked up her son's wooden horse and gently nestled it in his hands as he slept.

She slept with Benny until just after midnight. His sleep was deep and unconcerned. She envied him for that. Taking only one small bag that she packed earlier in the day, she left her children in the care of her companion whom she could trust to be their father. She took with her memories. She took with her an unborn child while taking from Benny what was his. She left behind what could have been the rest of her life had she been able to see that far.

When she delivered, she did not want to see the baby, did not want to hold it. The midwife told her it was a boy before Hellenia could tell her she did not want to know anything about the child. When asked who the father was, Hellenia said that she didn't know, leaving the midwife to draw her own conclusions about the exhausted young woman before her. When asked if she wanted to name him, Hellenia hesitated before responding. "Benjamin Wade," she whispered. The midwife, not understanding her, asked her to repeat the name. "Benjamin Wade," she said as her voice cracked, and the tears fell uncontrollably. Her sobbing could be heard in the next room of the little shack nestled in the trees that lined the bone-dry soils of the creek bed, patiently waiting for the winter rains to fill it and to quench the parched Santa Clara Valley's soil.

2016

The valley meadows were beginning to lose their lush pallet of green shades, giving way to golden shimmering grasses as the sun set behind Half Dome. The chill that fell onto the valley floor was sudden as was the growing darkness of the evening. Pete started later than planned, arriving in the park after dark. He had reserved a cabin in Curry Village for a week's stay. If he needed to stay any longer, he would. His thinking remained positive, and he fully expected that if she wasn't already there, she would be any day now.

Long past his concern about her reaction upon seeing him, he felt confident that when they connected, it would be okay. He had enough time to work through numerous scenarios as he drove east, always coming back to the most positive one.

Because of the hour, he decided to get a good night's sleep and check in with the park rangers in the morning. He knew that the situation had not changed or he would have heard. He only hoped that his being here would somehow send good vibes her way, bringing her back home sooner than later.

Even though he was sure that Zeke didn't want to hear from him, Pete had made sure to text him before he left, letting him know that he was heading back to Yosemite. With no response from Zeke, he let the issue between them take a back burner for now. The next move would have to be Zeke's anyway. Well, maybe not if…no…when Kit showed up. It was only right to let Zeke know. And maybe her parents? He wasn't so sure about that. The more he thought about it, the more he convinced himself that if anyone should contact them, it should be Kit. And he was certain that that was not going to happen. But it was none of his business. He could live with that.

The ranger on duty didn't have any information for him but told Pete to come back in a couple of hours. The officer who had information would be on duty then. But he reassured Pete that the Park Service was doing what they could within their jurisdiction.

Pete took advantage of the time to grab some breakfast

and then hike the Bridal Veil Falls trail, making sure to get back down in time to check in at the desk. He had forgotten how beautiful and treacherous this trail was. The last time he did it was at least ten years ago with a group from school. As he placed one foot in front of the other, noting the wettest rocks and avoiding them if he could, he felt the cool mist coming off the falls, covering his face and body in miniscule droplets of relief. Late October into early November this year saw some good storms come through the area keeping the falls fuller than in years past. As he considered this, his thoughts went to Kit. Had she got caught in any of the storms? Could that be a reason why she was late returning? He hadn't even considered the obvious until hiking this wet trail.

Looking at his watch, he decided that he wasn't going to make it up and back in time. As he headed back down the rocky trail, he imagined how easy it would be to slip, to lose his balance, to fall down a ravine or to hit his head on the rocks underfoot. Maybe sprain or break an ankle? He stopped, holding onto a small tree trunk for balance, all the while fighting off the negative thoughts that prevented him from going forward. Kit was playing with his mind, he knew. Taking many deep, slow breaths, looking up and all around him to center himself, she vanished. The path before him was doable if he kept his wits about him.

"What information I have is not much, I'm afraid." The officer pointed to a chair in the small office, inviting Pete to sit down. Pulling out a file drawer from his desk, he thumbed through the manila folders. "Okay. Here it is." Opening the folder, he studied it before addressing Pete any further. "Oh, wait a minute." He reached into his shirt pocket and pulled from it a small notebook, laying it next to the folder. "Okay. So, what I can tell you is that we haven't found her or any real sign of her." He stopped and looked back down at the folder.

Pete picked up on his word choice. "What do you mean by 'real sign of her'?"

"Yeah. I see where your confusion could be. Sorry about

that. No sign of her, is what I should have said. However, when I was up there a few days ago, I came across a couple of hikers and I questioned them. I met several folks heading off the PCT. None of them had seen Ms. Eagan or anyone matching her description. But this couple, well there was something about them. I can't put my finger on it, but I can tell you that they weren't being forthright with me. Can't prove it. Just a feeling."

"What makes you think that?" Pete controlled his growing frustration with the guy.

"Well, it's not a professional statement to make but they seemed nervous, anxious to be out of there. The young woman seemed especially nervous. I took some notes of my impressions of the two." He picked up the notebook, fanning through the worn pages. "Here. Yeah, like I said, nervous, female especially. Not clear about their whereabouts on the trail. Weren't sure where they were when they decided to turn around. Said somewhere near Lassen/Shasta area. I've got the conversation on my Body Cam."

"Can I see it, the video?"

"Sorry, no. Evidence if we need it." He closed his notebook and shoved it back in the shirt pocket. Taking out a pen, he turned to a blank page in the folder, dated it, and looked up at Pete. "So, if you don't mind, I've got some questions for you." He held the pen over the paper.

"Of course not. What do you need to know?"

"When you reported Ms Egan missing, you said that you left her. Is that right?"

Pete felt a sudden burn working its way through his body. Was he being accused of something? "Yes, that's right. I told the officer the background, I mean, what led up to me deciding to go my own way. Don't you have that information there in that file?" He tried to control himself, but he didn't like the position in which the officer was placing him.

"Something about not keeping up with her, I remember reading? Independent and could take care of herself, I think you told him?" He flipped through the first few pages of the report.

"Well, yeah. We planned the hike, but she was going on

it well before I met her. She kind of accommodated me, I guess you could say. That's what I meant by independent and taking care of herself."

"Okay. That makes sense. So, let me ask you this. Where did you leave her?" The officer did not look up but readied his pen.

"I think that is in the report. I remember telling the officer that it was somewhere around the Lassen/Shasta trail junctions. I remember hiking back down to a sign post and then heading west. I don't remember where I came out, but it took me about a week, I think. Yeah. A week. I hitched a ride to the rest stop on 5 before the 505 cut off and got another ride into the Bay Area."

"Did you hitch your first ride above or below the Shasta/Lassen area? I mean, did you pass Mt. Shasta on your ride south? You can't miss it." Now the officer was engaged with full eye contact on Pete.

"I really don't remember." Pete was panicking. He could feel his brain shutting down on him and he wasn't sure why.

"Who did you hitch your ride with?"

A simple question and one that brought Pete back to his senses instantly. "Eric, a truck driver." It was as though he was sitting in the cab next to Eric. The sounds, the smells, the highway running out in front of them for miles. "No wait, Eric… I can't remember his last name, but he gave me his address in Shasta City. Yeah, that's right. So, I must have hooked up with him north of Shasta because we were talking about where we were each from and he said that we had passed it." Pete suddenly felt at ease, that the truth he had been revealing to this officer might finally be convincing enough for him.

"Okay. That's helpful. Places you, in my mind, where the file indicates."

"I don't understand. Why is that helpful?"

"Well, it seems that that couple I mentioned to you did a turn-around in about the same area as you last saw Ms Eagan. You didn't see a male and female, in their early twenties up there, did you?"

"No, I didn't see a soul after I left her. Not until I got off the trail and hitched my ride with Eric."

"How long are you going to be up here, Pete?" He sensed a softening in the officer's voice.

"A week, at least. But I don't want to get in your way or anything. I mean, if it's better for me to be back home, then I can do that too. I just thought that when Kit comes in, I wanted to be here." He felt a tightening in his throat that took him by surprise.

"Good. You aren't going to be in anyone's way. I understand the need to be here. Of course. And it's your decision. Just let us know if you are going to head back so we can keep you informed."

"Yeah, of course. Thanks. And thanks for the information so far. So, do you think that this couple has something to do with Kit's not showing up?" He had held on to this question, afraid to voice it aloud but the officer had put him at ease.

"Well, we can't rule anything out." He said no more as he closed the file, placing it carefully into the desk drawer. "I know you already were asked, but I'm doing it again. If you think of anything that would be helpful, get in touch immediately. Even if you don't think it means anything. It could be the key to the whole mystery." As he stood, he reached out his hand to Pete. "Understood?" His palm, cold and dry, surrounded Pete's warm, damp skin in a firm shake. "Keep the faith, Pete."

1950

The midwife knew someone who knew someone else who might have work for Hellenia. Was she willing to settle down farther north? Up in Oakland? She wasn't sure what kind of work, but it had to be better than what Hellenia had now, fully aware that Hellenia had used her last cent to pay her. If she was interested, this someone up in Oakland could arrange travel there for her.

Hellenia, still weak from the birth, knew she had no choice. She had created a situation for herself that had no way out without help. Coming back to the Santa Clara Valley to have this baby was a purposeful decision. Distancing herself from Benny and her beautiful children who, in her mind, were no longer hers, a result of her decision to abandon them, was the only reason for coming here. No. Not the only reason. This was the only home she knew, and she longed to be cradled in the valley's fertile arms. And Joe? She would never consider seeing him again or the land she had been raised upon. By her own doing, she had soiled not only her own life but that of four other people. Joe and Benny would survive her transgressions, but she worried about her son and daughter, still too young to understand and so vulnerable to others' interpretations of their mother's decision. This new baby, at least, would have a fresh start with no knowledge of his biological parents, a decision Hellenia had signed her name to. And she agreed to have no further knowledge of him. A clean separation, unlike before. Yes, she would be grateful for any work. Going north did not concern her. Her desire to be in the valley, even for a short time, had been met and Oakland, a place she had only heard of, might not be that bad. She was not in any position to do otherwise.

*

No one had seen Joe for weeks. The last time he came into town was to buy supplies as he always did. He shared pleasantries with the shop keepers and a passerby or two who recognized him by name, but he never lingered for long, eager to head back to the ranch, it seemed. By now, most of the locals had heard about Joe and Hellenia and what she had done to him. Taking his babies right out from under his nose, leaving him alone. The poor fella. Never asked for help from anyone. Where she went was still a mystery. Some say that she stayed right in town while others knew she had left the valley. No one knew the truth, but the story of her and the children's whereabouts was beginning to have the makings of a real legend.

When Joe was found by the police, his shotgun barrel still imbedded in his gaping mouth, the intrigue that fueled this couple's woes turned on its heels. Shock and disbelief with a good dose of guilt became the story of the day, one that didn't have staying power, not like a legend, so disturbing was it. So, the locals did not speak of the couple again and if asked by some stranger who wanted to know if what he had heard was true or not about a suicide on the ranch down on Lawrence Station Road, they all agreed to respond the same way. "Guess you'll have to ask someone who knows."

*

The headline caught her eye as she passed the newsstand. Stopping to read further, the young boy reminded Hellenia to purchase the Oakland Tribune. No freebies. She did and stood to the side of the stand. "Santa Clara Valley Rancher Takes Own Life". She had no reason to read further. But she did, knowing full well that her life was about to unravel once again.

2016

She would never be able to tell anyone why she made the decision to head toward the wilderness isolation area of the park. Kit had been within a mile of her destination, her ending point, of what had been the longest trek she had taken so far in her life. But she knew that what she had started was not finished. There was more to the trek than just the miles racked up. Every step she took was one more opportunity to heal herself.

When she reached Tuolumne Meadows, she took stock of herself physically and mentally. Strong and tired, but with a decent rest, she knew that she could go on. She had to go on. The healing was not done. The longer she was alone, the weaker the façade of her own creation became but not enough to collapse it so that what would finally remain would be nothing more than Catherine Eagan. Catherine, before she knew how to hurt people so deeply. Catherine, before she had let time seal so completely the walls that enclosed her, separating her from everything she knew to be right and true and from those whom she loved. She was not ready to face them. Any of them.

It briefly crossed her mind that not showing up at the lodge as planned would be of concern. She didn't allow herself to consider the consequences as she knew what they would be. Pete and Zeke were unsubstantial encounters along her life journey, and she convinced herself that she was the same to them. They might hang out for a while, but would make their assumptions about her, all negative, she was sure, and head back to the valley. And there was no one else of any real importance to consider.

Making the decision to head out once more, she needed to resupply. The campers' store was nothing more than a stop-over point to do just that, and it gave her the opportunity to have a decent meal, non-dried food, and to purchase a topo map of the isolation area. Checking the weather reports, she was told that the storm season was here and that heading out there was not advised unless you were a seasoned trekker. Even then, not such a smart decision. But the trails were not closed yet and, yes, there were a few folks still out there. She was told to get a permit before going in.

There was only one person who saw her last. The store clerk was helpful as the officer questioned him. Checking the records of all permits registered for all areas of the park, the officer had confirmed that a Catherine Eagan carried one for the PCT portion and, most recently, had registered for the wilderness isolation area. Date of departure and date of return in order. Relieved to know that she was still in the park and alive, he had enough information to report good news to Pete.

Upon hearing that Kit's whereabouts was known, Pete was relieved. He held his tongue, though, when the officer informed him. Just like Kit, true to herself and no one else. He refused to let this good news, ironically ruin his day.

"Well, that's really great news. Thanks for all your efforts. I guess I'll just wait to hear from her when she gets back." He knew that he wouldn't hear a thing. And that was fine with him. Time to get on with his own life.

THE MURPHYS

The Santa Clara County birth records recorded that Benjamin Wade, born on March 10, 1950, was adopted by James and Barbara Murphy on March 20, 1950. His biological mother was Hellenia Wade. No known biological father. The Murphy's were childless, unable to have their own, and were thrilled to take baby Benjamin home with them to their ranch whose acreage spread for miles, north, south, and west at the base of the east hills within an easy drive into the town of San Jose.

Now a well-established spread, dating back to the early 1800's before California joined the union in 1848, it began as a two-room cabin used for hunting the plentiful wildlife in the area. Deserted for many years, the cabin remained standing and was part of a land deal made by Edward Murphy, young and single, venturing west to seek his fortune in gold. He carried with him his inheritance money from his father and, unlike so many others, wisely invested in land first before seeking further fortune. He soon married the love of his life and a small flock of children followed. As was the case for many of the land holders in the valley at the time, upon the death of one or both parents, the land was passed down to the oldest child which, in this case, was a son. The ranch thrived under the careful eye of Edward's eldest son and his wife as well as their own flock. The Murphy ranch continued to grow with each passing generation.

Now James and Barbara Murphy found themselves struggling to maintain the ranch in the 1950s, an era in the valley that had one foot in the past while the other was testing the waters of the future. The couple was painfully aware of what was happening to some of the other ranchers in the area. The temptation to sell out to builders of tract homes that were beginning to dot the valley spreading into the west foothills and out along Lawrence Station Road, was more than some could resist. The promise of more money than they had seen in a lifetime of farming and ranching convinced many of them to give up, to abandon what had been in their families for generations. Besides, their own children had no interest in caring for the land that was their birthright. Other careers called to them, both in the valley and far away. This was true for their son, Benjamin, who wanted to go to college. He had his heart set on becoming a doctor and his parents understood. His adoptive paternal grandparents, Lucas and Tilly Murphy, had set aside plenty of money for their only grandson, perhaps having the foresight, at the time, that so many did not seem to possess.

With that money, Benjamin became of doctor of internal medicine and along the way, met and married Martha (Marty) Aimes. They, too, had only one son, before they tragically lost their young lives in an auto accident in 2000. Their son was only fourteen when they were taken from him. The only willing relative to care for him was his mother's sister, Aunt Emily, who adopted him without hesitation. Peter Wade-Murphy, devastated by the loss of both parents, was saved by Aunt "Emee", who silently struggled with the loss of her sister and her sister's best friend. Together, Peter and Aunt Emee survived so that Peter went to college and was now finding his way in the world.

2016

He climbed up into the cab. He was already missing the time he had spent at home, a short three-day respite from the road. It was an unsettling feeling for Eric. Usually, he was ready to get back on the road, a sense of adventure luring him along. But not this morning. Physically, he felt rested. No aches. No pains. The leg would take him, once again, to the Long Beach docks, a run made so many times before. A piece of cake, he would say to himself. But something nagged at him, and if he believed in this kind of thing, premonition or something like that, he would have taken the time to think things through. But he wasn't one of those young folks in town who believed in the spiritual and mystical path to living. Granted, he lived in a place that drew people like that to it, and he even knew the folks who owned the gem and mineral shops on Main Street. But a believer he was not. Anyone in town would tell you that no more a practical and pragmatic fellow could you find among the residents of Shasta City than Eric Terner.

Whatever was bothering him, he pushed aside as he started the engine. His stash of sodas and pretzels in place, he slowly pulled out of town heading south on Interstate 5. The next time he would be home would be at least two weeks. He had managed to tag on another run midway on his way back north after he delivered in Long Beach. The extra money always came in handy. Not a spender, more frugal in his approach, his bank account reflected a comfortable savings balance, just in case. Enough to get by on for a year, at least, he figured, if he needed.

With the seasons changing, the mountain passes could be treacherous. An early winter rain storm in the flatlands could bring a heavy snowfall in the Siskiyous. It had been more than once that he had had to pull over, chain up, and lose time either waiting for the worst to pass or continuing south but with an abundance of stressful driving ahead of him. He knew his rig and could handle it in these conditions, but he couldn't account for the other guys on the road. Not really any different, if he thought about it, than driving in beautiful dry and sunny weather on the LA freeways. The weather reports did not indicate anything but smooth sailing for this trip, and he was grateful for the good timing.

The kid came to mind as he pulled into the rest stop. He hadn't thought about him at all until this moment. Recalling having shared his food with him, Eric wondered if he ever did get a ride to where he was going. Most likely. Nice kid, just starting his young life. So far on the other end of it all, Eric felt suddenly sad. Regretful. If he could do it all over again, how different would his life be? Completely, he was sure. But he couldn't and all that he had left now was the time allotted him. Not enough time to accomplish anything, he figured.

His father had done everything he could to give Eric and his sister a normal life. Besides growing up in a small town so far from the action, it had been safe, comfortable, and healthy. He and his sister, along with their friends, would spend hours outside before and after school. And in the summer months, if their father didn't need their help with house chores, would be out playing right after breakfast until home for dinner. The evenings were family time. Stories were read aloud, mostly by their father but many times, he would hand the book to either his sister or Eric and they would continue the reading, many times late into the warm evenings or until one of the listeners started to doze. He had so many good memories of his father. When he was young, his friends would ask about his mother. Did he have one? Why not? Where is she? How could you have been born then? Kid questions that his father had taught him the responses to. You have a mother, but she died when your sister was born. You had only just turned three when she left us. She is up in heaven with God. With those responses given, their friends were satisfied.

His sister grew to hate everything about growing up in "the sticks" as she referred to her childhood home. She couldn't wait to go off to college and make something of herself. She assured her father that she would not be coming back to the mountains to live. To visit, of course, but never to live here again.

Her father understood her need to see the world, but the hurt that she caused him settled deeply into his heart and only festered. With no visits, no calls, no indication that she even cared about him at all, he considered her dead, as she must have considered him. Eric had tried to console his father. He had tried to do the right thing by not abandoning the man who had nurtured him, cared for and loved him deeply. And Eric could not understand his sister's behavior. He had an even harder time forgiving her for what she had done to their father, to him, to their family. And so, Eric found himself staying with his father. He took care of him, as any child should. He let the world pass him by because family was more important. His resentment and anger toward his sister grew as the years went by, and he finally understood why his father considered her dead to him. Eric believed the same. When his father died, the town mourned his loss along with Eric. Their support and love were akin to his own father's love for his children, so rashly thrown away by his daughter, so fervently cherished by his son.

The rift in this little family never healed. The last time he saw his sister was in the summer of 1966 as she left for college. A boy she had met at some high school gathering was giving her a ride south to San Jose. She had purposely kept him from her father and Eric, only to intensify her departure even more for her small family. No long hugs, no kisses. Just a dramatic statement, something about being "glad to be out of this hell-hole" accompanied her slamming of the front door. Neither Eric nor his father moved to open the door and call to her one last good-bye. What was the point?

1951

She was grateful for the job in the laundry. It paid barely enough for her to get by, but she managed. The woman who ran the boarding house took a liking to Hellenia and after every dinner meal, would purposely keep some extra food aside for her tenant. She said that she was concerned about her health. So thin and pale. She told Hellenia that she needed meat on her bones so that she could go to work to pay her board. Hellenia never refused, silently worried about her weakened body after the birth of the baby. This birth had been difficult and had taken its toll on her. She did not eat or sleep properly after she signed the papers, lying awake night after night imagining her little boy crying out for her from some other woman's arms. The only sleep that came to her was out of pure exhaustion, her tears and stifled sobs subsiding for a while.

She knew that she wasn't happy. The burden of guilt that she carried was of her own doing, and she feared making more mistakes to add to what was becoming an unbearable weight. She moved through each day the same way. Afraid. Afraid of turning a corner in this busy town only to run into Benny dragging behind him her abandoned children. Or to see Joe sitting in a coffee shop, staring out the window, making eye contact with her, freezing her in place. Or to hear a baby's tortured cries as a new mother, awkwardly attempting to sooth him, silently pleads with Hellenia to take him back.

The newspaper fell from Hellenia's shaking hands to the sidewalk and the strong winds off the bay caught it, whipping it up and down until separate sheets blew in multiple directions with no possibility of easy retrieval. She didn't hear the newsstand boy yell at her or the quarrelsome traffic just feet from where she stood frozen in place. Unaware of the people all around her rushing to work, as she should have been, Hellenia, became an obstacle in their path. It wasn't until a woman bumped into her as she avoided a large man coming the other way. The human contact brought her to her senses, propelling her from the past into the present. She turned to apologize but the woman had moved half way down the block, her rushed pace no more so than all the others who knew where they were going.

It would only be a matter of time, she was convinced, that someone would approach her. After all, how many Hellenias could there be? Such an unusual name. She had not revealed anything about her past to anyone. Not since she left Benny. Using her maiden name, she convinced herself that she had taken precautions. But she was naïve. When she read the article, she gasped to see "...his wife, Hellenia Terner formerly Hellenia Wade..." in print. Still trying to comprehend that Joe had taken his life, she panicked, but her body would not cooperate with her decision to flee. A decision all too familiar with one difference. She had no control. It was not a decision of her own making. This was forced upon her, abruptly and unintentionally.

She did not go to work but returned to the boarding house, surprising the landlady who insisted that she go right to bed. She was convinced without Hellenia saying a word that her prediction about Hellenia's health was ringing true. Did she want any hot soup, tea? Hellenia politely refused the concerned woman's offer and said that she just needed some sleep.

As the afternoon grew long, Hellenia gathered what little belongings she had acquired slipping them into a small cloth bag that she had taken from the laundry. Timing her exit from the boarding house while the woman was in the kitchen preparing the evening meal, Hellenia came quietly down the stairs, slid out the front door, and momentarily stopped on the sidewalk wondering if going north was better than going south. She chose to go north.

2016

At one time in her young life, Kit would have told anyone who asked, "How far are you going?", that she had no idea. She would know when she got there. Looking at the topo map and the options she had, she suddenly felt old. Not old as in ancient but tired old. Her third decade had caught up to her faster than she ever imagined it would, and the passing of time suddenly weighed heavily on her. She knew that she could complete what she was setting out to do, but this time she accepted that it might be more of a challenge. Granted, having hiked over twelve hundred miles and now adding to it at least another hundred or more, her body had every right to complain, not to mention her common sense. And, for once, she took the time to listen. But she found herself between another rock and a hard place, not an unfamiliar place for her. She wanted to be sure of herself. Another shocker to her system, she realized. When had she ever questioned her confidence in decision making?

Her reasoning told her that she should go for it since she was already here. The trailhead was in sight, her pack resupplied, and her body physically in good shape. Some fatigue still lingered, but she reminded herself that she was at a higher elevation than she had been on the PCT. She would have to acclimate slowly.

As she set out on the trail, she ignored an unintelligible nagging that bubbled almost to the surface of her consciousness only to simmer, nonthreatening.

*

She didn't tell her husband about Peter's call. She knew what his reaction would be, and she didn't have the strength to battle him once more. Her daughter was no longer her daughter. Kit had made that perfectly clear. And Jean Eagan's stubbornness was fueled by an unspeakable hurt by and a resentment of her only child. The two of them were too much alike.

David Eagan was trapped in a marriage that had turned viciously sour. He was not allowed to love the two women in his life who meant everything to him. He crossed the line with Jean when he reached out to his wayward daughter. In retaliation, Jean removed herself from the marriage in its truest sense while refusing to permanently leave it and David behind. David accepted the situation offering no defiance. All the while, they kept up appearances. None the wiser, their acquaintances and friends enjoyed the company of the lovely couple and looked forward, as did her parents, to Catherine's visit, hopefully sometime soon.

In the early hours of the morning, long before sunrise and long after David had fallen asleep, Jean, once again, rose from their bed. Silently slipping out of the room, closing the door behind her, she made her way to the living room. Still in the darkness, she arranged the throw pillows, slid the afghan over her as she reclined on the couch, the pillows caressing her head against the couch's arm. She waited, staring into the blackness of the ceiling. She waited. And when Catherine appeared, the infant was nestled in Jean's arms. As Jean lay on the couch, she folded her arms around her, feeling her baby daughter's warm body against her own. She rocked from side to side, silently humming a lullaby until the tears formed, burning her lids, until she could do nothing but let them fall as her baby girl vanished from her arms into the darkness of the night.

*

    The semi, unseen because of the raised highway on the southbound side of Interstate 5, and the Valiant, on the lower northbound portion, simultaneously passed by one another. Eric's rig was just another semi on the highway heading south through the mountain passes. Hellenia's Valiant was just another old clunker heading north through the same mountain passes. Had this happened ten miles north or south, Eric, if paying attention and not reaching for his soda and pretzels, would have taken notice of the old Valiant.

*

The weight that had Pete in its clutches was lessened by the ranger's latest report. He sat in his car deciding his next move. It was hard to leave this valley in Yosemite when he thought about where he needed to be. In another valley where his work was, where his current life was unfolding, where open wounds needed his attention. He had no choice. He needed his job. He needed to be a responsible adult. He had done the right thing by coming up here but there was no more he could do here. He could not avoid what he had not done right any longer. Before calling Zeke, he felt obligated to call Kit's parents with the update about their daughter. He couldn't believe that they wouldn't welcome the call, no matter what her mother's detached impression would imply.

Her father answered. He asked Pete to call back on his cell and not use the landline. The conversation between Pete and David Eagan was brief. Her father was overjoyed to know that she was all right, that she was still in Yosemite. Pete asked him to let her mother know since his last call to her was upsetting news. David Eagan, avoiding a direct response, thanked Pete once again and hung up.

Still sitting in his car, Pete's second call was to Zeke. He had toyed with the idea of texting him but felt on a roll having just gotten off the phone with Kit's father. Pete was ready to hear Zeke's voice. His call went to voicemail. Pete played with the idea that Zeke was not answering having seen who was on the other end. So, he called again. And again voicemail. He redialed several times, a growing anger within, as he imagined Zeke holding his phone while purposely aggravating Pete. His imaginings now his reality, he decided not to play Zeke's game, never leaving a voicemail. He was done with this. Zeke could make the next move.

As he drove west, away from the park and back to the valley, he tried to relax and enjoy the time alone. His mind wandered as the miles passed by. Coming down the final grade into the San Juaquin Valley, a sudden urge to turn around and head back into the mountains surprised him. Not because of Kit. He was sure of that. And he almost did until he saw the sign for I-5 North. A stark reminder of his reality.

As Pete entered the freeway, he did not see Eric's semi barreling down the southbound side. He wouldn't have recognized it if he had. But the fact was that this freeway, stretching from Washington state's border with Canada to the California border with Mexico, provided three souls a passageway to their individual destinations, not only binding them together as fellow travelers, but also, momentarily, to their shared past. They traveled unaware.

*

Kit had been hiking less than two days, taking it slowly, until her body gave her a sign that she was acclimated enough to continue. She made a promise to herself to go no more than a week on this extra leg but was now having second thoughts. The beauty of the high country astounded her. In the presence of massive granite outcroppings, so near that she could touch the cold hard surfaces, to those in the distance, she felt not only alone and isolated from the world below but also insignificant. She likened herself to a creature smaller than an ant and even then, not small enough in comparison to the immensity of mother nature's creation. She was sobered by her surroundings. For a moment, she toyed with the idea that God does exist.

A lingering headache was her only complaint. It started in the morning as she was heating water for tea. Assuming it was a symptom of the altitude change and her acclimating to it, she took two aspirin from her med kit and swallowed them down with water from her bottle. But as the day wore on, the throbbing in her temples intensified. Forced to stop early, she found an area off the trail that would serve her well for the night. An almost flat surface surrounded by three granite outcroppings, all of which were at least fifteen feet tall. A perfect sheltered area, she marveled. Her head hurt her too much to think about eating. She dug the med kit out once again and found the small container of Advil. She took three, more than the dosage called for, but she was becoming desperate to have this ailment gone. She would sleep it off, she decided.

As she stretched out on her back in her bag, she closed her eyes willing the Advil to flow quickly through her blood stream and attack the enemy within. Unable to lie on either side as the pain in her temples intensified when she tried, she returned to her back and waited. Taking deep breaths to calm her body, she tried to let her mind drift to a stark white blankness. No thoughts were allowed to enter the clean whiteness. And when they tried, she forced them away by substituting more whiteness. She felt herself drifting off into a murky darkness, an unseen weight pushing her farther and farther down into the dark.

She never felt it. Had she been upright, hiking, or preparing her evening meal, she would have noticed something was not right. Perhaps her hand would refuse to hold the spoon as she stirred her soup. Perhaps her arm would refuse the command to move it away from the flame. Perhaps her mouth would refuse to close after falling open. But in her sleep, her brain slowly flooding with blood, the aneurysm shut down her life slowly but surely.

1951

"Have you ever been north of here, Hellenia?" the older woman asked. She had worked at the laundry for over twenty-five years, starting when she was younger than Hellenia. Born in Oakland, she had regaled Hellenia with the history of the place, the changes she had seen so far, and the mixed feelings she had about those changes. If she could, she would get out of here. Find someplace "real quiet and peaceful. I'd like to die in a place like that," she mused as the steam from the iron presses filled the space between them.

"Is there a place like that that you have in mind?" It passed the time to converse with her, all the while keeping an eye out for the floor supervisor.

"If I had the money, I'd quit today. Buy myself a bus ticket to Dunsmuir. Up in the mountains. I've seen pictures of it. It's a busy little town but there are places to buy hidden away off the highway and away from town. But not so far that you can't just walk to town when you wanted to." Through the steam, Hellenia could see her eyes light up.

"Is it far from here?" Everything seemed so far from anything she knew.

"No, not really. Real close to Shasta City. You ever heard of it? Or Mount Shasta?"

Hellenia felt her legs give a little as she grabbed onto the edge of the press for support. "No. I don't think so," she lied. She knew that she was going to be sick, the nausea intensifying with every heavy breath she took.

"Honey, are you alright? You don't look so good." The woman, afraid to leave her station, leaned over as far as she could towards Hellenia. "I'll call the supervisor."

"No! No. Just haven't eaten today and not been sleeping all that well lately. It will pass." Hellenia forced herself to take even shallow breaths as she moved out of the steam's heat. She didn't care if the supervisor saw her. Grabbing a towel tucked into her apron, she wiped her forehead and face, keeping the towel in place for a moment. She needed to regain her control.

"Are you sure?" The concern in the woman's voice was sincere.

Feeling a sense of normalcy returning, Hellenia reassured the woman. "I'm feeling much better now. Just needed to cool down, I guess."

"And you need to eat, young lady. Here." She reached into her apron pocket and stretched out her arm. Her hand held a small orange and apple. "Take 'em. Quick." She made an urgent but slight shoving gesture towards Hellenia. "Take 'em!" she whispered.

Hellenia didn't think twice but reached for the fruit and tucked them into her own apron pocket. "Thank you. But what are you going to eat?" Hellenia was truly concerned for her.

"You never mind about that. I ate today. And anyway, got more stashed under here." She looked down toward her plentiful chest. A wry smile appeared through the puffs of steam. "You be sure to eat them at the next break, you hear me?"

"Of course. You are very kind."

"Better get back to work or neither one of us will get a break." The woman turned away from Hellenia, focusing intently on the heated monster in front of her.

*

If asked, Hellenia could sum up who she was with little thought - a person with no staying power. Unreliable, selfish, and not one to be given a chance to prove otherwise. As Hellenia purchased the Greyhound bus ticket, she reinforced this description. She didn't deserve anymore chances, she convinced herself. Sneaking out of the boarding house without giving the woman the curtesy of a "thank you" and without paying what she owed for the week, nagged at her. Buying the ticket to Dunsmuir with the woman's rightful money, however, was Hellenia's only way out, once again. This time, though, the danger she felt was very real. They had given her no choice.

She asked at the ticket counter. "How far is Dunsmuir from Shasta City?"

The agent told her just a little less than ten miles. "Spitting distance," he laughed. "You want a ticket for Shasta City instead?"

She thanked him, but no. Dunsmuir was her destination. As she sat in the bus, waiting for its departure, mixed feelings raced through her mind. What on earth did she think she was doing? Was she just asking for trouble? So close to them. So easy to be discovered. Why was she taking such a chance? But she knew. She knew what was drawing her back and she was sure that the laundry woman was a sign. She was put in Hellenia's path to show her the way. It all made perfect sense until she played an imagined scenario in her head of seeing them again. Of trying to explain herself but finding she didn't need to because they accepted her back with open arms and love. That was the version she longed for, she realized, but the second version was her reality. There would be no welcoming, no tears of joy, no forgiveness.

As the bus pulled away, her body tensed. She started to get up, willing her legs to take her down the narrow aisle to the driver and demand that he stop the bus. She needed to get off. Instead, she stared out the window as Oakland, her betrayer, slowly passed from view.

1949

Benny made his decision. He would ask Hellenia to marry him. In the time that they had been living together, he never considered marriage. Without word spoken between them, he accepted their arrangement without complaint. But everything was different now. They had shared his bed and consummated their relationship. Hellenia did not go back to her sleeping area after that first night together. Although no words of love passed either of their lips, Benny knew what he felt. For the longest time, he was afraid to tell her of his growing love for her. He was afraid that she would do to him what she had done to Joe. But he reasoned that this relationship was different He knew the right thing to do despite his unreasonable fears.

He awoke earlier than usual to find that Hellenia had awoken even earlier, her side of the bed empty. His excitement about the day ahead had not let him sleep soundly. He had dreamt so many scenarios in his mind of his proposal, all ending with her saying "yes". He wondered if he had forced her out of the bed with his tossing and turning. He made his way to the children's room to find them fast asleep. As he moved down the hall to the kitchen, an uneasiness descended upon him, so quiet was the house. In the first moments of the morning, he fought off what he feared was the inevitable.

As the morning wore on, the children at his feet asking for their mother, he felt as if he was caving in upon himself. He no longer heard their crying for her. Did not feel them tugging on him for comfort. When the evening came, with no word from her, and no one in town having seen her that day, he struggled to accept the reality he now faced. Through his tears, he managed to make out Eric and Jean, cuddled together on the living room couch, having cried themselves to sleep in the dimming light of the long day. Benny watched them, envying them their peace, fleeting as it would be. He sat down next to them, exhausted and destroyed, and before closing his own eyes, he picked up the wooden horse that had fallen from Eric's small hand and tucked it between the sleeping babies.

2016

Pete answered his cell. The officer who had dealt with Pete about Kit's whereabouts spoke gently and slowly. Any official tone was humanely avoided as he let Pete know that Kit's body had been found. Unable to immediately respond, Pete sat down heavily into his office chair. His words formed slowly. "What do you mean? Her body? What do you mean?" He knew but could not fathom his meaning.

"She, Kit, was found just off the trail. It appears to be by natural causes. No sign of foul play or animal attack. She appeared to be asleep in her bag until someone checked on her on their way north. I am sorry for your loss, Pete. The authorities have taken her body to the coroner's office in Merced. I can meet you there, if you like. Does she have any next of kin that we should contact?"

It was unreal to him. He felt completely separated from the officer, his message, Kit, as if he was reading about a stranger in the news who had come to unfortunate end. He couldn't engage the way he knew he needed to and it frightened him.

"Pete? Pete? Are you still there?" The officer's concerned voice got through to Pete.

"Yes, yeah."

"Good. Okay. If you can tell me any next of kin?"

"Yeah, sure. Her mom and dad." He fought the confusion that insisted on cluttering his thinking.

"Good. Their names? Phone numbers?" The officer's voice was patient and steady.

"Uh, their names…uh, uh." All he could remember was the sound of their voices.

"It's okay. Take your time." Still reassuring and kind.

"David and Jean Eagan. I've got her dad's cell number." Pete brought up the number and gave it to the officer. He suddenly remembered his last call to the house and her father's request that he not call the landline. "Yeah. That's the best way to reach them." He could only imagine the devastation on the end of the line when her father learned the news.

"Thanks, Pete. I need to get ahold of them right away. Will you be coming up to Merced?"

"I'm not sure." He hesitated before he spoke further. He wondered if her parents would go. And if they did, he didn't want to be there. "I think it's best that her parents are the only ones there." He hoped he was right.

"Of course. I'll keep you informed if anything else turns up or is needed from you. I really am so sorry, Pete. You take good care, then."

"Yeah. Thanks. Thanks for your call. You too."

As he walked to his car, all his senses still numb, he stopped short in his tracks. The moving shadow overhead drew his attention to the sky. Looking up, he was blinded by the sun's light and blinked away its offensive intrusion. Then he heard it, a screech so familiar yet so out of place. It continued for minutes, growing in its intensity and nearness, until Pete turned away from the sun's penetrating sting, focusing his eyes on the sky all around him. It appeared just above him, swooping and screeching, again and again. The red tail hawk, not an unfamiliar sight further into the hills that surrounded the valley, was a rare sight in the busiest part of downtown San Jose. But there it was, just above him. In the terrain where it should have been, its behavior would be explained easily. Protecting a nest close by from predators only it could see. But hawks didn't nest in the city. At least that is what he thought. But maybe he was wrong. When the bird swooped down so close to him that he felt the air move against his face, he ducked and stayed low. The bird was attacking him, he was sure. He covered his head with his arms. His instinct to flee did not kick in. He had the opposite reaction. He stayed in place, still, anticipating the wild bird's next move.

The unexpected occurred, however. The screeching stopped. The air around him became deathly quiet. He lowered his arms, propping his crouched body on the asphalt, and slowly looked up. It was nowhere in sight. It was as though none of this had happened. He slowly rose and approached his car. As he opened the driver's side door, he froze. There, on the hood, lay the red tail hawk. Its rust colored tail wing still outspread, it caught the sun's light and appeared almost golden. Its eyes were opened seemingly startled by its rude resting place. It lay on its side, unnaturally positioned, the result of its inability to control its landing.

Pete sat in the driver's seat. He closed the door. He had not moved the bird from the hood. Instead, he let it be. Pete observed it through the glass windshield. He studied its fading beauty, its still body. Each feather lay perfectly in place, those that he could see, the rest hidden under the bird whose impact against the steel hood must have destroyed them. He closed his eyes and silently sent a prayer somewhere for peace. Peace for David and Jean Eagan. Peace for Zeke. Peace for Peter Wade-Murphy. Peace for the wild bird. And peace for Catherine Eagan.

1951-1996

Hellenia found almost fifty years of peace and anonymity in Dunsmuir. She shortened her name to Helen but kept her maiden name. She found work where she could get it. In the first few years of living here, she struggled with the inevitable restlessness that had plagued her in the past. So many times, she almost left the town, but something held her back. She began doubting that there was any other path left for her but what was right in front of her. But as she aged, the struggle diminished. The longest she worked anywhere was at the Roadside Inn. Cleaning up after other people's messes, making their beds, and wiping down the showers became mechanical to her. But something about the routine of each day, never changing, always monotonous, appealed to her. She knew what to expect and what was expected of her.

She kept to herself or tried to. There were always the men who tried to get her into their beds and the women who wanted to be her best friend. But Hellenia kept them at a distance, especially the men.

The one-bedroom house that she rented was set back in the mountains that surrounded the town. She had no need to come into town other than her work and groceries. Spending time by herself away from others was time that she treasured. It gave her time to think; something that she did not always welcome. But as she aged, she found her memories were of a much younger Hellenia, a child again, a young girl, a married woman, her children. She allowed herself to wonder about the children she left behind, about the child she never knew, and she convinced herself that they were better off without her, without any knowledge of her, without her ever seeing them again. She whispered little prayers for each one of them during these private moments.

She had been tempted in her weaker moments to take a ride north. She would only drive through town and only after dark. She even convinced herself that it would be okay to drive by the house, just to see it one more time. Benny probably still lived there, but she figured the children had grown up and gone their separate ways as these modern young people do. And what would she do if Benny happened to see her drive by? Would she stop? Would she go to him with apologies and request forgiveness? No, she knew that she would not, could not. It was best to leave it all alone. To leave it as she did so long ago.

The manager pulled her into the inn's office after her shift. He informed her that she was no longer needed, that, due to her age, the work was too difficult. They had taken notice of her "sloppiness" because several guests had complained about their rooms. The manager assured her that she was well over the age to collect social security. Why she hadn't done it sooner, he couldn't figure. "But there you are," he informed her. "Best of everything, Helen," he pronounced as if giving her a final blessing.

2016

Zeke did not take the news about Kit well. Surprised by his emotional reaction, Pete didn't know what else to say to him. All this time, Zeke had seemed disinterested in Pete's and Kit's relationship. Any time Pete had mentioned Kit, Zeke had remained aloof and had managed to change the subject. It wasn't that he didn't like her, Pete realized now. It was that she was a threat.

Pete stayed on the line waiting for Zeke's sobbing to stop. And when it did, Zeke chose not to have a conversation "right now." Pete, sensing a tiny window of opportunity to make things right between them, suggested getting together. Maybe over a meal? To Pete's surprise, Zeke agreed to meet. He suggested the place where they had shared their last meal. Once again, Pete was taken aback. The last place he would have thought Zeke would want to go was back to that place. But nothing was making much sense to Pete lately.

Zeke was waiting for him at the same table. Two untouched beers waited also. Pete had put some thought into what he would say but even that minor effort seemed wasted as he approached Zeke. Zeke was slight of build but as he sat at the table, hands on his lap, his body relaxed and open, Buddha came to mind. Pete's lopsided grin at the thought did not go undetected by Zeke. Standing now, he reached his hand out to Pete. Pete did the same.

"Good to see you, man." Pete released his hand from Zeke's grip.

"You too." Zeke motioned to Pete to sit.

Words of any substance were not spoken immediately. Instead, each one took a long drink from the plastic steins in front of them. And then a few more. A waitress prolonged their separation as she asked for their order.

Zeke's strained voice, almost at a whisper, broke through Pete's numbness. "I'm really sorry about Kit. And I'm sorry about my behavior on the phone when you called. I don't know why I reacted that way. Sorry if I upset you even more." He only looked up after he spoke.

"No worries," Pete responded, catching Zeke's eye. "Nothing to be sorry for. Pretty shocking news to hear over the phone, or any way, I guess."

"Yeah. Right. Have you heard anything more since we spoke?" Zeke no longer avoided Pete's eyes.

"No, nothing. I thought that maybe her dad would let me know about any funeral arrangements. I mean, he was nice to me on the phone when I let him know that she was all right. You know, when we found out that she was still up there doing her thing."

"Maybe it's too soon. It's only been a couple of days, right?"

"Yeah, only a couple of days." To Pete it had been an eternity and he saw no end in sight.

"Who let her parents know? Please don't tell me you had to do it."

"The park police." Pete didn't want to rehash his conversation with the officer. As a matter of fact, he didn't want to talk about any of it ever again.

"Oh, right. Guess that makes sense. Got to be a horrible call to get."

The conversation ceased as both men fell back into their own thoughts. When the meal arrived, they consumed it in silence, breaking it only when Pete ordered two more beers. Feeling more relaxed as their buzzes deepened, it was only a matter of time until one of them found the courage to face their real issue.

"Pete?" Zeke leaned in to him. "You've been through a lot lately. I mean with the hike and separation and now Kit's death. So, I don't want to burden you more. I just want you to know that I've had some time to work things out." He paused, and Pete wondered if he should say anything. He chose to wait. "I was selfish not to be honest with you. And I was selfish when I walked away from you. But I'm not a bad person."

"Come on, Zeke. I know that. Why would you want to say something like that? Why would you even think it?" But Pete knew why, and he suddenly felt a strong connection to Zeke. His throat tightened unexpectedly as he asked the questions.

"For a long time, Pete, since I can remember, I knew that I wasn't like you or the other guys. Even when I was young, I knew. But I watched my dad and his friends and figured out how I was supposed to be. He always used to say that I was a quick learner, and I was, but not about what he wanted me to learn. I learned quickly how to act the part. In junior high, well, that was its own little hell. When I got to high school, I had to learn new lines, new choreography, new personas. You guys were great teachers, I've got to give you credit. And then something changed for me. When I met you, I felt good. I felt like I could handle this façade that I created to survive while secretly knowing that someday you and I might be something more than bros at the beach."

Pete had questions, but he knew to be silent, to let his friend release what had been held in for so long.

"And I spent most of the time scared to death that you would find out who I really was. And that made me try even harder to be the wise-ass, the jock that my dad is, the acceptable way to be a man." He took a long drink of what was left in his glass. "Another?"

Before Pete could say no, feeling no pain, Zeke jumped up from the table and headed towards the bar. Placing the full mugs down in front of them, Zeke continued.

"I don't hate my dad. But my dad hates me. Ever since I told him off. Not to mention telling him about who I am. Kind of put the icing on the cake."

Pete wondered when Zeke revealed the news to his father but remained patient.

"So now, I don't have a father and I'm not sure if I still have a friend." He stopped, picked up the mug and put it back down again without drinking from it. Looking up, he asked, "Do I still have a friend? No strings attached. Just a friend?"

Choosing his words carefully, Pete began. "Zeke, I have always been your friend." The temptation to remind Zeke that he was the one who tried to make contact when they parted ways, that all his phone calls and texts had gone unanswered, bubbled just below the surface, but his common sense and reasoning prevented him from plunging them both deeper into the crevasse from which they needed to ascend. "It doesn't matter to me who you are." His words stung them both. "No, that's not what I mean. I mean that you should be you. That is what matters to me the most. Just be who you know you are. Be yourself. It's not going to stop me from being your friend."

There was more to be said, Pete knew. He was aware of Zeke's calm, physical aspect but was frightened by what he could not see. What impact his words were having on the man sitting across from him. What he should be saying but hadn't thought of it yet. Zeke remained silent, just as Pete had done.

"But you need to understand that that is all I can be for you. Whatever you might think of me, know that much to be the truth. I can never be what you want me to be, Zeke. I am sorry." There. He had made it as clear as he could. He had no more to say.

Zeke remained silent long enough for Pete to consider the futility of his efforts.

"Pete, I know you have always been my friend. I knew it all along, but I refused to accept the reality of my own existence. I blamed you for everything, I guess. Guess when I did that, I couldn't see any truth in anything. But you know, there are more important things in life than being angry with yourself or anyone else. I was hurt, for sure. You were kind of the final slap in the face. But that was all my problem, not yours. I want you as my friend, Pete. That's all. I know that now. When you told me about Kit, something kicked in with me. Life's too short, man. Life's too precious to screw it up. If my life means that you and I continue to be friends, then that's precious to me." He stopped. Wiping away tears that he freely let fall, he waited.

Pete's tightening throat released in an audible heave as he realized that tears were welling in his eyes. Who was he crying for? He knew. For his own parents, for Zeke, for David and Jean Eagan, for Kit, and for himself. Zeke's words had penetrated deeply even through the buzz that had transformed into a state of drunkenness. But he knew it wasn't the beer that opened his heart. It was the realization that his young life was indeed something to be preserved, to be cherished, to be loved. His friend had just unburdened himself of his life's trials that Pete would never really understand. His own scars and recent wounds would remain concealed. Pete knew that he was not as brave as Zeke. Yet the two men found themselves finally on the same path; a friendship tenuously rebuilt, whose thin foundation was that of appreciation but not of real understanding. And only each man knew what that truly entailed and how far they each wanted to go.

1999

She didn't celebrate her seventy-fifth birthday. The day came and went just as the last five had. She did not lose count of her years. She did not forget her birth date. But she realized when she turned seventy-two, the last year that she worked, the year that she was reminded of her age and inability to do the job properly, that her time was running short. What she wanted to do with the rest of her life was the direct result of the mess she had made of it. She decided that she would keep to herself, live out her remaining days as she chose to do, and any human contact would be of her own choosing.

No longer able to afford the rent, she moved out of her little house tucked away in the hills of Dunsmuir. She considered herself lucky to have lived in the place for so long. The landlord had died five years ago, and his daughter took over the property. That was the only time in fifty years that her rent went up. And even then, it was still within her budget, but she knew that she was tempting fate by staying there. What kept her from living on the streets was her health but with each passing day, even that insurance was weakening. She could feel it. With no work to supplement her social security payment, finding a new place was impossible at her age. She couldn't afford it. She never complained to anyone about her predicament. It was no one's business but her own. She told the landlord's daughter that she needed to move on. And the daughter did not try to convince her otherwise. She had plans for the house. She wished Hellenia well and watched Hellenia drive away with what little belongings she owned stacked in the front and backseat of the white Valiant.

As time went on, Hellenia whittled down her property to only the bare necessities. Her belongings were neatly concealed in the trunk except for two boxes she kept on the back seat. She had every intention of finding another place, but her heart wasn't in it. So, the Valiant became her home as she joined the other homeless wanderers on the backroads and highways of northern California. The only connection she still had with Dunsmuir was the post office and the bank. Once a month, she collected her government check from her mailbox. Then she walked across the street and cashed her check leaving half of it in her savings account that she opened over fifty years ago. And each time, a cashier would try to convince her to do a direct deposit to ensure that nothing happened to her check, but she politely explained that she liked the way she did it. Been good enough for fifty years. It was good enough now. What she didn't tell them was that she secretly enjoyed the once-a-month visits to town. It was the only anchor she had to anything normal.

2016

For weeks after the funeral, he dreamed about Kit. Every night, she came to him. Sometimes, she was the girl standing in line the day Pete met her. The girl who made him laugh. The girl who seemed to have so much in common with him. The happy times. Most of the time, though, she was the girl heading up the trail without him; without a voice, without a face, without concern, without compassion. In his dream, he tried to catch up to her, his arms outstretched to grab her back, but he could never reach her as she turned a bend. In her place, his parents appeared coming down the same trail. His arms, still outstretched, were always ready to embrace them, to hold on to them. But they walked by him as if he wasn't there. No matter how loudly he yelled for them to stop, to see him, to embrace him, they walked on and disappeared around a bend. He tried to follow them, but his legs were motionless, lead weights. The fatigue he felt as he dreamed overwhelmed him and each time this dream appeared, he woke up from it, heart racing, as panic, frustration, guilt, and overwhelming sorrow so profound consumed him.

His work suffered. His concentration was limited, and the mistakes were beginning to be noticed by his supervisor and colleagues. At first, questions were diplomatically voiced, and his response was always the same. "Trouble sleeping." True statement, but he was told that it was not their concern. He needed to figure it out and get back in the game or he was no longer a player. The pressure of this ultimatum only added to his stress. He confided with no one at work, afraid that his questionable mental state would then be grounds for letting him go. Instead, he made the decision to leave. In good graces, his work history with the company reflecting his strong quality of work, creative contributions, and willingness to be a team player, he asked for referrals which were generous in their praise, while compassionately ignoring his most recent performance.

He considered seeing somebody about his state of mind. Each time he did, however, he reasoned that he knew what his issues were and that he needed to clear his mind, not confuse it even more with a professional's suggestions. Time heals all wounds, he remembered hearing. What Pete didn't realize was that his wounds were deeply imbedded, deeply imprinted beginning at birth. He had no reference to this as the sub-conscience can hide its secrets. What he did understand was the sudden loss of his parents and of Kit. That was enough for anyone to have to deal with, he reminded himself. He could work through this. He was sure of it.

With time on his terms now, he decided to go south for a week or two, to the desert. It seemed to him the right place to go to think, to clear his head, to find himself again. While repacking his backpack, he discovered the piece of paper, completely forgotten, tucked into a side pocket. The scribbled name did not ring a bell for Pete, at first. Not until he read the address. Shasta City. The truck driver who had given him a lift, shared his lunch, and some conversation with Pete now appeared as clearly as if he were right in the room with him. Suddenly, the desert wasn't inviting. Pete didn't believe in stuff like this, but he wanted to. The piece of paper was a sign. Long forgotten, here it was in front of him, offering him an option. No, more than an option. He was meant to head north, and Eric was there to guide him. He shoved away any logic that would insist on coincidence and, instead, made up his mind.

He waited patiently through Eric's greeting, anticipating that he would have to leave a message. He was probably on the road. He hoped that Eric would remember him and not delete his call.

"Hello?" The familiar voice surprised Pete.

"Hi. Hello. Eric?"

"Speaking."

"I don't know if you remember me but I'm Pete. Pete Wade-Murphy?"

"Who?" Eric's voice competed with the engine noise in the cab.

"I'm the guy you gave a lift to from up north to the rest

stop near 505. I was headed to the Bay area?" Pete began to wonder if he had made a mistake in calling.

"Hey, man! Pete. 'Course I remember you. You'd been hiking, right?"

"Yeah, that's right."

"Well, how the hell are you?" Eric's warmth, even through the phone, put Pete at ease.

"I'm doing fine," he lied. "How about you?"

"Can't complain. Heading back north right now. Home for a while." The fatigue in his voice was unmistakable.

"That's good. To be home, I mean." Pete's plan seemed to be dissolving before he could get it off the ground. The last thing the guy needed was someone bothering him at home.

"You're damn right. This last one was a long haul. Looking forward to some peace and quiet. So, what are you calling me for?"

Pete hesitated, wondering if he should end the call now. He didn't want to hear what he supposed was inevitable. "Well, I don't know if you remember, but you gave me your address and phone number."

"Sure, I remember. How else would you have gotten ahold of me?" Eric's laughter was light, gentle, like a father's loving correction of his son's innocent mistake. It gave Pete the confidence to go on with the call.

"When you gave it to me, you said that if I was ever in Shasta area, to come by." He paused, sure that Eric would interrupt him, reneging on his offer.

"That's right. I did. So where are you now?" his voice, still gentle and kind.

"Well, I'm in San Jose but I was wondering if you would mind some company? Just a day visit. I understand if it's not possible." He hoped that it was.

"You thinking in the near future or a ways off?"

"Well, I was thinking of heading out today. Maybe come by tomorrow or whenever works for you."

"Give me a night to recoup. What's today?"

Pete was quick to respond, his heart beating excitedly. "It's Thursday."

"Thursday…Okay. Why don't you come by on Saturday? Work for you? That way I got some time to do laundry and get the house in shape for a visitor."

"Saturday's great, Eric. Please don't go to any trouble for me. Just a visit. No overnight. I'll take you out for dinner." His generosity took him by surprise.

"No, man. You can stay with me. Save you an over-priced hotel room. And I make some damn good ribs. You a rib man?"

"Yeah, sure. That's really nice of you."

"Well, I guess I'm just a nice guy." His laughter was even warmer.

"So, I'll see you on Saturday. I'll call when I'm past Redding."

"Sounds good, Pete. You drive safe. Watch out for the other guy, okay?"

"Thanks, Eric. Will do. See you soon."

Pete hadn't felt this good in weeks. His excitement grew as he unpacked his desert gear. The desert would be there, he reminded himself. Another time. His new path was set. For once, he felt that he had some direction. He couldn't put his finger on it, but the connection he felt with Eric was comfortable and compelling. It would never occur to him that Eric would be more than the guy who once gave him a lift.

*

He had not had a single visitor in his home, other than the parade of neighbors who were allowed no further than the front door, offering him home cooked meals and desserts when his father passed away. That lasted for a good week or two. Eric couldn't remember how long now. He appreciated their efforts at the time but wouldn't be lying if he admitted that he was ready before the two weeks was up to be done with answering the front door. Eventually, he was left to himself, only seeing neighbors off and on when he walked down Main Street. Just enough to confirm that he was still alive and upright.

The thought of sharing his home with Pete was not threatening or disagreeable to him, much to his surprise. Having a young man in the house for a day or two would be a pleasant reprieve from the rut he knew that he had comfortably created. Besides, maybe he could get Pete to help him with some unattended to jobs, jobs he had been meaning to do since his father's passing. Heavy lifting and such. And the basement. He had stored all his father's belongings down there, including one sealed box with the crude lettering "Private" scrawled across the top. He just never got around to taking care of the stuff. Never home long enough to get started and too tired when he was home, was his excuse. Out of sight-out of mind.

His father's bedroom would be the guest room. The chest of drawers was empty as was the closet. Just a few empty hangers left on the railing. From the cabinet, he pulled out the set of sheets that had once been on his father's bed. Washed and stored, he still detected a musty smell to them. The blanket's smell was even stronger. The last time he touched this bedding was almost fifteen years ago, right after his father's burial.

Now, he began to smell the mustiness throughout the unused room. He opened the two windows that faced north and left them open until darkness fell. He did the same the next day. When he was satisfied that the freshly washed bedding smelled better and that the room was aired out, he made up the bed. How many times had he done so when his father was alive in the last few months of his life? Before placing the sheet on the worn mattress, he ran his hand over its surface, feeling the depressions, the high spots that once gave way to the form of his father's aging body. This bed knew Benny well, even after all this time.

*

Once a month, after she collected her social security payment, she headed north of Dunsmuir, about ten miles north. She had been doing this for the past seventeen years, without fail. Never in the daytime. Too easy to be recognized. Although no one who had known her then would, if they were still alive, know her car as she purchased it in Dunsmuir years ago. Besides, no one would recognize her, not any more. Too much life stacked up behind her. But she took no chances, just in case.

In the darkness, the Valiant slowly moved through town to arrive on his street, once their street. She slowly drove by the house. Never a light on, never a sign of life, she dared not linger as memories flooded her thinking. Passing by, she continued onto a side street and down an alley. Once a month, she parked for the night making sure that she left long before the first citizens of Shasta City rose. She was on the highway well before sunup.

But as time went on, her visits became more frequent. Nothing had changed as far as when she arrived and where she stayed for the night. Nothing had changed about departing in the darkness before dawn. What had changed was her need to be there. To be there for her babies, for her Benny. She was not so consumed with this need that she became lax and outstayed her visit. A watch could be set by Hellenia's arrival and departure. She wondered, once, if anyone had seen her approach and slow down in front of the house. She also wondered if anyone had noticed her baby parked in the alley. But as nothing had ever come of her visits, she assumed that she was invisible, untouchable, and very much alone.

She was unaware that someone had noticed the old Valiant, had noted its coming and going, had wondered who occupied its worn interior, homeless and, perhaps, alone among so many.

*

As promised, Pete called Eric as he passed the last exit for Redding. Everything was going fine, he told Eric. He should be up to him soon. Everything was ready for his arrival, Eric had assured him. Looking forward to seeing you, both agreed.

Pete had no trouble finding the house. It was almost impossible to get lost here, so few roads in town. He had been captivated by Shasta far in the distance as he drove north only to be upon it so soon, its perfect volcanic shape as he had imagined it. Snow still clung to its uppermost ridges in complete contrast to its stark dark volcanic surface. He had seen numerous pictures of it but none of them did justice to it.

Eric directed him to park along the street. He had been waiting on the front lawn for Pete. When Pete saw him, something inside of him softened, relaxed, and he took a long breath, slowly breathing out as he pulled up. Foolish to think it, he tried to dismiss the thought, but it lingered; that he was home.

The bedroom was stuffy, even though Eric had opened the windows. But Pete did not say anything, of course. Eric explained that it had been his father's bedroom. Pete didn't pry. Eric hoped that Pete would find the bed comfortable enough. Of course he would, Pete replied. It was still early enough for Eric to suggest a walk through town.

"Just don't blink or you'll miss it."

As they passed one storefront after another, Eric nodded to a few neighbors but didn't bother to introduce Pete even though the passing neighbors made a point of slowing down enough to do so. Pete gave them a tentative smile but never spoke. He followed Eric's lead.

Eric stopped in front of the double doors of a shop whose entrance was deeper than most of the other stores. "So, are you one of those folks who's into rocks? Gems?"

"Not sure what you mean by "into" but mother earth has always interested me. So, I guess you could say "interested", yes."

"You want to go in? There are some beauties in here. But only if you want to. To be honest, not much else to see along

here other than the sporting goods store, but that's closed early."
Eric waited.

"Sure. Why not?" He was enjoying Eric's company.

As promised, the shop's owners were experts. Pete had never seen so many "rocks" of so many varieties. Beautiful colors, shapes, and consistencies on shelf after shelf. If he had been a rock hound, he would have been in heaven. As it was, he was having a hard time leaving until Eric reminded him that he was probably hungry. Thanking the owners, they headed back down Main Street.

"You should come down here by yourself before you leave. Do some wandering around. Nobody bites around here." There was that laugh again. "This place is deep into crystals and spiritual stuff that I don't begin to understand. We get plenty of folks who do, though."

Pete didn't know anything about that either but something about the spiritual side of rocks intrigued him enough that he decided he would come back to the shop.

"Folks say that she has powers." Eric pointed toward Shasta Mountain that loomed over the city. "Can't say if she does or doesn't but I have to admit that there is something about this place that keeps me coming back. I miss it like hell when I'm on the road. As soon as I take that exit into town, everything else just melts away." He stopped talking, embarrassed that he had said too much of nothing.

"I get it, Eric. Some places are just like that. Have that power over you. Yosemite's like that for me. You been?"

"Yeah. Went once, a long time ago. Took my dad. Didn't get to see much of it though. Early rains made everything miserable, so we turned around and came home. But the pictures I've seen look mighty awesome. Maybe someday I'll try again."

They were approaching the house. "You know, when that day comes, I'll be glad to show you around."

"That's real nice of you but at my age and my pace, I'm afraid I'd send you around the bend."

This time, it was Pete's turn to laugh. "No worries. I'm not known for my superman pace either." He caught himself as

Kit flashed in front of him.

"Well, then. Maybe we can manage it together. Sounds like a plan there, Pete."

He felt Eric's arm lightly wrap its length around his shoulders, momentarily, and his touch brought Pete back.

"Great," Pete managed to respond.

Eric was right about his ribs. They were mouth-watering. He joked that it was the only dish he knew how to make and saved it for special occasions, like this visit. Then he joked again that he couldn't remember the last special occasion and surmised that he must make the dish more than he remembered just because he remembered the recipe without even looking it up. Trouble with living alone, sometimes, he commented, is that stuff gets jumbled up in your mind. Time, events, people, places. But none of it really matters as long as you remember to get up in the morning, go to work, and go to bed at night. He wiped the remnants of barbeque sauce from his mouth and hands. "More?" He shoved the plate across the table to Pete.

"No thanks. It was great, but I'm done. So good, Eric." Pete meant every word. He was so full that he longed to leave the table and find some relief. But Eric grabbed the plate back and dug his fork into the remaining three ribs.

"Can't let them go to waste."

"Of course not." Pete shifted in his seat slightly feeling uncomfortable. Eric might not have a good pace for walking, but eating was another story. Pete had never seen anyone devour food as quickly as Eric could.

With clean-up done, Pete excused himself, eager to close the bathroom door behind him. When he came back, Eric had moved out onto the front porch and was comfortably lodged in a wooden rocker. Its companion next to it remained still.

"Have a seat, Pete. You want a soda? Some pretzels?"

Pete felt his stomach turn at the mention of more food. "No, no thanks. I'm okay." He sat down in the large rocker, a bit surprised by its comfort and deep rocking motion.

"Good. Glad you're doing okay."

Silence fell between them as each rocked back and forth,

each moving deeper and deeper into their own thoughts. After a while, Eric broke the silence.

"So, Pete. Besides going back into town, anything you want to do while you're up here?" Eric looked straight ahead, still rocking at a steady pace.

"No, not really. Just came up to get away from stuff for a while and to spend some time with you, if that's okay."

He knew that was partially the truth. The first part. He hadn't considered that he and Eric would get along so well, so comfortably. He came up to pay a visit and then head out on his own to start his healing process, whatever that was going to be. But he suddenly understood that there was no rush. Not right now. He wanted to enjoy the moment up here in the rocky world of gem shops, the slow pace of a gentle walk down Main Street, the deep consistent rocking of a well-made rocker, the evening and morning air, the mountain's presence that could not be ignored, and, most surprising to him, the company of an older man who made everything feel okay again.

"That's sure okay, Pete. Sure okay." Silence followed other than the intermittent creak of the wood runners on the porch floor.

*

The idea came to him as he lay awake in the dark anticipating the next run to Los Angeles. He had trouble sleeping since Pete arrived. He figured that it was natural, having gotten used to being on his own since his father's passing. Pete wasn't to blame. He knew that. As a matter of fact, he enjoyed his company. And maybe that's how he got the idea. He didn't know what Pete's status was, but he figured there was no harm in asking.

"I got this idea, Pete, in the middle of the night. Thought I'd pass it by you." Eric sipped the hot coffee that Pete had prepared along with a pancake breakfast.

"Oh yeah? Okay."

"I don't know what your plans are after you leave here and it's not any of my business. But if you don't have any, what would you think of staying here for as long as you want? I'm heading down to LA tomorrow morning and I'll be gone four days. You've got a place to stay and would be doing me a favor. I mean having someone in the house. Keeping up appearances, as they say. I always worry, just a little, about coming back home one day and finding the place not the way I left it." Eric set his coffee mug down in front of him, wrapping his hands around it.

Pete was surprised. He hardly knew the guy and the guy didn't know him at all. Not really; not the reason he came up here to begin with and not the mess his mind was in. And he had no intention of Eric ever knowing. Not that he wasn't a nice enough guy but because he was a stranger and because Pete needed to know that there was one person in his life who only knew Pete Wade-Murphy as Pete Wade-Murphy wanted to be known.

"Well, that's an interesting proposition. I mean, I guess I could. Kind of starting on an open stretch on my life path. Kind of weird that you should ask." Pete corrected himself immediately. "I mean it's a coincidence seeing as how I am at loose ends right now. Sure, Eric. If you really are okay with it. You might want to give it more thought. But I'm good with it."

"No more thought necessary. Great, Pete. That puts my mind at ease. Like I said, you can take off whenever you want. No hard feelings on my end. It's just a convenient arrangement for both of us, I guess. And by the way, weird? Maybe. Remember where you are." Eric laughed, picked up his mug and toasted the arrangement between the two men.

Eric took the time to show Pete around his small home. Where the important stuff was like the water heater, the gas turn-off, the trick to properly shutting a couple of the age-worn sash windows in the back rooms, and the extra keys to the house. His pantry was stocked, enough to keep Pete fed. From Eric's perspective, not that much to explain about the place and Pete silently agreed.

He didn't hear Eric leave the house in the dark well before sunrise. But he awoke to the sound of the truck's engine and lay in bed, half awake, as he listened to Eric back it out and head down the street, the low rumble of the massive engine at work. He strained to hear it as it faded in the distance until there was only silence.

When he awoke again, the room was already stuffy and uncomfortable. Shoving the covers off, he shielded his eyes from the bright sunshine filling the room. It felt late. Checking his phone, he swore out loud. How could he have slept until 10 in the morning? And he still felt tired. Collecting his thoughts, he remembered Eric's departure sometime in the dark. And that was it. And now he had the place to himself. He could stay in bed all day and who would know? His better sense kicked in and he slowly got up.

He was not comfortable in this room. He felt that he was trespassing. He knew that Eric had tried to make it welcoming, but that didn't prevent Pete's imagination from taking hold. He was sleeping in a dead man's bed, putting his stuff in a dead man's drawers, and walking the floors where a man, now dead, once walked. Maybe, he thought, given time, he wouldn't let that bother him. After all, he wasn't planning on staying with Eric forever! Just until he got back.

He planned on taking a walk into town after he ate and

before it got way too hot. Instead, he started looking around Eric's house. He could see more when Eric wasn't there, and his curiosity was in high gear. He started with the kitchen, sitting at the table finishing his breakfast. Eric was a neat freak compared to himself. Maybe he should pay some attention to Eric's organizational skills and when he got home, make some needed improvements. Forgetting this fleeting enlightenment, he put his dirty dishes in the sink and moved into the living room.

Small, as the whole house was, Eric had managed to cover one wall in the living room with bookshelves, floor to ceiling. Pete, of course, noticed them when he first arrived but from a distance and briefly as Eric led him into the kitchen and then to his guest room. But now he had the time to stand in front of them and check out the titles. What he found was an eclectic assortment of books whose subject matter ranged from the ridiculous to the genius level. Titles that made him laugh, titles that he knew from his own childhood reading, to titles that he could not pronounce. Subject matter that was completely foreign to him, in most cases. It got him wondering who this Eric character really was. Certainly not just a truck driver who never did anything with his life.

The framed photos were few and judging by the discoloration of the cheap metal frames, had been around for a while. Faded by the sunlight pouring on them over the years, the images were still visible but damaged. He carefully picked each frame up and examined the subjects. Two children stood together in one of them, a boy and a girl. The boy looked a bit older but not by much. Pete estimated that he was no more than five or six years old. The girl, he figured, was probably around three or four. Pete was captivated by their expression or lack of. Their little faces were hollow, almost transparent. Their eyes were void of life, it seemed. The girl held the boy's hand. The boy's other hand was holding something, but Pete couldn't make it out. Were these Eric's kids?

The second frame almost fell apart in his hand as he picked it up from the small table next to the couch. He quickly tightened his grip to keep the four sides in place. The image was damaged even more than the children's and Pete, to see it more clearly, moved to the window and drew it closer to his face. The woman was young, maybe in her twenties, and she was beautiful. Her hair was twisted on the top of her head while tendrils of the chestnut threads escaped all around her face, down her neck, and onto her shoulders. But like the children, her expression was void of any emotion. Pete carefully placed the weakened frame on the table where he had found it.

The last framed photo in the room sat on a high shelf of one of the bookcases. Pete stretched his arm and carefully picked it up, fully expecting it to fall apart in his hand. But it didn't. Instead, it felt firm and stable. Again, he moved to the window to get a better look at it. He noticed that the frame seemed much newer than the others. The man who stared back at Pete from the photo was older. Older than Eric, for sure. Balding and standing with the help of a cane, his eyes, not looking directly at the camera lens but somewhere off in the distance, reflected pain as did the rest of his face. The effort to smile seemed strained. It was disturbing to Pete but not as disturbing as the first two photos. And he wondered about these strangers. He would ask Eric about them, he decided, if the moment felt right.

Within this one small living room, Pete had gathered information about Eric that only left him with many questions. What he thought he knew was that Eric was a reader of just about anything. Pete guessed that he must be smart. Just one of those guys who keeps it to himself. Not a braggart. Pete liked that quality in Eric. Not certain, of course, but assuming he knew, Eric had family. Maybe a wife and kids. Maybe the old man was his father or grandfather? What he didn't know bothered him. Why did everyone looked so unhappy? He wasn't even sure "unhappy" was the right word. Something, though, was off in those images. The more he thought about them, the more depressed he became. Determined not to allow his own problems to be influenced by those of these strangers, he left the room and headed outside. He needed air and a good walk.

He thought about heading back to the rock shop but changed his mind as he crossed the street. The sports store that had been closed was now open. Entering it, Pete felt like he was back in the Bay Area. The place was busy with young and old alike engaged in preparations for treks. The staff, young and experienced, who knew everything there was to know about the area and beyond, was friendly and eager. A middle-aged man stood behind one of the counters deep within the store surrounded by trekking and camping gear. A large topo map lay open on the counter as he talked through the terrain that a young couple was considering attempting. Pete lingered by them, pretending to be interested in the "sale" rack of convertible pants. The man was explaining the dangers of hiking up the volcano, the best time of year to do it, and the only side to ascend if you wanted to make it to the top unscathed. Pete hadn't even considered climbing Mt. Shasta. If anything, a gentle flat hike through the forest was enough for him now. But he couldn't help feeling a bit of envy. He was envious of their youth, their excitement, and their naiveté. The ignorance that prevented them from having second thoughts. The ignorance that propelled them forward. The ignorance that assured them that they were invincible.

He needed to get out of the store. It came on suddenly but not unexpectedly, he realized later. The images froze him in place and he reached out to the clothes rack to steady himself. The young girl's voice was no longer hers but Kit's. The topo map was no longer on the counter but in Kit's hands. And as the man described the climb, Pete only saw Kit's body ascending the steep trail in front of him, as if she were floating ahead of him.

He shut his eyes tightly, ridding himself of the images. Letting go of the rack, he reopened his eyes and headed straight for the doors. Once on the sidewalk, he took long, deep breaths to calm himself. Not wanting to go back to Eric's yet, he decided to keep walking and found himself in front of the rock shop.

*

In the still and dark of the early morning hours, as Eric approached the alley, he took a double look. The old car was running. Headlights and rear back-up lights were on. Whoever was in the car was heading out again. But as he passed the car, the lights turned off. The car was almost invisible in the darkness. He wanted to stop the truck and let his curiosity get the best of him. Instead, he continued toward the south bound entrance onto I-5. Just before the entrance, he pulled into a gas station to fill up. Something nagged at him to keep an eye on the road in front of him. To watch for the old Valiant. To see where it was going. Maybe catch a glimpse of the driver.

The Valiant crawled along the road and started to slow as it approached the gas station. Eric saw it as he was turning to place the hose back in its stand. When he turned back, the car was nowhere in sight. Had the driver tried to avoid him? Twice? And why? Disappointed that he had come so close to solving the mystery of the old car and its occupant, he climbed up into his rig. Pulling out of the gas station, he chuckled to himself. Where was his head? Better that he focus on the journey ahead.

He crossed the overpass and entered the I-5. At this hour of the morning, the roadway seemed surreal. Empty expanses of concrete lanes ribboned their way in front of him. Darkness concealed the landscape other than what the headlights revealed, a fleeting glimpse of partial tree trunks that he knew towered over the road. He liked getting such an early start because he had the whole highway to himself, at least for a while. But he didn't like the illusion that the darkness and headlights created. He depended on his memory to provide the daylight images. He had seen them enough to know what was there in the dark. But he still felt uncomfortable not seeing the whole picture.

*

Hellenia heard the truck before she saw it in her rearview mirror. Quickly, she turned off the headlights and the car. She waited for it to pass the alleyway, her heart beating heavily. She loosened her grip on the steering wheel after the truck passed and darkness engulfed the old car once more.

It was early, much earlier than usual for her to leave but she could not sleep. She lay awake throughout the night, staring at the worn ceiling of the car, a hundred thoughts appearing and colliding, each one leading to another and another until she could stand it no longer. It bothered her that she couldn't say why such a night occurred, considering that she had spent so many nights here in deep, restful sleeps, unhampered by her past.

Wide awake now, she made the decision to get on the road. She knew that she would collapse at some point as the day went on, but there was no sense staying here now. She knew all the good rest stops going both north and south and would make use of them. But today, she might not give anyone a lift. She was not in the mood. Besides, there were plenty of truckers who could. She felt badly about her decision. It went against a promise she had made to herself a while back. A promise that she had fulfilled each time she was on the road. She promised that she would help someone in need each day that she had remaining. She understood clearly the guilt that she carried. The guilt that sustained this promise. If anyone asked her who she made this promise to, she would, without hesitation, state that it wasn't to God. No, she had betrayed others much closer to her. And to all those people, she promised repeatedly, each night before she closed her eyes and each morning when she opened them, that she would not let them down again.

*

Without Eric, Pete took his time wandering up and down the aisles of the shop. He lingered over rock samples whose labels indicated their ages; some dating back millions of years. The hand printed signs, small and fading, said not to touch. But where there were no signs, Pete picked up the rock, holding it in the palm of his hand and examined it as if he knew what he was doing. He hadn't a clue, but he wished he had. Just as his brief first visit to the shop had overwhelmed, so did he feel the same this time. But this time, he wanted to take all the time he needed to examine and admire the earth's samples all around him.

The selection of crystals from all over the world captivated him. Some were as transparent as air while others' milky compositions hid their secrets. There were crystals whose delicate miniature spires clustered closely together but maintained their individuality. Pete did not pick them up fearing that they would crumple in his hand. On another shelf, crystals the length of his forearm stood erect from their earthen base, each spire a different height, solid and strong.

He lingered for a long time in their presence. Their indescribable beauty, strength, and mystery captivated him. No single crystal was identical to another. He remembered reading that snowflakes possessed the same quality. And Pete wondered how that could possibly be. How could anyone be that sure? Of all the crystals and snowflakes ever created, not to mention those that had not been created yet, how can it be said that they were each one of a kind?

Impossible. But he couldn't deny that the idea intrigued him. Enough so that he purchased one of the larger crystal clusters. If he chose to believe it, then he had something no one else in the whole world possessed. And this excited him. The owner asked him if he had a collection as this newly purchased example was a "beauty". Pete confessed that he had never purchased a rock before, let alone something like this. The owner smiled, confirming to Pete that he had made a good decision for the first time out. He boxed it carefully and slipped in a sheet of paper. He told Pete to be sure to read the information about crystals and, particularly this kind. It would give him a whole new meaning as to why he purchased it in the first place.

The box was heavy and grew heavier as he made his way back to Eric's. He started to doubt himself. He had just spent a good amount of money on a rock that was now slowing him down and becoming a burden. What was he going to do with it anyway? Weakness had gotten the best of him, he figured. Could have used the same money towards something that he really needed, like a new car. He considered turning around and returning it, making up some ridiculous story as to why. Instead, he plodded up the small hill until Eric's house was in sight.

The midday heat was building. Hot and sweaty, Pete put the box on his bed. He went to the kitchen and opened the refrigerator door. Standing in front of it, letting the chilly air embrace his body, he reached for a beer. There was no air conditioning unit that Pete could see. He wondered why. True, it got darn cold up here in the winter, but he knew that the summers could be uncomfortable. Maybe, because Eric was on the road so much, he didn't bother with the expense. Driving an air-conditioned cab during the day and sleeping in air-conditioned motels, he could probably bear the day or two at home in the heat of the summer.

Pete realized that he forgot to pull down the shades before leaving. The eastern sun had bathed the back rooms all morning and was just shifting toward the west, about to drench the small house in the hottest heat of the day. He opened all the windows in the back of the house, the way Eric had shown him. He did the same for the front of the house. Drawing the thin drapes over the front windows, he hoped that there would be some relief by the evening. So far, there was not one hint of a breeze. A fan would help, Pete thought. He searched but found nothing. Not surprised, he resigned himself to wearing as little as possible, finding some big shade tree, and parking himself under it for the remainder of the afternoon. Why not? Nothing else to do. Later, when the sun was lower in the sky, he would head back to town and get a bite to eat in an air-conditioned restaurant.

He stood in front of Eric's bookshelves scanning the titles. With so many books to choose from, he tried to remember any author's name. Someone familiar to him. Jack London, John Steinbeck, Earnest Hemingway, Herman Melville-the guys who his English teachers forced him to read. Some of their works he remembered but only bits and pieces of the others. He focused on finding some Steinbeck or London. He had enjoyed these authors, he remembered.

He ran his fingers along the bindings of the shelved books, hoping to come across his chosen authors sooner than later. As he did so, his fingers felt the gap between books before his eyes saw it. He focused on the indentation. Pushed back against the back wall of the shelf and only half the size of the books that surrounded it, was an untitled book. Pete reached his hand over the top of the books and coaxed the small leather-bound book from the shelf. It was not a book. It appeared to be a journal. The mustiness of its old leather was strong as Pete gently opened the front cover. The internal pages, yellowed and edges dusty, added to the powerful musty odor that invaded his nostrils. Every page in the journal was filled with someone's handwritten entries. And each entry was dated. The first entry was dated January 1, 1934. Pete gently flipped to the last pages and found the final entry- June 5, 1999. On the inside cover's faded paper lining, Pete tried to make out the owner's name. One or two letters were slightly legible. Not enough to make sense of though. Curious but understanding that he shouldn't pry without Eric's consent, he placed it back between the books leaving its binding protruding from the edge of the shelf. He wanted to find it again once Eric returned.

He continued his search for reading material and was about to call it quits when the Jack London book titles appeared one after the other. He had no idea that London had been so prolific. Eric must have a complete collection! Pete only knew a few titles; *White Fang, The Call of the Wild, The Sea Wolf*, and a short story, *To Build a Fire*. He tried to remember what the connection was between the first two books. His teacher had made a big deal of it when he had to read both books in freshman literature class. Something about the dogs. They both had dogs in them. And then he remembered. In *White Fang*, the dog was wild turned tame. In *The Call of the Wild*, the reverse. Buck. That was the dog's name. Buck. In *The Call of the Wild*. He remembered feeling so badly for the dog when it was kidnapped from its home. No longer the king of the "sun-kissed Santa Clara Valley" ranch where he was born and raised, he was taken into the Yukon to become a sled dog, learning the ways of unkind men lured by the promise of gold and of mean dogs beaten into submission but whose instincts to survive remained. A good story. Pete took both books off the shelf. He looked forward to rereading them, especially since his perspective on life was much more jaded than it had been at fourteen. Would he understand London's perspective better? He figured he would.

Heading for the kitchen, with the books in hand, Pete decided to pack a light lunch. He imagined the coolness of a tree's shade, the stillness of the air, and the peace and quiet under its umbrella branches, as he ate his small meal and then settled back against its trunk to greet Mr. London after such a long absence. He had in mind a small park set back from the street that he passed as he made his way toward Main Street. He had made a mental note of its location as it looked inviting, but he had been eager to get back to the house, his crystal growing heavier with each step.

Locking the house, as Eric had instructed, Pete made his way to his afternoon's destination. He hoped that he would have the place to himself but would not be surprised to see others there with the same idea. To his surprise, he saw only an open green expanse of grass, bordered by the old shade trees that beckoned him to them.

He had fallen asleep for a while before opening the book. The light lunch had evolved into a substantial meal enhanced by snacks that Pete had found in the pantry. Mostly pretzels, but Eric obviously had a soft spot for chocolate, which Pete shared, he realized, as he finished off the last Reese's Cup in the bag. It was no wonder that he had fallen into a comatose state. As the afternoon wore on, he lost track of time, absorbed in *The Call of the Wild*.

Far from hungry but noting that it was close to seven o'clock, he was surprised how quickly the time had gone. The air was still warm and still no breeze brought any relief. The evening insects had been serenading him continuously, but he only tuned in to their song as he noted the time. His body was in full sunlight as the sun, now below eye level, slowly began its crawl before slipping below the horizon. The book in his lap lay open and he noted the page where he had left off. He didn't dare dog-ear the page as he had always done with his own books. He would just need to remember. It was the part when Buck's "instincts, long dead became alive again." Where Buck's "domesticated generations fell from him." Pete found the full passage, and before packing up, reread it aloud.

> "... In vague ways, he remembered back to the youth of the breed, to the time the wild dogs ranged in packs through the primeval forest and killed their meat as they ran it down. It was no task for him to learn to fight with cut and slash and the quick wolf snap. In this manner had fought forgotten ancestors. They quickened the old life within him, and the old tricks which they had stamped into the heredity of the breed were his tricks. They came to him without effort or discovery, as though they had been his always. And when, on the still cold nights, he pointed his nose at a star and howled long and wolflike, it was his ancestors, dead and dust, pointing nose at star and howling down through the centuries and through him. And his cadences were their cadences, the cadences which voiced their woe and what to them was the meaning of the stillness, and the cold, and dark.
>
> Thus, as token of what a puppet thing life is, the ancient song surged through him and he came into his own again; and he came because men had found a yellow metal in the North, and because Manuel was a gardener's helper whose wages did not lap over the needs of his wife and divers small copies of himself."

Pete did not close the book but let it rest, opened to the final paragraphs in Chapter II, *The Law of Club and Fang*. The words stayed with him and he played with their meaning. He understood London's obvious meaning; that of a creature, once domesticated, now returning to its instincts, to its roots. But Pete wanted to understand what these words meant to him. Why he could not leave them alone. He reread the passage again and again. On the final reading, he saw what he was looking for. "...it was his ancestors, dead and dust, pointing nose at star and howling down through the centuries and through him. And his cadences were their cadences, the cadences which voiced their woe and what to them was the meaning of the stillness, and the cold, and dark."

As he sat under the umbrella tree, he watched the sun set through blurred vision as he let his tears fall freely to the open pages in his lap.

*

"Will you come with me today?" David Eagan knew his wife's answer before she spoke. It was always the same.

"Not today. Maybe tomorrow," Jean would always respond, conveniently never making eye contact with her husband.

"Fine. Maybe tomorrow," David would mumble as he walked toward the front door. "Be back soon."

"Fine," Jean's voice barely audible.

This exchange had become a daily routine for the Eagans. David never pressed his wife to accompany him, and Jean's mantra meant nothing to her. And not to David, for that matter. He had long given up on his wife and her unreasonable attitude toward their deceased daughter. He had tried, for her own good, for her mental state, to change her mind for days after they buried Kit but with each attempt, he felt that he was fueling whatever fire his wife kept raging inside of her. He could not reach her. He accepted that she did not want to be reached.

Kit's grave stone was prominent among the other stones. Its shape would indicate to the uninformed eye that the stone was unfinished, roughly honed, and an eye sore among all the others. But David had intentionally demanded that the granite stone be a true symbol of his daughter. Its craggy edges and off centered pointed peak was David's homage to his adventurous child. To the many mountains she had climbed, to the rugged terrain that never frightened her but spurred her on, and to her unfinished climb, her unfinished life.

As David kneeled next to his daughter, he saw her ascending and then descending the miniature jagged rock face that shadowed her grave. He ran his fingers over the surface of the unpolished granite face, tracing the name of his only child engraved in simple font. Then he laid his fully open hands on the peak of the stone, straining to hear his daughter's voice once more. And he stayed with her, waiting for her to speak, until he bore her silence no longer. Each day, without the mother of his child, he visited Kit. And each day, he asked for her forgiveness, for not being the parent he should have been. For silently giving her permission to be the adult among the three of them. For holding back his love for her because he was too weak to go against his wife. Somehow, he knew that she would, one day, accept who he had become and forgive him. And because that day could be any one in the time he had left on earth, he vowed to be by her side, to hear her voice, every one of those days.

*

Before Eric got back, Pete had finished *The Call of the Wild* and *White Fang.* Just as he suspected, with age and experience, he was lost in London's narratives that sucked him into places and times that intrigued him. It seemed to Pete that so much of what London wrote was an education about humanity, with all its faults and wonders, an education that he had never received in school. He found himself rereading passages, trying to commit sentences to memory, emotions on edge as he wept for four legged creatures, for humankind, and in the next moment feeling rage toward others in the novels. But the satisfaction he felt when the antagonists got what was coming to them made him smile.

Jack London was sitting right next to Peter Wade-Murphy, silently enjoying the reader's reactions. Pete believed this to be the case, so strong was his growing attachment and admiration for the author. He wanted to know Jack. He decided that he needed his own copies of the novels and Jack's biography. Looking through the collection on Eric's shelf more carefully, he was sure he would find such a book, but he found nothing on the man's life. Pete decided that he would need to start his own collection of London's works, beginning with the biography.

He found a collection of short stories and began with a familiar one, *To Build a Fire.* It had been so long ago that he had read it. His mind was blank as he read the first paragraph and then it came back to him, a sudden rush of images and emotions. "The man" whose name London purposely did not establish, sent a chill through Pete's body. "The man" who was not impressed by all the signs around him of impending danger, life threatening danger. Pete read the sentences aloud that loomed from the page.

> "But all this-this mysterious, far-reaching hairline trail, the absence of sun from the sky, the tremendous cold, and the strangeness and weirdness of it all-made no impression on the

man. It was not because he was long used to it. He was a newcomer in the land, a *chechaquo,* and this was his first winter. The trouble with him was that he was without imagination. He was quick and alert in the things of life, but only in the things, and not in the significances. Fifty degrees below zero meant eighty-odd degrees of frost. Such fact impressed him as being cold and uncomfortable, and that was all. It did not lead him to meditate upon his frailty as a creature of temperature, and upon man's frailty in general, able only to live within certain narrow limits of heat and cold; and from there on it did not lead him to the conjectural field of immortality and man's place in the universe. Fifty degrees below zero stood for a bite of frost that hurt and that must be guarded against by the use of mittens, ear flaps, warm moccasins, and thick socks. Fifty degrees below zero was to him just precisely fifty degrees below zero. That there should be anything more to it than that was a thought that never entered his head."

Pete turned to the imagined author sitting next to him once again. "You are speaking to me, aren't you, Jack? You knew Kit long before I did."

Pete closed the book, drawn away from his unfinished conversation as he heard the rig pull onto the property, the sound of its heavy labored engine chugging loudly through the walls of the house. The whoosh of the air brakes followed by the stillness of the silenced engine, the thud of the driver's door shutting on yet another run for Eric. And Pete guiltily wished that Eric was still on the road.

*

She always waited until she was sure he was driving away. Only then could she breathe deeply, clearing her head of the fog that oppressed and depressed her. The house was quiet, still, and as she moved through it, she heard her breathing and felt her breath leave and enter her body. David never missed a day. He always invited her. She always declined. It had become so well-choreographed, their inconsequential exchange, that if either one should misstep, well... she wasn't sure what the result would be. An argument, more likely than not.

During David's daily absence, Jean allowed her past to be present only to be quickly shut away when she heard his car pull up the driveway. Entering her daughter's childhood bedroom, a room that she had prohibited David from disrupting, she stopped just inside the doorway. From this point, she examined the contents of the room. Once sure that nothing had been disturbed since the day before, she moved to Kit's bed. Resting her hand on the quilt as if just under its warmth lay her sleeping little girl, Jean smiled. Assured that her only child was sound asleep, she sat down on the edge of the bed and held onto the footboard. The deluge of memories that came threatened to pull her under so that if she let go of the footboard, she knew she would be swept away. But the past's current was much stronger than her, and each time, she let herself drown in it.

The memories never came in any order. Rather, brilliant images played in and out of her mind's eye while dull, unfocused yet strikingly familiar images took their place. She could never identify these, however, not like the digital sharp memories. The vivid ones brought her newborn child into her arms, brought her toddler's hand into her own, brought her young gangling, awkward daughter to her side, brought her so close that Jean could feel her pubescent daughter's shy kiss on her cheek. She searched for more of these memories, but they were few. As she sat on the bed, she focused on her daughter's bedroom, hoping that an object, a picture, a book, or a long-forgotten toy would call up the good ones. Instead, other memories overwhelmed her that she could not determine to be hers, but the familiarity about them frightened her. An overwhelming sadness accompanied them. And still, no matter how often these came to her and no matter how hard she tried to make sense of them, they remained out of her reach.

Rising from her daughter's bed, she slowly made her way to the door. As she did, she saw Kit, now a young woman packing for college. Excited, happy, and anxious, her daughter telling her mother that she could pack on her own. No need to "hang over me like some vulture". Jean felt the sting for the very first time as her little girl betrayed their bond. Standing in the bedroom doorway now, listening for David's car to pull up any second, Jean's heart pounded in her chest. Instead of the car, all she heard was her daughter's ugly voice rejecting her mother and, yes, her father, as she stubbornly refused their help. The void of all the years that followed without hearing her baby girl's voice, without seeing the woman she had become other than in her own imaginings, had taken its irrevocable toll on Jean.

As she closed the door on Kit's bedroom, she swore out loud at her daughter. She swore out loud at her husband, and she swore out loud at herself. The only reality that Jean accepted each time she shut the bedroom door was simple. "What goes around, comes around."

*

She kept her word. And she felt badly about it. The young hitch-hikers' faces haunted her as she made her way back north. How many had she passed by? Too many. She didn't keep count. Besides, she was driving a strange car on the return trip and one stranger at a time was her limit.

What was to have been her daily ride stretched into a night away from "home". She knew that her "baby" was out of sorts as soon as it tried to ascend the first mountain pass heading south. It felt tired under her foot and the problem only grew worse. Downhill, she made up some time, especially on the long grades, but those were not enough reprieve for her dying "baby". Just outside of Redding, Hellenia pulled over to the shoulder. She knew that her "baby" could go no further. As she turned off the labored engine, she gave the dashboard a gently pat. "You did real good. Don't you worry. I'll get you fixed up and we'll be on the road in no time."

Raising the hood, she quickly backed away letting it fall shut again. The heat and smell of the engine compartment slapped her hard in the face. She tried again, this time ready. But she couldn't reach in to release the hood support rod much less hold the hood up for long to do so. For a second time, she let the hood drop.

She saw the highway patrol car approaching about a half mile away. Its lights were on, and she could see it slowing down until it pulled in behind her. A wave of relief washed over her, and she thanked her lucky stars that he had stopped. The irony of the moment was not lost on her, however, as she recalled the folks she purposely passed up earlier in the day.

Her "baby" was towed into Redding to a repair shop that the officer suggested to Hellenia. He reassured her that they would take good care of her and that if they could fix it, they would. Had his own car in there several times. Good guys and trustworthy. He did remind her, however, that her license was going to expire on her next birthday, just a month away. "Don't forget to take care of this, ma'am. And congratulations on your clean driving record. Wish I could say the same about other folks on the road, much younger than you."

She thanked him and told him that her motto was to "watch out for the other guy." Always had been. He helped her into the tow truck, a climb that Hellenia was not prepared for. "You have a better day, ma'am." The officer closed the heavy door, stood back and nodded toward Hellenia. She did the same.

"We can get her on the road again, but it won't be cheap. We're looking at some expensive repairs here, ma'am. I'll work up the estimate for you. Then you can decide what you want to do." The man stepped away from the counter and slid behind a laptop. Hellenia knew before she saw the figures that she couldn't afford to fix her "baby". A panic set in as she realized that she was about to be stranded. She was too old for this kind of shit, she thought. Now what?

And she was right. The amount didn't matter. A million dollars? A thousand dollars? A hundred dollars? She didn't have it and told the unconcerned man so.

"Well, I am sorry, but that's the best we can do. Can't put you back on the road in a car we can't give some guarantee to. You understand that?"

His condescending tone struck a note. A bad one. "Do you think I was born yesterday? Of course I understand. Just because I look old…" She stopped in her tracks. Her laughter threw him off and he looked quizzically at her. "Well, for God's sake, I am old."

The man's face softened, and he smiled. "Tell you what. Are you willing to part with this car? If so, I might be able to find something for you. Probably can't give you much for it, not in its present condition, but I know a guy who collects these vintage cars. He might make a trade. You want me to call him?"

Give up her "baby"? The thought was not new. She had considered the possibilities as she sat next to the tow driver, her "baby" being dragged behind her. Hearing what she expected to hear, she'd already considered that this had been the last ride with

with her best friend and companion. She just didn't have a solution.

Now, it was in front of her. And maybe it would just turn out all right. She had no choice.

"Well, seeing as how I'm stuck between a rock and a hard place, I would appreciate it. Can I get my belongings out of my "ba…" She corrected herself. "Out of my car? I got my whole life in there." The finality of it all came crashing down on Hellenia. But she wouldn't let this stranger see its effect on her.

"Of course you can. Let me call my friend first. Let's see what we can do for you. Give me just a minute."

She needed to sit down. The fatigue came on suddenly and, for a moment, she felt faint. Looking around, she saw a beat-up leather couch in the corner of the room. "I'll be right over here." She didn't wait for the man to acknowledge her.

"Ma'am?"

Hellenia heard him through the fog of sleep but couldn't respond.

"Ma'am? Excuse me. Sorry to wake you up."

She felt herself rising above the fog. Slowly opening her eyes, she adjusted to her surroundings. It took her a minute to remember where she was.

"Ma'am? Can I get you some water?"

She nodded slowly. The liquid was cold and refreshing, enough for her to fully come to. "Thank you. Must have nodded off there. This heat gets me every time."

"Yes, ma'am. It's darn hot today, that's for sure. Well, I've got some good news for you. My friend wants your car. And he'll do a trade for it. An older car but I can guarantee you that it is working fine. One thing I do know is that Al takes good care of his cars. He doesn't usually do this, sight unseen, but I described your car to him and he wants it. What do you think?"

Hellenia worked to make sense of the news. "So, he will give me one if I give him mine? Is that up and up? Sounds a little fishy." She wasn't going to give in so easily.

"Yes, that's what he's proposing. And there's nothing

fishy about Al. I've known him for going on thirty-five years and in all that time, the guy's been a saint. He's helped lots of folks in pickles like yours. And he'll help you with the DMV. Get you through the transfer of ownership without you having to worry."

"Okay, okay then." She heard her voice but wasn't so sure she had produced the words. Surprised by her response, she thought about retracting her words but what she said, she meant.

"Great. I'll make the arrangements for the cars to be transferred. We can do that tomorrow. Al will take you to the DMV tomorrow and make sure everything is legal. You'll be on your way by tomorrow afternoon, I expect."

"Tomorrow? You can't do it today?"

"No, ma'am. Al's real busy but he can give you the time tomorrow."

"But…I don't have a place to stay tonight. I don't have a place…" Hellenia stopped. She wasn't willing to let this stranger know that the only place she had was her "baby".

"I can call you a cab. We've got plenty of motels and such in Redding. I can even recommend one to you, if you want." She could see that he meant well.

"Where is my car?"

"It's back in the yard."

"What do you mean?"

"Behind our garages. The tow truck always drops them there until we are ready to work on them. Oh, right. You had some belongings in there. I can get one of our guys to take you back there so you can get them."

Hellenia almost agreed until she realized that there was no possible way she could take the boxes and belongings with her. "Can I get my stuff tomorrow when we trade cars?"

"Well, I don't see why not. Guess that makes more sense, doesn't it. So, do you want me to call a cab?"

She didn't have the money to throw away on a cab. She didn't have the money to throw away on a motel room either. Her social security payment only went so far. Not sure what she should do, she didn't answer him right away.

"Do you need a place to stay tonight?" He sat down next to her on the couch. "I don't mean to pry, but my wife and I would be pleased to let you stay in our son's room. He's gone and married with kids of his own. We use the room for guests."

"I can't do that. It's mighty kind of you to offer, but I can't." Hellenia felt his sincerity and it shook her.

"It's not a problem. Would it make you feel better if I told you that it wouldn't be the first time we've helped stranded folks? It's just something we can do. Wish you would reconsider?" He stood up and faced her, waiting for her response.

What was she going to do if she said no thank you to his offer? She didn't mind being alone in her car at night but the thought of being alone on the street somewhere was out of the question. She wasn't that far gone, she thought, to understand that the idea was dangerous and stupid.

"I don't even know your name." She would say yes but in her own time.

"Sorry. Of course. I'm Benjamin Drake. Benny, most people call me. Wife's name is Peggy.

If the ceiling had fallen on them both just at that moment, it wouldn't have surprised her more than his revelation. Benjamin. Benjamin. Benny. Hellenia grabbed the worn arm of the couch, her ancient hand gripping it tightly.

Benjamin watched her reaction, suddenly alarmed. "Ma'am, are you okay? Are you having a problem?" He was sure that she was having a heart attack or something. "Ma'am?"

Hellenia, still digging her fingers into the thinning leather, tried to breathe slowly and evenly. She needed to respond. "I... I am fine. Fine. Nothing to worry about. Just been a long day." She felt her body relaxing and she pushed herself forward to the edge of the cushion. Benjamin reached out his hand to her and helped her to stand.

"Of course. Just want to make sure you are okay. More water?" He didn't let go until she nodded her head. "You okay standing on your own?"

"Yes, yes. Thank you."

She drank the cold water slowly, feeling it slide down her throat and into her chest. It was enough to bring her to her senses.

"I am embarrassed, you see. I've never had to ask for any help before. Not like this," she lied.

"Please. Don't be. Everyone needs help at some point in their lives. I'm just glad that the one time you needed it, I could oblige. So, you are saying yes?"

"Yes, thank you. I don't know how I can pay you back for your kindness." She tried but could not say his name aloud.

"No need to worry about that. Not doing it for the payback. Let me call my wife and let her know. I'm off in about 30 minutes, if you want to wait in here. I'll take you home with me and bring you over to Al's tomorrow morning. Does that sound okay?"

"My stuff in my car? Will it be alright out there?"

"Absolutely. We lock up the yard when we leave, and it stays locked until my guys get here in the morning. Do you need anything out of there for the night? We've got toiletries at the house and anything else that you might need. Anything in particular?"

She tried to go through her nightly ritual and realized that all she needed was her front seat, a blanket, and the darkness. "No, no. Let it be. I appreciate your kindness, Benja...Mr. Drake. And your wife's."

"Good. Have a seat. Can I get you a magazine or something? More water?"

"No thanks. Let me just sit here. Maybe take a nap."

"Sounds fine. Won't be long, Mrs. Wade."

*

Eric was relieved to be off the road. Lately, each trip took a little more out of him, and he was noticing it. Stiffness in his joints made itself known as he climbed down out of the cab. He had to take a minute to adjust his stance before taking a step forward. And when he did, his legs didn't want to work together immediately but insisted on taking a few awkward steps forward until they felt familiar to Eric. The thought of retirement was even more appealing but not realistic, he knew. A few more years, if his body held together. But moments like this made him wonder if a few more years were in the books for him.

He hadn't forgotten that Pete was staying in the house, but he was still surprised to see lights on. Every window was illuminated. He would remind Pete that power was not cheap. As he walked up the front steps, it dawned on him that he hadn't checked the alley as he drove by. He always checked the ally, but it slipped his mind. It wasn't a big deal but just another hint that he wasn't getting any younger. Judging by the hour, almost eight, the Valiant would be there. He was sure of it.

"Welcome home." Pete was waiting in the living room, the book placed face down on the small side table.

"Hey there, Pete. Haven't heard that greeting in a long time." Eric didn't stop to chat but went into the kitchen. Emptying his freezer chest, his routine never changing, he opened the refrigerator and placed the leftover cans of soda on the top shelf, ready for the next run. The bags of pretzels were long gone. He dumped out the lukewarm water into the sink, turned the chest upside down, and let it drain. After a good hot shower, he would put the dried-out freezer chest away. It was all in the timing, he reminded himself. Routine was good.

Remembering his house guest, he went back into the living room. Pete hadn't moved.

"You don't mind, do you, if I just take a shower? I'll be with you shortly." He didn't care if Pete minded.

"No. Of course not." Pete felt uncomfortable as if he were in the way. A man likes his privacy. Especially a man who's been living by himself all these years. "Don't worry about entertaining me. I'm okay."

"Wasn't worried and wasn't planning on entertaining anybody," Eric commented as he walked toward his bedroom.

Pete was getting to know this man. His humor, his sarcasm, his dry wit. As he turned back to the open book, he realized that he was smiling. Somewhere, deep within, Pete noticed a stirring, some attempt to bring forward a familiar yet unidentified knowledge and with that stirring, he thought he recognized a confusing and unsettling fact; that he was closer to home than he had ever been before.

*

Mr. Drake, as Hellenia insisted on calling him, even in the solitude of her "new" older car, was a saint by her reckoning. Someone or something had been keeping a good eye on her as her "baby" died. Had placed her in the compassionate hands of Mr. and Mrs. Drake. And of Al, the collector.

True, the car she was driving north was not her "baby". It didn't run like it, didn't respond like her "baby" knew to do, and was not as comfortable. But it ran. And its big front bench seat appeared to be sufficient for her needs. Her two boxes fit on the back seat with some room to spare. And the possessions she had in the trunk had room to roam. She couldn't remember the name of the car. Something about a deer? A big boat on the road, she noted, as she passed one or two other smaller vehicles. As she peered over the steering wheel, the front end looked like it went on for miles in front of her. And when she looked in the rearview mirror, the back end seemed to do the same but in the opposite direction. It would take some getting used to, she acknowledged silently, as she reached up to readjust the review mirror one more time. She wondered how her "baby" was doing without her and it made her sad to think about it.

With reassurances from Al and Mr. Drake, if she ran into any trouble she was supposed to give them a call, one or the other or both. They would make sure she was taken care of. "Good people," she commented out loud. "Real good people. Mrs. Drake made Hellenia feel like she was in her own home. Well, if she had a real home. A house to call her own. The dinner meal was more than Hellenia could eat, but she tried knowing full well that the probability of getting a home cooked meal in the near or far future was nil. The son's bedroom was a mix of teenage boy with a mother's feminine touch. Unwilling to change it completely, Mrs. Drake had made sure that both her boy or a guest would feel at home. The twin bed was comfortable enough, but Hellenia couldn't sleep. Her own little boy insisted on visiting her, coming and going throughout the night. When she finally fell into a short sleep, only deep, dark blackness filled her mind.

Her baby boy was nowhere in sight.

She was later than she had ever been pulling off the interstate, driving slowly through the town until she maneuvered her "boat", as she decided to call it, into the alley. It occurred to her as she turned off the lights, then the ignition, that she might be in trouble. The neighbors who kept to themselves when it came to the old Valiant parked for the night were bound to raise questions with the sheriff's office. She knew that they would not approach her first. The owner of the strange car would be trespassing as far as they were concerned. And worst yet, whoever was sleeping in it was not someone they "knew". She had made a mistake coming here. It was, to her, as apparent as the nose on her face. The car was a god-send but also her certain demise, she was sure of it. She couldn't stay here, not tonight. Maybe never again. But the thought of leaving frightened her. Not because she was in a strange car that she didn't know well enough yet and what to expect of it. Not because she would be driving through the night searching for a place to rest. But because she could not say goodbye to a part of her that possessively gripped her heart tightly demanding that she pay attention to its need; not to forget her past. She had never felt so close to her past as she did in this alley. Perhaps her luck would continue, just for one more night, she hoped, as the fatigue of the last two days suddenly caught up with her.

*

He had been staying at Eric's place for close to a week. The thought crossed his mind that he should be saying thanks and good-bye now that Eric was home for a while. Based on Eric's comments as he headed in for a shower, Pete could interpret them one of two ways; you are a big boy so no need to entertain you or you are a big boy who needs to get on with his life. He'd prefer to believe Eric meant the former but was not so sure that the latter didn't apply. True, Eric was probably tired and on edge having just come off the road. It was possible that Pete was misinterpreting everything because of his own hang-ups. In any case, he probably should be thinking about moving on. No need to wear out his stay. He liked it here. He liked Eric. And he especially liked his library. To ensure another invitation to Eric's home, Pete knew it was time to go. However, if Eric tried to convince him to stay, he would.

"I see you found something to read." Eric had entered the living room without a sound. At least that is what Pete thought, so engrossed was he in London's short story.

"Yeah. You've got a great collection here, Eric. Really great."

Eric moved to a chair that faced Pete. "It's something darn special to me. These are my friends, every single one of them." His eyes focused on the bookshelves as they scanned up and down, left and right. "Every single one of them," he murmured. "What friend of mine did you find?" he asked as he pointed to the open book on Pete's lap.

"One of my favorite writers. Jack London. This is *To Build a Fire*."

"One of the best," Eric noted as he sat back in the chair. "You read much of his?"

He could fib and say yes, but he knew that Eric could read him like a book. Pete silently enjoyed his own wit, straining to keep the grin from appearing, just in case Eric couldn't. "Not really. Just what I had to in high school. But rereading his stuff makes me wish I had paid better attention to what Mrs. Rosen was teaching us about London. About the stories."

"I think most of us who came to loving literature later in life have the same regret. I know I do. But, hey. I was just a kid in high school with a lot more on my mind than some dead guy's literary career. You know what I mean."

Pete knew what Eric was implying. But Eric's implication was so far from Pete's reality. He knew that without his parents in the picture, he couldn't keep his mind on anything but running away from everything he had known that was no longer there, gone in the blink of an eye. He knew that if it hadn't been for his Aunt Emily and Zeke, he would have dropped out in his freshman year. He hadn't thought about her in a while, and his emotional response to his memory of her and how she saved him from himself momentarily overwhelmed him. He had to look down, avoiding Eric's eyes. Composing himself, but not looking up, he responded, "Sure. Sure I do."

"You are welcome to read whatever I have here, Pete. Got to tell you, it's a relief seeing your head in a book and not glued to a device. You and I have that in common. I spend hours in here reading. You are welcome to join me. Kind of like our own private library, right?"

Pete understood what Eric was saying without him saying it. An invitation to stay. That was what Pete heard. He debated whether he should ask for clarification or just let it be. He decided to be sure. "Eric, I appreciate you putting me up like this. I've been here almost a week, far longer than I had originally planned to be. I don't want to take up any more of your time." He couldn't believe the round-about way he was speaking. "I mean, I should be heading back. You have been really kind, sharing your home with me. Thanks."

Eric did not respond immediately but rose from his chair. He moved to the section of the book shelf that held London's works. Reaching for one of them, he gently removed it and held it up. "Did you know that this is not, what you see on my shelves, a complete collection of his work?"

Pete had thought it was. "No, I didn't. I thought that it might be. That's a lot of books for one author to write."

"You bet it is. Mr. London wrote fifty-one books. Between 1900 and 1903, he wrote seven books alone! Imagine that!"

Pete was observing a trucker turned literature buff right before his eyes. He knew nothing about this man.

"And if you are really interested in London, you need to read one of the many biographies that have been published. You are in for a treat. Did you know he was an oyster pirate? A sailor? A journalist? A gold seeker? A rancher and an innovator?

None of Eric's facts rang a bell other than the "gold seeker" description. He vaguely remembered Mrs. Rosen telling his class about London's northern journey and that a replica of the cabin he lived in while in the Yukon was erected in Jack London Square in Oakland.

"So, when you finish that story, help yourself to more." Eric was glowing. His enthusiasm for London was obvious but there was more than that at work.

Pete was speechless. He would never judge a book by its cover again. Too awe struck by Eric's words and demeanor, Pete didn't even register his own humor. "Are you saying that you don't mind if I stay a bit longer?" He needed to get this question answered.

"Of course not. I already told you that you can stay as long as you want. But right now, I'm heading to bed. Stay up as long as you want." With the London book still in hand, Eric was heading toward the hallway when he stopped. Turning to Pete, he said, "Just remember to turn off the lights you're not using. My electric bill will be sky-high if you don't."

Pete hadn't realized how many lights were burning in the house. Not until Eric mentioned it. Embarrassed by his laziness and inconsideration, he started to apologize, but Eric had already shut the door to his bedroom. He would apologize in the morning.

Lifting the story from his lap, he refocused on the words before him. But his mind kept wandering. Something about Eric's admonishment. Pete felt badly about it but, at the same time, welcomed it. As he thought about it, letting the book fall to his lap again, he struggled to sort out his confusion. And then he remembered.

When he was ten years old, his father had caught him in a lie. Pete remembered it as if it happened yesterday. It was sometime after his tenth Christmas, maybe in January, when the heavy rains of winter were relentless. The thirsty dried creek beds that carved their way from the east hills and the San Francisco Bay through the Santa Clara Valley drank the heavenly rains until the ground was saturated and could swallow no more. That was when the creeks raged, full to the brim and overflowing their banks. The numerous wooden bridges constructed as footpaths for short-cuts between neighborhoods and neighboring streets were off limits during this time. Off limits to anyone with even an ounce of common sense. But to some ten-year-olds, it was an invitation for adventure. Pete and his friends fell into that category, but only once.

He had asked his father if he could go to a friend's house for the afternoon. The rains had stopped for the time being, but the sky indicated that more was to come. But Pete only saw the breaks in the clouds, the brilliant blue sky in slivers between the darkening storm clouds. He convinced his father that he could get to his friend's house before the next rains started. He would be careful, though, and go the long way, avoiding the wooden creek bridge. He would stay on the roadway. He knew his father was going against his better judgement when he gave Pete permission. But he was to call home when he got there and for a ride home if the afternoon rains continued. Not to even think about walking home in the storm. Pete triumphantly accepted his father's decision.

As he approached the wooden bridge, he could see his friend waiting for him on the other side. Between them, the angry muddy waters raged, filled with debris from the low hanging trees that stretched for miles along the creek's course. Branches ripped from their mothers and small logs collided with an assortment of trash that once sat undisturbed, someone's dumping ground, at the bottom of the dry bed. Pete knew that what he was about to do was going against his father's command, but his ten-year-old mind didn't care. Before he knew it, his legs were running under him as he hit the first section of the bridge. He felt the cold, filthy water invade his shoes as the crashing water almost submerged the wooden path. He reached out, at one point, to grab hold of the wooden railing to regain his balance, so shocked was he by what was beneath him. But he could not stop, nor could he turn around as his friend kept yelling at him to hurry up. And before he knew it, he was standing on solid ground, his friend quickly side-stepping to avoid a collision with Pete.

The rains continued into the evening and through the night. The forecast was for rain throughout the week ahead. Returning home, Pete sat in his father's car, avoiding saying anything until his father asked him if he had had a good time with his friend. Pete, unaware that his father knew exactly what he had done, said that he had. The long silence home was torturous.

When his father turned onto the street that crossed the creek, he pulled to the side of the road and turned off the engine. He opened his door and got out of the car. He gestured to Pete to do the same. Pete's legs wobbled as he stood next to his father's car. He watched as his father walked to the end of the street bridge, stop, and then turn to face Pete. Again, he gestured to Pete to do the same. When Pete reached his father, his father said nothing but walked back to the other side, passing the car. Again, he gestured for Pete to do the same. This oddly choreographed movement continued for almost thirty minutes. Back and forth. Back and forth. The rain was cooperating with his father's choreographed plan. With every step that Pete and his father took, the rain grew heavier and heavier as the wind grew in its intensity and the creek below the concrete surface of the street raged on. And after thirty minutes, drenched and tired, Pete watched his father gesture for him to get in the car. Not a word spoken in all that time, but Pete understood clearly his father's lesson. And he had never loved his father as much as he did on that silent drive back to the warmth and safety of his home.

As Pete sat in the warmth and safety of Eric's home, he realized that the confusion he was feeling had its source in a ten-year-old's mind, a memory long submerged until now. He loved his father, respected him, and missed him. As he sat forward in the chair, letting the book fall to the floor, the realization that he would truly miss Eric if he were not in his life, overwhelmed him with the fear of loss much like the raging muddy waters of the creek had tried to produce in him. At ten, though, he was only scared and did not comprehend the cost of one small slip on the wooden bridge slats that would send him into the unforgiving waters below him. He did not comprehend the loss that would follow in his absence. The lives he would leave shattered. He was only ten. Why would he? He had never revealed his fear to his friend or to his father. But he was older now. He had no excuses anymore. The fear he was feeling was real and demanded to be acknowledged. The losses in his life, his parents, Aunt Emily, Kit, and Zeke were enough. For some reason he couldn't understand, Pete accepted that Eric could not be another.

*

David Eagan sat across the breakfast table, his wife silently finishing her meal. The pleasantries of greeting had been exchanged. The last words spoken during the meal until David spoke again.

"I've been thinking a lot about Kit lately." He waited for any reaction from his wife. He saw nothing. He continued. "Not because of my daily visits, you know, but because I'm beginning to realize that we are not going to make it, Jean, if we continue whatever this is between us. When we had Kit in our lives, before she chose not to have us in hers, we were so happy. All of us. Don't you remember that?" He waited again for any reaction. About to continue, he barely heard her response.

"I remember," more a whispered communication, almost imperceptible.

David wanted to reach his hand across the table and hold onto his wife as she fought her way through the invisible barrier that was keeping them apart. He would not let go until she was safely by his side. But the thought was merely that.

"I know you do. And I often wonder if our memories are the same ones. We shared our beautiful child's life for so long. There must be some." His thoughts were rambling, and he tried to refocus on his original point. "Jean, I think...no, I know that we have to make the effort to save our marriage. I can't go on like this, living alone while living together. I can't believe that you want this either."

Jean shifted in her chair so that her body angled away from her husband.

"I don't," no longer a whisper but David had to lean in to be sure he heard her. "I don't, David, want any of this." She turned back toward her husband. "I don't want any of this, not any of it!"

David, taken aback by the clarity of her words and struck by their meaning, felt his stomach summersault wildly. His heart was beating rapidly. He refused to believe that his wife was not willing to try but was shutting him down so cruelly.

"Wait a minute. Wait…wait. Are you telling me that you don't want to even try? That everything we have shared and been through together you're willing to throw away just like that? Is that what you mean?" He couldn't gather his thoughts coherently to continue as his body's interior rebelled against her as well.

Jean stood slowly and moved across the kitchen, dirty dishes in hand. She put them in the sink and did not turn to face him as she spoke.

"No, David. That is not what I am saying. What I want I cannot have. What I need I can no longer need. What I have done I cannot undo. I don't want any of it. Do you understand?"

She did not move but held onto the counter's edge, gripping the cold tile so that she would stay upright. She did not trust her body to support her, so eager was it to betray her, she thought.

David wanted to go to her, as he had wanted to hold her hand. He knew that she needed his touch as much as he needed hers. But the distance was still so great between them.

"Jean, I do understand," he said, now standing but not moving. "My god. I understand. It's not your fault, it's not. It's not our fault what happened between us and Kit." He paused before he continued with what he had understood for a long time. "Maybe, it's all of our faults."

Jean turned and faced her husband, her face revealing traces of moisture, tiny rivers of salt water running nowhere.

"Blaming our daughter, our child, for our adult behavior? Are you doing that, David? I can't believe you would do that." She did not hold back. "That's ridiculous! I know who's to blame and it's not our daughter."

The cluster of words slammed into David who was not prepared for Jean's attack. The last thing that he wanted was an all-out fight infused with accusations and irrationality. But there it was. The first volley. He did not have to retaliate. But he did, and he hated himself for it.

"It's not? Are you that sure? And are you blaming me? You had nothing to do with it at all?"

"That's not what I'm saying! I know what I did! And I

know how you reacted. You, who just let me do it. You…you should have stopped me. You should have been the husband and stepped in to protect your daughter from me. But you didn't. You just kept you mouth shut. You gave your approval of my behavior and that of your daughter by not saying a word. I will never forgive you for that, David. Never!"

The tables had turned so quickly that David had no response. What could he say to combat her irrational thinking? But he finally understood why his wife would have nothing to do with him. Why she would not talk about Kit with him. Why she would not go to her daughter's gravesite. He was to blame for keeping Kit away. He was to blame for allowing his wife to do so. And what she said was true about not standing up to her. It was what he hoped that Kit would forgive him for each day when he spoke to her. It was what he knew about himself from the first day that Kit denied her parents' love. He was waiting for his daughter to forgive him even if his wife refused to.

"I need you to forgive me, Jean. You are right about me not standing up to either one of you. I accept all the blame for that. I can't undo what I've done any more than you can. So where does that leave us? Hating each other? I don't…I can't hate you. I can't even dislike you, Jean. I love you as I love our daughter. I won't stop loving you or Kit. I just can't." His body quivered uncontrollably, his breathing now short gasps between the pent-up cries of anguish finally released after all these years.

Jean Eagan froze, frightened by the emotional disintegration of her husband. His words had penetrated her angry thoughts. His love for her and for their daughter was undeniable. He was fighting for his life, for their lives, and she knew in her heart that what he said was true. Unable to let him suffer alone, she went to him. He allowed her. Their bodies sank to the kitchen floor as one, both holding on for dear life in an embrace of forgiveness and survival.

*

"You up for a hike?" Eric handed Pete a cup of coffee as they prepared their breakfast.

"A hike? Sure," Pete responded as he buttered his toast. "You got a place in mind?"

Eric handed Pete the strawberry preserves. "Thought we might try the base of Shasta."

"Seriously?" Pete heard the sarcasm in his voice before Eric reacted to it. "Sorry. I just mean…well, isn't that a serious climb? Aren't you tired from your last run?" Pete still was not on solid ground with his comments.

"Well, if you're not up to it, that's fine. Just thought you might like to get out of here for a while. Go exploring. Don't have to do it today. Probably be smarter to head down to the "Fifth Season" and get some info from the experts before we try it anyway." Eric sat down and started to eat.

"Sorry, Eric. That didn't come across right. But, yeah. I wouldn't mind trying it. Maybe get the info so we have a good time of it." He flashed on the PCT for just a moment.

"Okay then. That's the plan. How about after breakfast that's what we do? Then see where the day takes us. You up for that?"

It crossed Pete's mind that he was not going to be in charge of his day. With Eric home, he would need to shift gears. He said a silent good-bye to Mr. London for a while. "Sounds like a plan, at least the first part." He laughed, and Eric laughed with him.

"You know, I found in my lifetime, that the best times I've ever had were the unplanned ones. Too many times we get in our own way, you know what I mean?"

Pete understood completely and, once again, this man sitting across the breakfast table from him impressed Pete. "I sure do. Like the ride you gave me the first time we met. We wouldn't be sitting here if the old lady who picked me up after you, picked me up first." Pete smiled as he recalled Hellenia's purple hands gripping the steering wheel.

"What old lady? You mean at the rest stop after I left you?"

"Yeah. She took me all the way into San Jose to a few blocks from my apartment."

"No kidding. That was a lucky break for you, I guess." Eric chewed vigorously on a reef of bacon. "Totally unplanned. See what I mean?"

"Not only that but get a load of this. She grew up in the same area as me. Knew places that I knew. Just weird." Pete reflected on what he had just said. It was weird.

"Coincidence is what they call it. Bay Area has a lot of people in it, coming and going. More likely than not, you would have been picked up by someone familiar with the area. Both heading south, I mean." Eric paused in his chewing. "But I will agree that coincidences can have the trappings of weirdness, if you believe in that kind of thing."

"Well, all I can say is that someone was watching out for me that day."

"You would have gotten a ride eventually."

"No, I don't mean because I got a ride. I mean that this old lady was not all there. And her driving? Well, I'm sitting here because someone was taking the wheel, helping her along. I'm sure of it. It was wild. I thought for sure that my life was over when we entered 80 going west." He saw, again, her purple hand waving at the traffic while the other turned the wheel into lane after lane.

Eric couldn't help but laugh at his young companion's retelling. He'd seen his fair share of loonies on the roadways but from the safe distance of his cab and he had the height and weight of the semi in his favor. But he could understand how it might be as a passenger in one of those loony tunes' car and was glad he didn't have a similar story to share with Pete.

"Well, that's a good story, Pete. Next time you hitch, don't get in a loony tunes' car."

Pete heard the smile in Eric's voice before he looked up at him from his eggs. And he heard his father's voice, admonishing him yet again. And it was okay with him.

"No, you're right about that. I can't believe they even let old folks drive. How did she get her license? Not to mention the car she was driving. You ever been on a bench seat before?"

Eric burst into laughter and it took him a while to control himself. "What do you think you sat on in my rig?"

Pete realized his mistake but that wasn't what he meant. "Well yeah. Okay. But I'm talking about the older cars, maybe in the sixties or earlier, that had the front bench seat? You ever been in one of those?"

"Course I have. My dad owned a few of them. Learned to drive on one. So, you shared a bench seat with a loony old lady?"

"Yeah. All the way to San Jose. I guess she wasn't all that loony. Not really. We had a couple of good conversations, now that I think about it."

"Well, see. You can't judge a book by its cover, can you?" Eric scraped the last of the egg from his plate with his toast.

Pete smiled broadly. "No, I guess you can't."

*

"Will you come with me today?' David Eagan had waited for his wife to wake up enough before asking. They had lain in bed together, nuzzled in each other's arms, sluffing off the deep sleep that had mercifully taken them away, momentarily, from their waking hours. They had not made love, not physically. That would come.

"Yes," was all Jean Eagan replied.

*

The night had not been kind to Hellenia. It insisted on dragging on and on. Every time she awoke, she checked her watch only to find that mere minutes had passed since the last time she stirred. Her frustration only grew as her tired body demanded rest. But she couldn't comply with it. The seat, her bed, was comfortable enough. As a matter of fact, it was wider than her "baby's" and had more cushioning. It wasn't the car that was to blame.

In the darkness, afraid to shine any light within, alerting others to her, she sat up and reached over the front seat. She groped for reassurance that her boxes were right where she had put them. Yes, she felt them. Their solid sides, tops and bottoms securely in place. She toyed with the idea of getting out of the "boat" and checking that her other belongings were still safely stored in the trunk. But her better judgement warned her against it. Too dark, without any kind of light. Maybe it was the car, after all, that kept her from sleeping. She feared that she might never get used to it. It would never replace her "baby" who knew her so well.

Slowly lowering her body again, she turned to face the seatback, pulling the worn blanket up around her shoulders and neck. She closed her eyes and tried to imagine that her "baby" was nestling her in its familiarity. That when she awoke before daybreak, she would thank her lucky stars that she had made it through one more night.

*

Pete saw it before Eric noticed it, but Pete didn't say anything. Just a car. An old one, not so uncommon in this area. They were heading into town, the planned part of their day.

"Hold up." Eric stopped and turned toward the parked car in the ally.

"What's up?"

"Just a minute." He took some steps into the alley but did not go any further.

"Eric. What's up?" Pete could see nothing amiss.

"It's just that this car...well, it's not the car that's usually parked here."

"So? Is that a problem?" Pete wasn't connecting with his friend.

"No, I guess not."

Pete heard the hesitation in Eric's response. "What do you mean, 'you guess not'?

Eric turned and made his way back to Pete. "Never mind. Let's go."

As they headed toward town, Eric was deep in thought. Pete sensed that and left him alone. Whatever was on his mind was not his business. Eric would engage with Pete when he was ready.

The store was already busy with tourists and serious trekkers. Making their way to the counter, Eric acquired a trail map and got the information about the base of the volcano. The trail did not appeal to Pete in the least. He wasn't sure why, but he faked mild enthusiasm for Eric's sake. He could hang in there.

"So, what do you think. You still want to try it?" Eric held the door open as they exited the store.

"Yeah, sure, if you want to."

"That's not a resounding confirmation."

"Sorry. I'm willing." He tried to sound enthusiastic.

"Okay. Let's head back, get our gear and head out. Okay with you?"

Pete had no choice. "Yup. It's a plan. Let's do it."

The plan never came to fruition. The unexpected turn of events that morning for both men was about to change their lives forever.

*

Jane Eagan gripped her husband's hand as he led her to Kit's gravesite. She had not seen the headstone. It wasn't put into place until after the funeral, days after. Upon seeing it, she stopped and pulled her husband closer to her. He held her as she turned in to him. He held her until she was ready. And when she moved away from him, releasing her hand from his, she walked to her daughter, knelt beside the granite stone and reached out to it, running her hand along its unfinished surface. Then she reached out for David to join her. Together but apart, they each reflected on their memories of their little girl. No words spoken, no glances of reassurance, no physical contact with one another. One finally asking for forgiveness while the other waited for his daughter's response.

*

This time, on their way back to the house, Eric entered the alley and approached the car. He said nothing to Pete, leaving him at the foot of the drive. Not sure he should follow, Pete waited. He watched as Eric stood behind the car for what seemed minutes. Then Eric moved slowly to the driver's side, keeping some distance. He never looked back at Pete.

He watched as Eric gently rapped on the driver's window. He did it again. Then he saw Eric's hand on the handle. Unable to open the door, he watched as Eric went to the passenger side and attempted to do the same, but the door would not open. He watched in surprise as Eric leaned into the window and peered through the glass, this time banging on the window.

Pete watched as Eric quickly moved towards him. "Call 911. Now!"

Both men stood helpless as they watched the fire and rescue teams break open the car. Simple maneuver that Eric knew well but could not draw upon at the time. His adrenaline still coursing through his veins, he fought the urge to interfere with the uniformed men.

He didn't tell Pete what he saw in that car. Not at first. And all Pete could see was a drape placed over the back of the car, held up by two officers, as movement occurred behind it. The body was removed and placed on a gurney. They both knew that much as they watched an EMT push it towards the waiting ambulance. The sound of the gurney's collapsing wheel base as two men shoved it into the ambulance made Eric jump ever so slightly. Enough that Pete noticed his friend's sudden movement.

"Eric, are you okay?" He had no idea what was going on but whatever it was had shaken this man.

Eric did not respond but moved forward, closer to the yellow police tape hurriedly wound around the area where the old car sat. Pete followed him, not sure of anything.

"Eric, I don't think we should be this close." A sheriff's deputy apparently agreed as he observed the two approach.

"Sorry, back off, please." He stood in front of them, one hand resting on the handle of his gun. "This is police business."

"Okay, sure." Pete was already backing up as he spoke to the officer. But Eric stayed where he was.

"Sir, you need to back off." This time the officer came towards Eric and this was enough for Eric to react. He did not turn around but took a few steps backwards, all the while keeping an eye on the scene in front of him.

"Understood."

The officer nodded and returned, ducking under the tape.

"Eric. What's going on?" Pete had had enough of being in the dark. It was obvious that Eric knew something but was unwilling to share it with Pete. "Why don't we go back to the house. Nothing we can do here."

"You go, if you want. Go ahead. I'll meet up with you there." Eric did not bother to turn to Pete as he spoke. "Go!"

Pete knew better than to say another word. That much he was beginning to understand about Eric. He turned his back on the scene and headed back to the house, a million questions beginning to form in his mind.

Eric returned almost an hour later. He came in without acknowledging Pete who was reading in the living room. Pete had tried to focus on the story, but his mind kept wandering to the alley. To the car. To Eric. The uneasiness of suddenly not knowing, of being kept in the dark, was strikingly familiar.

When his parents were instantly killed in the highway crash, he wasn't told about it. Not until the end of the following day after his Aunt Emily had lied to him about their whereabouts. He went about his business, sat in his freshman classes, went to soccer practice wondering if his parents were having a good time on their spontaneous vacation. Something bothered him about this, but he would be the first to admit that he knew nothing about how adults functioned in marriages other than what they modeled for him. He had no reason to believe that they were anywhere else than what his aunt told him. She would be waiting for him when he got home. "Babysitting", he remembered her telling him with a forced smile on her face, until his parents returned. And when he opened the door of his home, he heard his aunt crying uncontrollably in the kitchen. She didn't hear him come in but must have sensed his presence. Quickly wiping her face with a dish towel, she turned to see her nephew standing in the doorway, uncomfortable and embarrassed for his aunt, unsure of what to do next.

Eric disappeared for a short time only to reappear holding two glasses of water as he sat down across from Pete. "Thought you might need this." He held one glass out to Pete.

Pete put the book down on the side table, closing the cover, forgetting to mark his place. It didn't matter. He took the cold glass from Eric and drank. Not knowing what to say, he braced himself and waited for Eric to speak. Pete's fourteen year-old-self fought to be present.

"Sorry about being so dismissive of you back there." His eyes were focused on Pete. "I need to explain."

Eric began by telling him about the old car in the alley, the one that he had seen there so many times before. He told him that it came in the night and was gone before the sun came up. He figured that whoever was in there was homeless and needed a place to stay. No one bothered the occupant because what harm was it? Sure, he had been tempted to find out, to offer help if it was needed, but he never carried through with it. And as time went on, it became a fixture, an accepted part of the neighborhood, a publicly unspoken topic that was only spoken about in the privacy of one's own home. He was sure of that because he had spent plenty of time wondering aloud to himself about it, so he was sure others did the same.

What had thrown him was that the old car was not the one that he approached today. And he couldn't be sure that the person found in the car was the same person who had been his silent neighbor for all this time.

"What do you mean?" Pete was intrigued.

"It's a different car. An Impala, probably early sixties."

"So?"

"So I don't know the car. I never knew the person, but

somehow I came to believe I did." Pete could see the worry on Eric's face. The confusion.

"Well, if it's not the same car, what was the other car?"

"It was a white Valiant, vintage sixties."

"A white Valiant? Are you serious?" He didn't mean to sound incredulous, but he did.

"Yeah. What do you mean, am I serious?"

Pete tried to calm the rushing waters of his mind. He saw her so vividly. Her white wisps of ancient hair, her tattered filthy knit hat pulled down to conceal the rest of her strands, her purple gloves gripping the steering wheel. He saw Hellenia and he wondered aloud.

"Who did they take out of the car?"

"I don't know who. I could only see the head. Some kind of wool hat pulled down so that I couldn't make out the face. Probably to keep the cold away. Whoever it was, was wrapped up in an old blanket."

Pete knew. He knew it better than he knew his own soul. He fought off the freefall that his body yearned for, that he yearned for. What he had felt as he walked home, the questions that he could not formulate had been answered in a matter of two simple words. White Valiant. He confirmed that it was Hellenia. The wanderer who traveled Interstate 5 day in and day out for who knew how long. The fellow traveler who had the heart to stop and give him a ride home. The woman who had lived longer than he knew he ever would. The woman whose roots ran deeply in the same place that his did. The woman who would "live and die in them there mountains." The same mountains that surrounded him at this moment. The woman who had haunted him every day since he first met her. A fact that only now he was aware of and accepted.

"Eric, I think I may know who the person is…was." He felt that he should not say, not give her away so easily.

"What do you mean? How would you know?" Eric sat down, ready for anything.

"Well, you said that the car came and went. Stayed here at night. And you said something about a wool hat? I know that you're going to think I'm nuts, but I think I've been in that car before. The white Valiant."

The silence between them was deafening.

"How? Why?"

"Okay. You remember me telling you that I hitched a ride after you left me at the rest stop?"

"Sure."

"So, the person who picked me up was driving an old white Valiant. There can't be that many still on the road, can there?" Pete was attempting to approach all this as logically as he could.

"No, I guess not. But up here lots of folks hold onto old beaters." He wasn't dismissing Pete's question, but wasn't entirely convinced either.

"Okay. That's possible. But I got to tell you, Eric, the old lady driving that car wore a knit hat. It was over ninety degrees that day when we came out of the mountains and into the San Joaquin Valley. Not only that, she had purple knit mittens on and kept them on the whole way to San Jose. Did you see any mittens?"

"She was too wrapped up in the blanket to tell." Eric was intrigued.

"And now that I think about it, her car was not a beater. She traveled from here south, sometimes as far as the Bay Area, numerous times during the week. She liked giving people lifts and she liked driving. But she was one crazy driver." Pete let a smile escape as he remembered Hellenia's antics on the freeway.

"So, you're saying that you could identify her? Do you know her name?"

"Yeah, I could, yeah. Her name was Hellenia, but she told me to call her Hell."

The name was so familiar, but Eric could not place it. A beautiful and unusual name. Maybe he was thinking of that town in the Napa Valley? Wasn't there a place called Helena or something like that?

"Don't know why but that name rings a bell. Think I might be thinking of that Napa town. You know the one I mean?

"Sure I do. St. Helena. I can see how you could mix up the names. Another thing I just remembered. When she picked me up, she told me to put my pack in the back seat but to be careful of her boxes back there. Did you see any boxes on the back seat?"

Eric tried to remember but all he could visualize was the poor woman's body. Everything else was a blank. "No, I didn't notice them if they were there."

"Well, if I didn't believe in coincidences, I do now. What are the odds?" Pete was starting to comprehend the enormity of the recent events.

Eric stood up and headed for the front door. "Come on. Get your ID and stuff."

"Where are you going?

Eric was half way through the door when he spoke. "Going down to see Willy."

"Willy?" Pete was up and searching for his wallet.

"The Police Chief. Chief William Burns to you. But Willy to me. Hurry it up." Eric was at the bottom of the porch stairs.

The ambulance was long gone. On its way to the city morgue in Redding. Pete wasn't sure what he thought he'd see when they arrived at the station. From the outside, everything looked normal. But when they entered, Eric in the lead, the place was bustling. Eric didn't wait for permission as he walked straight back to Willy's office. No one stopped him either.

"Eric!" He held up his hand indicating he needed a minute. His phone call done, he stood and came around his desk to shake hands with his best friend. "What brings you down here?"

"Willy. Good to see you." He turned to Pete. "Want you to meet Pete. A friend of mine."

Pete shook Willy's hand. "Nice to meet you officer…sir …Chief. Sorry." He was nervous, uncomfortable, not knowing where any of this might be going.

"You got a last name, Pete?"

"Pete Wade-Murphy. Sorry, yeah…Wade-Murphy."

He struggled to regain his composure. The last time he spoke to an officer was when Kit went missing. He felt his stomach starting to do flips.

"All right then. I say again, what brings you down here, Eric?"

Pete could see why they were best friends. The chief appeared to be a twin of Eric's. Not in looks but in his demeanor; open, friendly, and nonthreatening. Granted, he had only just met the man, but Pete could feel it.

"The incident this morning. The body found in the old car in the alley up by my house? Pete here thinks he knows who the deceased is. Thinks he's even been in her car before." Eric looked at Pete for confirmation and then back at Willy.

"Not that car but another one she had," Pete corrected Eric. "The white Valiant."

"Right. You're right, Pete. Stand corrected." Eric kept his eyes on Willy.

"Is that so? Well, this car is in compound and we won't know anything until sometime tomorrow. The body's been taken to the morgue in Redding. All personal property and identification will stay in compound for now. So, I can't tell you anything than what I just did."

Eric was growing impatient, Pete could tell. "I understand all that, Willy. What I'm telling you is that Pete might know the identity."

"Might is not good enough, Eric. You know that. We'll have confirmation of the facts tomorrow. And if Pete's info matches the facts, well then, good."

This time Pete spoke first. "I understand Chief, perfectly. We can wait." He didn't look at Eric knowing all he'd see was a look of disapproval.

"Well, you don't have a choice, now, do you?" He threw his head back and a forced laugh filled the space. "But I do appreciate you coming in. A situation like this is upsetting for everyone. Well, let's just say, the intrigue can be overwhelming."

Was he looking right at Pete when he said this? Pete thought so. "Excuse me, Chief. I just want you to know that I'm in no way intrigued by any of this. In fact, I am one of those who's upset because I think I know her. I know her name. I spent hours with her in her car. Not the Impala. The white Valiant. She came from the same place I did. I…" Pete stopped short cutting himself off from further humiliation. The Chief's hint of a smile and the wink of his eye directed right at Eric was enough.

"So, tomorrow. No sooner. Eric, you up for a bite tonight after I get off? Haven't shared a meal with you in a while." He glanced at Pete. "Are you staying with Eric?"

"Yes."

"Well, you're welcome to come along if you don't mind spending your time with two old men. Right, Eric?"

That laugh again. Maybe Pete had jumped too quickly to conclusions about the twins. The guy made him uneasy.

"Right, Willy." Eric turned to Pete. "It's up to you, Pete."

He didn't have to think about it. "Thanks, but I think I'll be on my own tonight. No problem."

"Okay, then. Settled. See you around 6 down at Elsie's?" He didn't wait for Eric's confirmation but walked back into his office. He turned and stuck his head through the doorway. "Good to meet you, Pete."

Pete just nodded and followed Eric out the door.

*

Eric left the house just before six but not before he made sure that Pete was still okay with it. Considering the day that they just had, Eric was concerned for his young friend. But Pete reassured him that he was fine. He'd catch up on his reading. Maybe even finish the story he had started. "See you when I see you," he told Eric.

The evening air filled the house. Pete had opened every window and door to bring the outside in. He wasn't concerned about the occasional flies or moths that flew in. They'd find their way out eventually. After supper, he had taken a short walk in the direction of the alley. He had no intention of stopping there. Besides, the police tape was still draped haphazardly marking the perimeter of Hellenia's last night on earth. Pete thought about that as he slowly walked by. He wondered where she was right now. Not her body but her soul. Was she still with us, standing next to him? Remembering him? Or was she moving up and down Interstate 5, an entity with no body but only memories? Was she finding her loved ones? Maybe she had already, instantly, he corrected himself, found her way back to San Jose. And if so, was she seeing the valley as it was when she was a little girl or as the modern city rat-race it had become? Or was she just dead? No soul, no heaven, no hell. Nothing but organic material, period.

He kept walking and found himself in town, so deep in thought about Hellenia that he was surprised when he looked around and saw the gem shop across the street. He had no need to go in and recalled his visit there. What had he done with the crystal? He couldn't place its location other than on the bed. He dropped the box there but couldn't remember doing anything with it. The thought crossed his mind that Eric might have moved it, but he dismissed it. Eric wouldn't disturb his stuff. He was pretty sure of that. Funny. He'd look for it when he got back.

Sure enough, the box was right where he had put it. Under the bed with his other stuff. He couldn't remember doing it, but it didn't matter. His mind had been elsewhere, he figured.

He lifted it on to the bed and this time, opened the box. The crystal was carefully wrapped. Sitting on top of it was the page the shop owner had printed out for him. Seeing it, he remembered that he was supposed to read it to understand his crystal. Sure. Whatever. New Age mumbo jumbo. But he had nothing else pressing other than Jack London waiting patiently for him in the living room. He would understand.

The title caught his attention first. "SELF-HEALED". He began reading and did not put the paper down until the last word was read. And then he read it again.

Your purchase of this quartz crystal is for a reason. Yes, your eye was drawn to it, but why? Crystals have grown in popularity but have been in use for thousands of years. They are considered to hold powers of healing. Perhaps you are in need of healing? Is the universe giving you a little prodding? No matter what your personal beliefs may be, you now possess the possibility of moving forward positively in your life, if you choose to do so.

Examine your crystal. Do you see that one end looks different than the other? On one end, it appears unscathed. But at the other end, it looks quite different. This part of the crystal was the broken end, injured end, if you will. Look closely and you will see what looks like stone upon stone. The reason your crystal is called Self-Healed is because this disturbed end has been overgrown with Quartz crystal; the crystal's attempt to heal its wound.

Perhaps you understand now why you are reading this? If not, more explanation is needed. Self-Healed Crystals can help you examine your life. We all have past experiences, some good, some bad, and some quite terrible. You are who you are because of them. And, like most of us, we work at submerging the uncomfortable experiences in favor of gliding through life, tentatively relying on the strength of the happier moments.

However, to help you heal from the uncomfortable experiences, you must find a way to accept them and to understand how you have grown because of them. Your crystal can help you achieve this.

(For more information, see "Meditation with Crystals")

Pete unwrapped his crystal and held it in his hand. He

examined it closely determining one end from the other. And he wondered if the coincidence of the explanation given and that of his own life was just that, a simple coincidence, or if he had in his hand a gift. As he held it to the light, turning it this way and that, the air on the left side of his body suddenly felt chilled and heavy. It passed as suddenly as it came.

"Is this from you, mom and dad or from you, Hellenia?" he whispered aloud. There was no immediate response.

*

Jean Eagan had found peace again and her sleep was deep and undisturbed. No longer did she wander the house in the early morning hours. No longer did she enter her daughter's bedroom and linger in the darkness, alone. And no longer did she swear at her daughter, her husband, or herself. If anything, she spent a good amount of time with her husband. When she was ready, she began to put away Kit's things and make the room into a guest room.

So, when she suddenly awoke in the middle of the night, heart pounding, she was frightened that she wasn't free yet. That the healing of her mind was not complete. She sat straight up, trying to breathe deeply and slowly, trying to slow down the pounding in her chest. An overwhelming sadness struck her. Her tears fell, and she covered her mouth to keep the audible gasps from her husband's slumbering body next to hers. Something was wrong and the only feeling that she could identify was a tangible loneliness, a terrible loss, and a longing for whatever it was to return.

*

It was not the next day, as Chief Burns had indicated, nor was it the second day that any news about the identity of the body was released to Eric. A full week later, Eric got a call from Willy to come down to the station. He had news.

"Eric, you know that I cannot release information about an incident to just anyone who wants to know. That's not how it's done. You know that." Willy did not take his seat but remained standing in front of his desk. Eric stood in front of him with Pete at his side.

"'Course I do. As a matter of fact, I figured that after a week of no news, it was none of our business." He looked at Pete who was about to remind them both that he knew the lady. But he kept quiet.

"I would like you both to come with me. I want to show you something that will shed some light on all of this. Won't take long." Willy did not move but waited for Eric to respond.

"Okay. Pete? You okay with that?" Eric had not forgotten what Pete had said about the other car.

It suddenly dawned on Pete that whatever was going on right now had something to do with them both or they would not be here. Why would Eric be involved?

"Pete?" Eric asked again.

"Yeah. That's fine." But Pete wasn't convinced by his own words.

They followed Willy through the building and down two flights of stairs finding themselves standing in what appeared to be a large storage unit. Pete had never seen so much stuff in one spot. The shelving went from floor to ceiling on every wall. Every shelf held mostly cardboard boxes with printed labels, some so worn that they were impossible to read while others looked as if they were labeled yesterday. On a long table in the middle of the room were two cardboard boxes, not the same as the ones surrounding them. They were old, well-used, and carried no labels.

Willy moved to the table. He placed one hand on the

nearest box. "These were found on the backseat of the deceased's car. Personal belongings." He stepped away, dropping his hands to his sides and did not speak for a moment, as if out of respect.

Pete remembered Hellenia warning him to be careful of her boxes as he threw his pack over the front seat. But not in this car where they found her. A queasy feeling tried to erupt in his gut as he concentrated on taking slow breaths, preparing himself for whatever was to come next.

Eric spoke, breaking the silence. "Willy. I don't understand. What are we doing here?"

Pete wanted to speak up, but it was not his place. Something within him was guiding him to remain quiet. To wait. To be there for Eric.

"That box," he pointed to it this time, "contains an envelope among other stu…items," he quickly corrected himself, "that indicate your involvement with the deceased." He could detect Eric's growing confusion. "I think it best, Eric, if I leave you two alone for a bit. Best that you take your time with the contents. As a matter of fact, we can get these boxes put in your cab so you can do this at home. Got your cab with you?"

Pete looked at Eric. He could see that Eric was not on solid ground. He took a chance. "No, we walked here but I could go back and get my car, Eric, if you want?"

Still focused on nothing else but the boxes, Eric remained silent.

"Eric, I'll have one of my guys bring these up to the house." Looking now at Pete, "You going to be there within the hour?" Willy sensed that his old friend was in shock. Seen it plenty of times before in his career. And he wasn't at all surprised by Eric's reaction, considering the letter inside the envelope. At this moment, he was the only one, other than a detective, who knew the contents. Best if Eric had someone with him when he read it, Willy surmised.

"Yeah. I'll make sure that we are." He did not look at Eric this time.

The walk back to the house was in silence. Pete didn't try

to engage his friend in talk. He knew better.

Within the hour, the officer brought the boxes into the house and Pete directed him to the kitchen table as Eric looked on.

Eric sat down on the couch. To Pete, he seemed strangely calm, unconcerned, and distant. Not at all the confused person who stood next to him less than an hour ago.

"You want me to leave for a while, Eric? Give you some privacy?" Pete hoped that Eric would say no to his offer. He didn't want to leave him alone.

He glanced up at Pete, then to the boxes. He walked over to Pete and placed his arm around Pete's shoulders. "You know. I'm not sure about anything right now. Well, maybe one thing. Whatever's in those boxes wants us both here. That I'm sure of, Pete."

*

Jean was up before David. She had tried to get back to sleep but she couldn't shake off the remnants of whatever had awakened her in the first place. As she sat at the kitchen table in the dark, sipping on hot tea to calm her, her place in time, at this very moment, seemed intangible. All her thoughts were not of the present but of somewhere very far away, long before Kit, long before David. So very far away but forcing their presence upon her now as she sat in her kitchen sipping her tea in the very early hours of the morning.

*

The boxes, like anything old, smelled musty and aged. Their once brown surfaces were now bleached and brittle, for years the victims of a beating sun through clear car glass windows. Eric first opened the one that Willy's hand had rested upon. He knew it by the number one that was written on its top. An envelope lay on top of the contents which were wrapped in old newspaper and tissue paper. He held it for a long time before opening it. Pete stood on the other side of the table. When Eric opened the envelope, he slowly took out a piece of paper that appeared to Pete to be handwritten. Letting the envelope fall to the table's surface, it landed face up. Pete read the scrawled writing: *To My Children, Eric and Jean.*

*

The images came quickly. She had no control over them. All Jean could do was focus on them, desperately drawing on her memories to interpret them. She could not go back far enough to do so, however. But something in the darkness of the images reached out to her, trying to hold on to her. She felt it, a comfort and security, as if she were wrapped up in someone's arms. Her tea, the mug still hot to the touch, soothed her internally but the sudden chill that descended on her, hovering next to the left side of her body, caused her to wrap her robe even tighter around her. And just as suddenly, it was gone.

*

He read it in silence. Pete did not move from the table, waiting for Eric to finish. He knew that Eric was reading it more than once, watching his eyes shift from the top to the bottom of the sheet numerous times. When he was finished, he carried the sheet with him to the living room and seemed to be looking for a book on the shelves. He began on one side of the shelving, methodically tracking every title with his index finger, as he moved across the length of each shelf. Those that he couldn't reach with his hand, he stood back and focused his eyes upwards, frowning as he tried to read the titles. Still, Pete did not interfere or say a word.

Eric stopped. His hand rested on the leather-bound journal that Pete had slipped back between the others, leaving just enough of it protruding for easy retrieval. He gently pulled it from its recently disturbed lodgings and turned to Pete.

"Did you read this?"

Startled not only by the question but also by the accusing tone of Eric's voice, Pete froze. Had he? He panicked. Stupidly.

"I...I...well, no. Not really." Eric's eyes focused on Pete's. "I mean I opened it and flipped through it but put it back. I figured it was personal. Something I should not be reading, Eric." Watching Eric's interrogating expression still unchanged, he remembered. "Oh, right. I understand. The reason it was out like that? I did that so I could ask you about it when you got back from your last run. I completely forgot about it, Eric."

Eric's face did not relax as he crossed in front of Pete and headed back into the kitchen. Pete didn't know what to do. Probably best if he just left for a while before he made things worse. He suddenly felt like a little kid in a heap of trouble waiting for his punishment.

Eric put the book on the table next to the boxes. Pete, almost to the front door, heard Eric call to him. "I expect you better be here when I open these up, Peter Wade-Murphy."

1934

He was disappointed when he first opened the small birthday gift. It was from his mother and father. Times were rough for the families in the valley. He was lucky to get any present, considering it was a luxury, not to be afforded but once given, not to be taken lightly. The blank pages added to his disappointment. What was he supposed to do with it? But he pretended to be grateful and thanked his parents.

"You start today, young man. You write down everything that happened to you today. No fibs, no lies, no exaggerations. Just the truth. You do that every day from here on until the last day you draw a breath. Don't forget to write the date at the beginning. That way you have your own record of your life. When you get to be our age and, if God is willing, older, every little moment will be right there," his father pointed with his weathered and dirty hand, slowly extending his arthritic index finger as best he could toward the leather journal, "right there for you to read."

Benny assured his mother and father that he would. That he would do this every day for the rest of his life. But a ten-year-old's life wasn't all that exciting to write about and as each short entry, one or two sentences long, began to fill the pages, unbeknownst to him, a life-long habit was forming.

2016

Pete wasn't sure how much time went by before Eric said anything more. To Pete, it seemed an eternity, left in the dark and completely unprepared for what was to come next. Nothing made any sense and he suddenly felt afraid.

Eric's sudden move startled Pete, so immersed was he in his own concerns. He watched Eric reach in and gently release a wrapped object from the many still in the box. The old newsprint he let drop to the floor. In his hand, lay a plastic horse, a child's toy. To Pete, it appeared quite new, possibly purchased recently. It was black with a fake brown leather saddle. Its jet-black mane made from thin silky threads lay on either side of its long neck. Other than rigid, it was rendered life-like. He could see how a kid would like playing with it, but he wouldn't have. Never was into horses.

Eric stood it upright on the kitchen table. He reached in again. Another plastic horse was freed from its wrappings. This time it was a deep chestnut brown with a black saddle. Like the black horse, it looked new. Eric stood it next to the black horse. Again, and again, and again, the yellowed newsprint revealed one more horse each time. Each slightly different from the rest. Some were miniature compared to their companions. A few towered over the rest. Most were what Pete thought of as "normal" toy horse size. As the pile of newsprint on the floor grew, so did the herd that Eric was creating. He would stop every now and then, focus on the group of equines, and then rearrange two or three of them. Pete watched, captivated by the scene playing out in front of him. The deeper Eric's hand disappeared into the box, the unwrapping revealed much older looking horses. Certainly not as sophisticated as the first ones and with each revelation, they seemed to grow larger. Fuller bodies, necks, and stout legs joined Eric's herd. More rearranging. And never a word spoken.

Eric lifted the second box and put it on the floor next to him to make more room for his growing herd, now stretching the length of the table and almost as deep as the width in most places. Pete lost count. There must have been at least thirty horses waiting patiently forever as Eric's hand disappeared into the box one last time.

When he lifted the last paper bundle from its old home, he held it for a moment before opening it. Pete watched as Eric's hand opened and closed over the newsprint, his fingers examining the contours of the object within. Carefully unwrapping the paper, Pete watched for the first signs of plastic-color but none appeared. Instead, as Eric released the last bit of newsprint to the floor, the shape of a horse was evident, but it was nothing like its companions. Its paint had faded over time so that its color was nondescript. The patches of bare wood, perhaps pine, seemed a blight on what once must have been a silken finish. It had no saddle but neither did some of the plastic ones. No threaded mane hung about its neck. One of its tiny wooden ears was partially missing, its tip broken off somewhere along the way. The painted eyes, an almost invisible greying of the original black, were slanted, reminding Pete of the Japanese wooden dolls he had seen in the shops in Japan Town when he was a kid.

Eric did not set it in place with the others. He held it gently, holding it up momentarily as if examining all parts of its body. Still, without a word to Pete, Eric left the room and walked down the hall, still holding the horse. He was in his room for a long time. At least it felt like that to Pete. Everything lately seemed to feel that way. Almost like he was caught in limbo unable to find his footing.

When Eric finally returned, he was smiling. In each hand, he carried a wooden horse. Gently, he placed each one on the remaining table surface in front of the herd. They were not identical now, but Pete was sure they must have been at some point in their history. The horse that came from the box was in better shape than the horse Eric had brought from his room. The second horse was well used. Chips of wood were missing on its body as if it had been knocked about in careless play. One ear was missing entirely while the other carried the same wound as its companion. Its immovable tail was only half the length of its original size, displaying a ragged wooden edge of wound. The wooden surface was almost clear of any paint so that Pete would describe it as a wooden horse, period. Nothing else about it indicated that it was anything more, other than its supposed companion who, now standing next to it, innocently showed off its fading beauty as if to say, "This is what you could have been".

Eric finally spoke. "It's something, isn't it?" His eyes surveying the collection in front of them.

"It's amazing, Eric," he answered cautiously. He would wait for Eric to take the lead and enlighten him, if Eric chose to do so.

Still absorbed in what lay before him, Eric continued. "This one here," he pointed to the wooden horse from his room, "my mother gave me. Guess I was around one or two. I played with it every day and slept with it every night." Eric sank into his thoughts again. "Got to be sixty-six, maybe sixty-seven years old. An antique." He laughed, but just barely.

The laugh was enough for Pete to relax a bit. Whatever the wall was that had descended between them for the last half hour seemed to be disintegrating. "What about the other one? They look like they were a pair?"

Eric picked up the second one. "They were. Guess they still are." He was gone again. Pete waited. "That one," he pointed to the wooden horse still on the table, "that one was my sister's." Another pause. "Appears that she wasn't as rough as I was with our toy."

What was Eric saying? Why did the old woman have something that belonged to Eric's sister? Pete didn't even know that Eric had a sister. Why should he? But that wasn't the point. Even in his confusion, Pete's instinct told him to keep quiet.

"And all these?" Eric swept his hands over the herd. "Never seen them in my life. But there they are."

Pete longed to ask the questions that were rapidly forming in his mind.

"Okay, let's see what we got here." Eric lifted the second box and carried it to the living room. He set it down on the coffee table in front of the couch. Pete followed him.

Neither box had been properly sealed. There were no signs of tape anywhere. The flaps had been tucked under on opposite corners, leaving gaps where dust found its way into the top layer of newsprint. Pete hadn't noticed it with the first box, but as Eric opened the flaps, a visible puff of dust erupted from its confinement and sprinkled itself in the air around the two men. Perhaps Willy or the detective didn't bother to open this one?

The old newsprint covered the contents, not crumpled up to safely cushion its content but laid flat in multiple overlapping sections as if put aside to read later. Eric lifted the sections from the box and dropped them to the floor. Nestled tightly within, Pete glimpsed three smaller boxes, one next to the other, just fitting in the space provided by the larger box. They appeared to be shoe boxes, but Pete wasn't sure. Eric reached in and gently jostled one of the boxes as he tried to gain hold of it. But it was wedged firmly into place, its aged sides bulging with unknown content. Pete was about to offer help, his hands smaller than Eric's, when Eric went to the kitchen. He came back with a cardboard cutter in hand, releasing the retracted blade as he approached the box. Pete watched as Eric, with the precision of a surgeon, carefully cut away the walls of the box so that, as they fell, one by one, the three smaller boxes remained undisturbed. And below each one was another small box. The six boxes, now easily recognized as shoe boxes, were each taped shut on all four sides. Eric lifted each one and gently slit the seals on all six boxes. Retracting the blade, he shoved the cutter into his back pocket.

"Well, might as well get started." Eric lifted the lid of each box leaving the contents subjected to the fresh air, long deprived of it, judging by the familiar musty odor. Two boxes were neatly packed with baby clothes. The other four held sealed envelopes, the kind for greeting cards. Each envelope was the same size, just right for the size of the shoe box. The uneasiness that Pete felt grew in its intensity as did his confusion. None of this had anything to do with him and he felt like a silent interloper. He wanted nothing more than to leave Eric to it. But that was not to be.

"Dear God," Eric mumbled.

"What is it, Eric?" Pete reacted without thinking.

"Well, I think these baby clothes belonged to my sister and me." He lifted a tiny shirt, its neckline and chest stained. He continued to pull out of the shoe boxes what appeared to be newborn clothing, some very old while others, like the horses, recent purchases.

His mind was working overtime trying to make the puzzle pieces fit. But Pete only grew more confused, not by the contents of the boxes but by the content of Eric's mind and what he was and was not telling Pete. If this was a game that Eric was playing, Pete did not like it.

Tucked in the corner of each box was a small blue velvet bag with a drawstring tightly knotted. Pete recognized the bags immediately having just seen them in the gem shop in town. But what their content was, he could only guess. Eric undid the draw string and drew from each bag a small quartz crystal. Pete held his breath. The same crystal that he had purchased but so much smaller! Self-Healed Quartz Crystal. He visualized the print from the copied page included with his purchase as clearly as if the paper was in his hands.

"Must mean something but not to me." Eric held the crystal out to Pete. "You got any ideas?"

"Yeah, Eric. I do. But I got to tell you that all this is just weird to me. All of this." He searched Eric's face for some indication of agreement so that he wouldn't feel so horribly alone.

There was none. It was as if Eric was just cleaning out a closet. "Do you want this, or that, or this old thing?" He suddenly doubted Eric's mental state.

Pete attempted to pull himself together. "I don't know how any of this is connected, especially to those boxes," he pointed to the shoe boxes, "but all I can tell you is what I know for sure. I know that I purchased the same kind of crystal…they're called Self Healed Quartz Crystals…down at that gem store in town. The one you took me to the first night I was here. The guy down there gave me printed information about them. What they're good for. What they mean. Mine's bigger than these two but size doesn't matter, I guess."

When Pete finally focused on Eric's face, an effort that he found difficult, Eric was smiling, a happy Buddha-like smile.

"Let's see what these are all about." He was lifting one of the envelopes from one of the shoe boxes. Sliding his index finger under the seal, the face of the envelope was visible to Pete. Eric's name was scrawled in the center, the same scrawl that he had seen on the letter's envelope minutes ago.

"Well, what do you know." It wasn't a question, more an affirmation that he had been right all along kind of comment. Eric opened the Happy Birthday card, read the contents, and then slowly slid it back into its envelope. He picked up another sealed envelope, opened it, read it, and tucked it away again. This went on until he was through two of the boxes. He did not do the same for the last two boxes. Instead, he placed those on the edge of a bookshelf. The examined envelopes he had carefully placed back in the empty shoe boxes.

When Eric put the lids on the boxes, Pete saw what looked like dates written in bold print. He stepped closer to the table. He was right. The first box that Eric opened was dated "1946-1980". The second, in the same bold print read, "1981-2016. Pete's patience and curiosity were working against one another. And then he remembered Eric's words. "I expect you better be here when I open these up, Peter Wade-Murphy". Why? And how far was Eric going to go before he answered Pete's silent question?

1949

As he had done every night, Benny opened his journal and lifted the ribbon page marker as the pages fell open. And as instructed by his father, he entered the day's date, January 15, 1949. His thoughts flowed quickly and easily as he laid pen to paper. A blend of guilt, regret, and overwhelming happiness flavored each description of the day's events, much like the previous two weeks of his life. Three years ago, he had lost his dear Savannah but in the last two weeks, the weight of her loss had been slowly lifted and a contentment he had not felt in a long time was present again. Now Hellenia had come into his life with her two babies. He had taken her in knowing full well that her legal husband and father to the babies was nearby. He never questioned how far he wanted to go in this new relationship. He saw no need to do so.

2016

Pete felt completely invisible. Had Eric forgotten that he was even in the room with him? Wherever Eric was, he had not taken Pete along. He had left him in the present. Instinct was nagging at Pete to pay attention. If Pete had allowed himself to do just that, he would have remained patient, biding his time until his friend returned. At some level, Pete acknowledged that he needed to be here right now, in this room, with this man and his history. But at another level competing strongly to rise to the top of his logical reasoning scale, Pete wanted nothing more than to be elsewhere. Anywhere but here. The confusion frightened him. He should never have come here to begin with. He should have stayed in the valley and faced his failures head on instead of running away to the mountains.

He wasn't prepared to hear Eric's voice as his own internal voice was actively at work. Pete visibly jumped at the sound.

"How are you doing?" Eric's voice was loud and forceful.

It took no time for Pete to shut down his own thoughts, so relieved that Eric was back. "I'm okay, I guess," a lame response, he thought, considering the recent chaos in his head.

"Tell you what. Let's go out on the porch. Grab some beers from the fridge, would you?" Eric was headed to the front door. "And...well, no need to tell you. I can see it in your face. Your confusion. Your questions. That's okay. Everything in good time. Meet you out there."

The feeling was the same one he had had when he said yes to Kit. Committed himself to the hike. Couldn't worm his way out when the doubt set in the worst. He wondered if Kit had read his face, like Eric, but had ignored it. Had known all along that his heart wasn't in it. That, given time, he would either hang in there or he wouldn't. That it was no skin off her back if he didn't. And he hadn't. As he opened the fridge door, he hesitated. Again, the same feeling. Follow her up the trail or turn around and never look back? That moment of his indecision on the trail descended upon him now with the same weight of guilt and betrayal. He could join Eric on the porch or he could grab his stuff and leave out the back door. He had been unwilling to carry through, to do his part, on the hike. She had lost her life. He had not. Now he was unwilling to go any farther with whatever this relationship was with Eric. But not for the same reason. With Kit, it just wasn't what he expected it to be and she ground him down so that he had nothing to look forward to. But something else was at play here with Eric. Something that Pete could not identify but only sensed deeply. Was it fear? Of what? He thought he trusted Eric. Eric had done nothing to betray any trust. A real nice guy. A good friend. Fear. It was fear, just not identified, Pete realized as he closed the fridge door, two cold beer bottles in each hand.

"Need any help?" Eric's voiced boomed from the porch.

Pete passed the kitchen table, the silent herd grazing on the imagined field of grass, while one of the baby garments lay on top of the old cardboard box, as if on display in a shop window, and the three shoeboxes hid their contents from view. The leather journal was nowhere in sight.

"No…no thanks. I'm coming."

"January 15, 1949

There is lightness in this home again. Hellenia and her children have made me forget my loss. Today, little Eric followed me out to the woodshed intent on helping me carry logs back to the house. He was patient as I put them, one by one, in the wagon but I knew he wanted to do the same. Instead, I gave him a log to carry on his own. My goodness! Did that boy's eyes light up! Proud as could be. And he carried it all the way back. I let him take it in the house so his mother could see before he dropped it on the hearth. Last night was trying on me. On Hellenia, of course. Little Jean would not take the breast and cried through most of the night. I felt helpless but dear Hellenia assured me that there was nothing I could do. She apologized for keeping me awake while she walked the floor, rocking the little thing in her arms, quietly singing to her. This morning, the baby had a fever. I called the doctor and he came out. Some kind of baby illness that's not serious. Gave Hellenia some medicine and reassured her that little Jean would be better by tomorrow. As I write this, little Jean is sound asleep after her nursing. Hellenia is exhausted, I can tell. I put Eric to bed tonight. He couldn't find his little horse anywhere and wouldn't settle until it was beside him. Fortunately, I found it behind the chair in the living room. Amazing how something so small and insignificant to an adult can mean the whole world to a little one."

"April 12, 1949

We made the decision today to move up to Shasta City. Hell surprised me with her eagerness to do it. We discussed taking the children away from the only place they've known. Neither one of us spoke of Joe but he was on my mind. I can't believe that he wasn't on her mind as well. But there has been no sign of Joe. I admit that I'm worried about what could happen. I mean with the law and all. But we can't stay here and make a go of it. Anyway, I miss my hometown. Hell will be happy there and so will the children. Planning on moving up there in the next month. Got to call someone about putting the ranch up for sale. Do that tomorrow."

"May18, 1950

In the middle of the night Hellenia walked out the door. I don't know what I was thinking. Taking her and the babies in was just asking for trouble. No, I don't mean that. I mean that nothing good could come of it. It was wrong on both our parts. I don't know what to do. I don't know where she's gone or if she's coming back. And the babies, Eric and little Jean. How could she just up and leave them? What kind of mother would do that? What does she want me to do with them if she doesn't come back? Give them back to their daddy? To Joe? If he had wanted them, he would have come looking for them. For his wife. Searching for them the day they left him. If he wanted them. But he didn't. Never saw him after Hell left him. Maybe I do have trouble now. I asked for it and I got it. Now I'm paying for the wrong I did to Joe. Damn! But I love her and I thought that she loved me. Her kids? Does she love them, even a little? Dear God, help me. Help me. I need to know what to do. Dear God, help me, please."

"February 22, 1951

Joe Terner died yesterday down in the Santa Clara Valley. Took his own life. My God! I am so sorry, so sorry, Joe. I know I'm partly responsible. If I hadn't taken them in. If I hadn't been so foolish, so cowardly. I know you'd still be with us if I had done the right thing and sent them back to you. I'll live whatever days I have remaining asking for your forgiveness, Joe. But I can't tell anybody about you, Joe. Not even up here, so far from where everything went wrong. I guess I can't even tell the kids. Too young to understand and I guess they didn't even really get to know you, did they? Especially Jean. Just a babe in her mother's arms. Maybe one day, Joe, when they're old enough to start asking questions. I can't speak for Hell. Haven't seen or heard of her for almost a year now. I expect that I never will again. That's why I made the decision to adopt them at the end of last year. I wrote to you and told you. Not by mail. In this journal. Sometime around the end of July. They're rightfully mine now. They know no different. I spend a lot of nights wondering why you gave them up so easily. But I can't be judging you, Joe. Only God can do that. And I guess whatever his judgement is you have no choice now but to abide by it. My time will come. I know that. Joe, I want you to know that your children are okay. They're safe and happy.

I'll take good care of them for you. For Hell. Who knows? Maybe their mother will come back some day. And if that day comes, I want them to be here to meet her all over again."

Eric was sitting in one of the rockers on the porch. He didn't look up when Pete handed him the beer bottle. A slight nod of the head was all the recognition Pete received. He understood why. The opened leather journal lay on Eric's lap, its ribbon dangling from its binding between his legs, gently shifting left to right in the afternoon whisper of a breeze. He feared that Eric was elsewhere once again. Pete wished he had left the beers in the fridge.

But he sat down in the other rocker, molding his body into the chair's contours, and sipped on his beer. He waited, not rocking because, he thought, that would look like he was content, and he was not.

"Been quite a few days, hasn't it Pete?"

Pete glanced at Eric who was looking straight ahead. "Yeah. It sure has." He wasn't sure what else to say. He would take his cue from Eric.

"There's a lot of stuff here that needs explaining, Pete. Stuff that I thought I'd never have to explain to anyone ever. But here you are and here I am. And then there's all that stuff." He lifted his beer bottle and, with it, gestured to the inside of the house. "And there's this." He looked down at the journal. "You already made its acquaintance."

Pete was about to defend himself again about the journal when Eric spoke.

"This journal belonged to my father. Not my real father. My adopted father. And every day since his tenth birthday, he wrote an entry. Imagine that. Every day he disciplined himself enough to do it. I haven't found one single day missing, date-wise. Right up until the day he died. He made an entry on the day of his death." Eric fell silent.

The breeze was enough to move the wooden chime that hung from one of the porch beams. What once must have been a pleasing sound was now only a dull clunking of dried up old wood. But it was enough to fill the stilled space between the two men, an almost deafening sound. A rude intrusion, Pete thought.

He needed to respond. "That really is something, Eric. I don't think that I could ever be that disciplined."

"You could, if you had something to say."

Pete felt the sting of Eric's words. Stupid, he thought. That can't be what he meant.

"I mean to say, Pete, that we all have something to say. It's just how much we want to say it. Maybe that's what I mean." He took a long draft of the beer.

Had he read his mind? Again? All too weird, Pete mused.

"My adopted father's name was Benjamin Hopkins. My real father's name was Joseph Terner." He turned to Pete. "And my mother's name was Hellenia Wade."

If the earth's surface suddenly yielded under his feet at that moment, its agitated surface no longer stable enough to keep him upright, violently throwing him to the ground; if the rumbling of the earth grew with such intensity in volume he could no longer hear his own cries; if the mountain, awake again, exploded darkening the sky so that day suddenly became night; none of that would have had the resounding impact that Eric's revelation had on Peter Wade-Murphy.

"April 20, 1934

Today is my birthday. I'm ten years old now. My mother made a strawberry cake, my favorite. My father and mother gave me a present. It is this book. My father calls it a journal and I have to write in it every day. That is why I am writing in it today. This is my first birthday here. My best friend lives too far away to come to my birthday. He's in Shasta City. His name is Rusty. I miss him. I miss our old house there. My mother says that I will make friends here but I don't think so. That's all I have to say."

"April 29, 1934

Today my new friend and his parents came to visit us. His name is James Murphy. He lives on a ranch next to ours. It is a long walk to his house. They drove their car to our house today. We live on a ranch too. But we don't see them very much because it is so far. I get to see James in school, though. My school is half-way to James' ranch. That is what my father says. So it is not so far to walk there. I don't like walking so much. In Shasta City, my school is just down the road from our house. And houses are a lot closer than here. When I tell my father this, he tells me to stop talking about it. This is our new home and I better get used to it. Tomorrow, James and I are going to play together at recess. He said he was going to bring a baseball to show me. That's all I have to say."

Somewhere in the distance, Eric was speaking. Pete tried to focus on what he was saying but he couldn't decipher any of it. His mind was working at a frantic rate, sorting out the most recent occurrences that found him here on Eric's porch.

"Pete?" He heard Eric's voice, louder and clearer than moments ago. "Pete!"

"Yeah, I heard you. Sorry." He didn't know what to say, what he was feeling, what anything meant anymore.

"I told you that there was stuff that had to be explained.

I need you with me the first time because I don't think I can go through all of this again." Eric's tone was demanding but Pete sensed a profound sadness as Eric spoke. Enough to alert him to pay attention to his friend.

"I'm here, Eric." He swallowed hard, afraid of going any farther but accepting that he had no choice. Not anymore. Lifting the bottle to his lips, he let the cool beer linger in his mouth before taking another sip.

Eric closed the journal on his lap and placed it on the small wooden table between them. "Do you believe in something more than what we see? Something bigger than any of this?" Once again, his bottle became a pointer and extending his arm forward, Eric made a large circular gesture, whose circumference indicated the sky, the earth, and everything in between.

The question lingered between them, Pete formulating an answer that, he realized, would be a very different answer if Eric had asked the question when they first met up on I-5. "I think I'm beginning to."

"Good. So what I'm about to tell you is meant to be told now. Here. Just the two of us, right now, right here. And none of what is about to happen would have happened if I hadn't given you a lift that day. That's what I mean about something bigger, Pete." Eric drank the last of his beer. "You ready for another? Never mind answering. I'm getting us a couple more."

"*November 23, 1938*

No school tomorrow because of Thanksgiving. I was hoping to get some extra sleep tomorrow but that won't happen. Mom told me I have to get up early and help get the house ready for guests. Dad is going to be too busy to help because he has to work the ranch like any other day. And she has to cook the meal. That leaves me to do all the chores. James Murphy is coming over. His mom and dad too, Lucas and Tilly Murphy. They're supposed to be bringing some food to help with the meal. Hope it's her apple pie. I won't ever tell my mom that Tilly Murphy's apple pie is far better than hers. But it is. James and I are going to go riding before we eat. I'm going to let him ride Lop Ears. She's gentle and James can't ride that well. I better get some sleep in now."

"April 20, 1942

It's my birthday. Finally, I'm eighteen. The war over in Europe has been going on and now I can help out. My mother doesn't want me to enlist but my father says it's my duty. So tomorrow, I'm going down to the recruitment center in San Jose. James already enlisted and he's at what they call a boot camp somewhere in the south. Maybe I'll get sent to the same one. When I get back from the war after we've killed all the Nazis and Hitler, I want to go to college. Father wants me to work with him on the ranch. Hand it down to me someday, he says. Keep it in the family. He won't hear of me becoming a college boy. I don't know. I guess I'll just have to wait and see what's in store for me. Tomorrow, I become a man!"

"April 21, 1942

This is the worst day of my life. They won't let me go fight. Something about my trouble breathing. Asthma they call it. I get winded real easy and sometimes it's really hard to catch my breath. But I didn't know it was a "condition". My mother knew but never told me because she didn't want me to worry. Just be a normal kid. My father knew too and went along with my mother. They told me this tonight at dinner. I can't believe it. I can't believe they lied to me. Well, not outright, but they should have told me. The recruiter thanked me for offering my services but with my condition, there was no place for me in the service. It was all I could do not to weep in front of the man and beg for an exception. Right now, I'm angry with my parents. I don't want to stay in this house. I don't care how much my father wants me here. I never asked for it. I don't want it. Tomorrow I start looking into college. I don't know how I'm going to tell Savannah. I won't be surprised if she dumps me for another guy, one in uniform and with lungs that work right!"

"*October 15, 1944*

My dear Savannah said yes to my proposal of marriage. I'm the happiest man alive! We'll wait until summer to wed. She'll be on break from her classes at San Jose State College and the ranch work will settle a bit in the beginning of summer. Maybe we can get away for a honeymoon. We'll see."

"*December 17, 1944*

Sad news today. Lucas and Tilly Murphy called to tell us that James was coming home before his time was up. He's been wounded in some battle in a French village. I don't remember the name. He'll be okay once he's back in the U.S. and getting better medical treatment than over there. But he can't go back to war. He's home for good. I wish it was me instead of him that got wounded. In any case, it will be good to have him home. I don't think he knows about Savannah and me. The Murphys tell us he should be arriving home before Christmas. Bless all those boys."

"*June 3, 1945*

I'm writing this while my beautiful new bride sleeps. The wedding was simple. James and his family came. A ranching family about two miles away, Hellenia and Joe Terner also came. They seem to be about our age, me and Savannah. Two families that I don't know that well also came. The wives are friends of my mother's. Savannah was a thing of beauty. I am beyond happy. Need to get back to bed and, well…not proper to go any farther here."

"*January 1, 1946*

Happy New Year! With the war behind us, the country really celebrated last night. So did we. So much so that Savannah could barely manage to keep up with the fun. We got together with James and his fiancé, Barbara, and the Terners. I can tell you that we sure did welcome in the new year. My head is killing me right now. A few too many. Better close for tonight. Anyway, I need to keep my sweetheart warm."

"September 12, 1946
  I am too sad to write. My Savannah died today."

Eric closed the journal marking his place with the worn ribbon. "I thought that you should hear these entries, Pete, before I tell you too much more. My father's words tell it far better than I ever could."

Pete had listened carefully to every utterance as Eric read aloud. But his confusion only deepened, and he was embarrassed. Only one name was familiar to him, that of Hellenia's. He remained silent.

"The woman in the car was Hellenia Wade, my mother." Eric released the words aloud. A peacefulness filled him. He was not surprised by it but nodded his head slowly as if accepting and then confirming the fact. He had somehow always known every time he passed the alley but was buried in his subconscious unable to be reached for verification. 'A feeling', he told himself each time. And when he approached the car, banged on the window, peered inside, he knew. No longer a feeling but a fact.

Pete was speechless. He knew he had to say something, but nothing would register as sensible in his thinking. He remained silent.

"And you were fortunate enough to make her acquaintance." Eric chuckled. He took a swig of the cold beer. "And I believe, she was fortunate to have met you, Pete."

Now Pete's words came rapidly. "Why do you say that? What do I have to do with any of this?" He knew the answer. But the murkiness of everything he had heard so far would not permit him a clear view. Nowhere close to a clear view. All he knew was that he had farther to go in order see what Eric saw.

"June 11, 1964

Eric graduated from high school today. Nice celebration. It was all I could do not to weep. Time has gone by so quickly. Just yesterday, he was a little boy playing with his baby sister. There are days when I see his mother in him. And other days that I wish I didn't. But he's not to blame. I love him like he was my child. He is my child. And Jean…well, she'll be out of school in two years. My little girl growing up much too fast. She's been bucking my will since she turned thirteen. Some days, it's hard to love her. She can be so mean to her brother and so disrespectful toward me. I wouldn't be surprised if she left this place as soon as she graduates. Lately, she complains about the small town with nothing to do. No, she won't stay. I'm sure of that. She's like her mother that way, I guess. Wish you could have seen your son today, Hell. You would be proud."

"June 30, 1964

Eric is trying to find some work here in town. Not much here. There might be a spot at Willard's Auto Repair. Eric's pretty handy with machines. He's always been interested in my tools in the shed. Spends hours in there fooling around with them. Hasn't broken one yet. And if he has, he's fixed it before I ever knew it was broken. Maybe Will can start him with something soon. We talked about college, but something is holding Eric back from going. I can't put my finger on it. It's not the money. I told him we can always find a way for him to go. But he doesn't seem that interested in anything that he can't get right here in town. We'll see. Give him some time. Maybe he'll surprise me and change his mind. Jean is driving me nuts. Now if she wants to go to college, and I know she does, I will help pack her bags and drive her to the gates of her chosen institution of higher learning. I love my girl, but she'll be happier away from here. Not to mention, me."

Eric finished off his beer after closing the journal once again. "You know, my sister is still alive. Jean. She lives in the valley with her husband. She did well for herself. They both did. I haven't heard from her...well, it's got to be going on forty years. I guess she could be dead by now, but somehow, I think I would have heard. For a while, she wrote to one of her girlfriends from school. She was real kind in sharing some of Jean's news with us. That's how we kept track of her but not for long. Never got an invite to their wedding. I don't even know when they got married or if they had kids. I've always wondered what I did to her to cause her to cut me out of her life. But maybe that's just Jean. When I think of her just before she left my father and me, she was always unhappy and mad about something. Didn't much matter what. I hate to say it out loud, but I was happy to see her go. I just didn't know at the time that I would never see her again."

"Wait a minute. So, Benny was your father, well, not your real father but the man who brought you up? Right?"

"Right."

"And you're telling me that your mother was the woman who gave me a lift? Hellenia?"

"That's right."

Pete was struggling to keep the facts in front of him straight. "This journal was Benny's."

"It is Benny's. Yes."

"So, who was your real father again?"

"According to Benny's accounts, his name was Joe Terner. It appears that Hellenia was married to him and had my sister and me by him." Eric, still trying to digest the information himself, refused to allow his own confusion and shock to muddy the waters between them.

Pete was starting to put two and two together but only barely. "What happened to Joe? I mean why did Hellenia leave him? How did Benny get involved?"

"Best as I can tell, she went to Benny with us kids because of something Joe must have done. Why else would a mother and her babies leave a marriage?" He had no answer to

Pete's question and this bit of reasoning didn't ring true to him either. He was maligning a man he knew nothing about. The voices they needed to hear were both gone.

"Okay. So, your mother, Hellenia, and Benny brought you both up here. Right?"

Eric realized that he had read Benny's account of Hellenia's disappearance without Pete present. He didn't have the will to read it aloud to his young friend. He didn't want to hear Benny's anguished words again. "No, not really. Benny writes about how my mother left in the middle of the night without any of us. Just walked out the door."

"What? She just left you and your sister with Benny? For how long?"

"Right up to the day she died. You were there." He kept his eyes locked on Pete's.

Pete recognized both profound sadness as well as cynicism in Eric's voice. He would need to tread lightly with his questions.

"Eric, did you know that Hellenia was sleeping there, in the alley? Did you have any idea that your mother was so close?" He hadn't heeded his own warning but there it was. So clear and unfathomable. How could something like this even happen?

Eric pushed himself up from the rocker and gingerly moved to the porch railing. He grabbed the rail with both hands and looked straight ahead. His shoulders rose to hunch about his ears while he let his upper torso lean at an angle over the railing. The silence was palpable and the longer it lasted the more frightened Pete became.

He did not turn around, did not relax his body; if anything, it seemed to Pete to grow more tense as Eric slowly and deliberately spoke. "I believe I did."

Pete bit his tongue. So many questions!

Still with his back to Pete, Eric continued but with less deliberation. "That must sound terrible to you. I don't think I can rightly explain it." He turned back to Pete, his eyes glistening with moisture. "Something kept telling me to keep an eye out for it. For the car. And every time I saw it sitting there in the alley, something else told me that everything was going to be okay. It was a feeling, Pete. Just a feeling."

Pete saw an opening. "I get feelings, Eric. You're right. They are hard to explain. But I still don't get why you thought it was your mother in that car. How could you ever come to that conclusion and not investigate it?" Judging by the expression on Eric's face, Pete knew he had gone too far.

"You have no idea. Pete, you can't judge me like that." A steady, even keeled voice that Pete recognized immediately as forced.

"You're right, Eric. I apologize." He would let it go.

"I was afraid." Eric's voice was barely a whisper, but Pete understood. "Sometimes the feeling was so strong that it frightened me. There was a time, just before Benny died, that I was sure she was here. But a person's mind is not in its right state in times like that. So, I talked myself into believing that I just wasn't thinking straight. Benny took a while to finally pass. And it took a while for me to think clearly again. But I can tell you now that the feeling stayed. Just not so intense. And then that morning, the feeling wasn't a feeling anymore. It was a fact. I couldn't ignore it anymore and when I tried the handle and banged on the window, I knew it was her. And you, Pete, you confirmed it for me. You knew who was in that car before her body was identified. The difference is that you told me, but I never told anyone. I guess I should resent you for having time with her before she died. But I don't. Of course not. It was meant to be, all of it."

Pete knew there was no reasonable answer to his original question. He wasn't going to try any further to understand what was seemingly impossible to understand. Eric was right about one thing. "It was meant to be, all of it." There was no other explanation.

"March 14, 1951

A real surprise today! Went to the mailbox and there was a letter from James Murphy down in the Santa Clara Valley. The last time I saw him was New Year's Eve, 1946, when he was engaged to Barbara. We just lost touch. But he tells me that he and Barbara are real happy even more so because they just adopted a baby boy. And what beats all is that his given name is Benjamin. Imagine that! Benjamin Wade-Murphy. A good strong name. Lucus and Tilly, his adoptive grandparents, as James identified them, are thrilled to welcome their first grandchild. Can't believe that my friend is a father. Got to write a congratulations card to them. Life is sure strange. Had someone told me that I would adopt two children and my friend would adopt as well, I wouldn't have believed them for a second. But there it is. Maybe I'll write him a letter telling him about my situation. Maybe."

Eric stopped reading aloud. He waited for Pete's reaction. He waited for the other shoe to drop. He would not go on until it had.

And it had. Pete could not respond immediately. His brain, working on overtime, was trying to catch up. Too much to digest. He heard his last name attached to someone he didn't know.

"Who is Benjamin Wade-Murphy?" That was all he could manage to produce.

Eric, relieved that he could now go on, sighed heavily. "Well, let's find out." He flipped through the next few pages and then stopped, placing the ribbon along the binding. "When I read this journal, long before you showed up at my door, and a while after my father's passing, not a whole lot of this made much sense to me. I mean, the people my father knew, especially James, I didn't know at all. So, reading this the first time was like skimming for stuff that interested me. Meant something to me. But now it all has a very special meaning. And like I said, there's a reason you're here, Pete. I don't pretend to know why or how this all works but I know that it's true." Eric reached over to Pete and laid his hand on Pete's arm, just for a moment, before he opened the journal and continued to read aloud.

"*December 21, 1980*

Getting close to Christmas and the weather this winter has been bad. And we've got months to go before it passes. The volcano looks darn impressive, though. The snow melt-off is going to fill the lake and rivers for sure. Feeling the cold in my bones a little bit more every year. I might not have a lonely Christmas this year after all. Eric tells me that he's not scheduled to drive his rig over the holiday week. Which means he'll be with me for Christmas. Would be too much to expect Jean coming home with her new husband. Well, not so new. Married two years ago. The only reason I know that is because she sent an announcement card. Not an invite. It hurt but what with all the wounds the girl has given me over time, what's one more?"

"*December 23, 1980*

Got a Christmas card from James Murphy today. He's been real good about keeping in touch with me since the baby arrived. My God! It's been thirty years. Hard to believe. Now he tells me that Ben is getting married. To a girl named Martha Aimes. They call her Marty for short. James says that he's never seen his boy so head over heels for a girl and he's had his pick. James thought he'd never settle down. Guess my Eric will be a bachelor for the rest of his days. What is he now? Thirty-four? Well, maybe there's still hope but if he's courting someone, he hasn't brought her across this threshold. A good son, taking care of his father like he has. A good son."

He didn't want to look at Pete. Not just yet. The moment was a private one. That is, if Pete understood what Benny's words revealed. So, he waited.

This time it was Pete's turn to stand up and move to the railing. But he didn't grab on, didn't seek its support. Instead, he turned and looked directly at Eric. "Those were my parents' names. You just read my parents' names." He fell silent.

Eric wanted to go to Pete. To put his arm around him. To reassure him that he was okay. That they both were okay. But he was paralyzed by the immensity of his father's words and what they meant to both men.

"I don't understand, Eric. I'm trying to, but I don't get it." Pete choked on his words. He tried to compose himself in front of Eric, but he couldn't. He was desperate to make sense of all of this.

"I know, son. Believe me, I know. I can try to explain it as best as I can. And I may not have all the facts straight. Just basing it on my father's accounts. Are you willing to hear me out?" He knew the answer as Pete wiped the tears from his face and sat back down.

"Yeah. Go on."

Eric inhaled deeply before he began. His young friend was in a vulnerable situation and depending on how well he kept himself together would determine Pete's getting through this.

"Pete, from what I can gather, your father was the baby adopted by James and Barbara Murphy, my father's friends. So, your adoptive grandparents were Lucas and Tilly Murphy. You remember me reading those names?" Pete nodded. "Your father, Benjamin Wade-Murphy, married Martha Aimes, your mother. And they had you."

"So, you're telling me that my father was adopted?" He was beginning to unravel the chaos of his brain. "Not only that, but my grandfather knew your father's friends?"

Eric was impressed by Pete's simplification. "Well, yeah. I guess that's exactly what I'm telling you."

"Okay. Okay. Wait a minute. So, this is just a great big coincidence. You and me? The only thing connecting us is two dead people? Not so unusual." He didn't mean to sound so flip and wished he could take back his words. Because, he realized, it was pretty darn unusual. "Sorry. Didn't mean it like it sounded."

"But you're right about that. Two dead people are in our combined histories." Eric was contemplating his words, a smile now appearing on his less strained face. "But I think that we have more in common than just those two folks."

"What do you mean?" And then it hit him, as if she had just walked up the front steps and demanded that he pay attention to her. Hellenia.

"Remember I told you back there that the woman in the car was my mother? And I told you her name? Remember?"

His brain was racing again to catch up. "You told me her name. Yeah, Hellenia. I already knew it."

"Right. You did. But I told you her name was Helenia Wade." They both said nothing, each taking in stride the truth about the old woman.

"Okay, Eric. I'm really confused. I'm trying to make sense of it, really. But I don't get the connection."

"Remember there was a sheet of paper on top of one of her boxes. I read it but didn't say anything to you. Remember?"

The boxes. He had completely pushed them out of his mind. Since the journal readings began, nothing else seemed to matter. Pete did remember Eric falling silent after reading it and his own fear of losing his friend.

"Yeah. I do. And those boxes, Eric. You told me about the baby clothes. I kind of get that. But what was with all the envelopes? And the horses?" He knew he was getting side tracked but he didn't care. As his thoughts unraveled, he needed immediate answers.

"That's right. I never did talk to you about them, did I? Well, I expect that my mother wanted to keep our baby clothes. You know, memory's sake. All I can figure is that, once in a while, she bought new ones because she missed her "babies." He paused before going on. "The horses. When I was a little kid, real little, probably around one or two, my mother gave me a wooden horse, the one I brought out from my bedroom. Can you believe that I've held onto it for all these years? She gave my sister one too. That one was in the box along with all the others. All I can figure is that she just kept on buying horses for her kids even though she had no kids anymore to give them to." Again, a pause but longer. He looked at Pete. "Are you still with me?"

"Yes, sure. And the envelopes?"

"The envelopes. Well, I opened every one of them. Read each one. Some were to me and some were to my sister. The first one sitting on top of the pile was to me and dated September 4, 2016. My birthday, Pete. And two days before she died. My mother wrote both my sister and me birthday cards every year from the day we were born until the day she died. She just never sent them."

Pete should have been taken aback by Eric's explanation. If nothing else, he should have been impressed by this woman's odd and estranged history from her family. But while Eric went on about the boxes, Pete's thoughts kept drifting back to only two words. "The connection". He needed that answer more than anything else. Suddenly, he was aware of silence. Eric had stopped talking at some point.

"So now you know. She physically abandoned us but, from what I surmise from these boxes, not in her heart. And it appears that in her later years, she was close by. All this time, just around the corner. Did I tell you that Benny told us kids right after she left that she had gone to heaven? That she was up there with the angels? So, all this time, I thought she was dead. And that feeling? It's been with me ever since I can remember. All I wanted for a long time was to have my mother come back. Not to be in heaven. As a kid, I thought that could happen if I prayed hard enough. That one morning, I would wake up and hear her talking to Benny. It was just confusing for me, I guess. And when the car started to show up in the alley, the feeling got stronger and stronger. But I was afraid to find out the truth. I wanted my mother dead. To stay dead. It had been too long without her, you see. Sounds horrible to say, but there it is."

Pete couldn't understand it. He tried. How could you want your parent to stay dead? He would give anything for his parents to be alive. He was beginning to think that he was never going to understand any of this. "No, I don't think it's horrible," he lied. He was at a loss for words.

"No, it is, Pete. And if I could change things, I'd do it in a heartbeat. You ever heard of the domino theory?"

"Sure. That's when you set the first domino in motion then all the rest will follow. Right?"

"That's the one. So, I figure that you and me and everyone living right this minute are not of our own making. I mean that who we are is everyone and everything they ever did going back in time to where ever we started. Like dominos falling one by one until the last one to fall feels the weight of them all. Guess what I'm trying to say, Pete, is that we are not ourselves. Who we would like to think we are. We are hundreds of pieces in a gigantic jigsaw puzzle that still isn't finished. Imagine all the pieces that are missing, lost, or hiding. Impossible to see the completed picture with pieces missing."

Pete listened to his friend's meanderings until silence fell between them again. Eric had a point, he confessed. What Pete did understand was that his own life was a prime example, a realization that weighed heavier on him as the afternoon wore on.

As the next few days passed, Eric was busy arranging for his mother's remains and internment. Pete and he did not return to the journal during those days nor did they discuss it. It appeared to Pete that Eric knew exactly what to do. Probably, he thought, because he had been through it with his father. Pete made every effort to stay out of Eric's way during this time. His questions still pressed him though, the conversation still not completed. But he knew to give Eric the time needed. To take care of business and to mourn. Pete remembered all too well, the feeling that he would never be the same again after losing his parents, that he would never heal from the loss. But he had. Enough to continue with his life and to appreciate his parents from afar. But in Eric's case, Pete would not begin to make the same comparison. All he could do for now was to be patient and to be there if Eric needed him.

On the morning of his mother's internment, Eric sat in silence as Pete sat across from him, trying to swallow cold toast. For the last few days, Eric had refused Pete's offer to make breakfast for the two of them. Instead, he only drank a cup of coffee. This morning was no different. As Eric left the room to get ready for the ceremony, he called back to Pete. "I expect you to be in attendance with me for my mother's service. You've got an hour to get ready."

*

Hellenia Wade's ashes sat in a plain wooden box on a patch of dried lawn as Samuel Harrington, the director of Shasta City's only funeral home, spoke the final words. There were only a few people in attendance; Eric, of course and Pete, Willy and one of his officers, and Benjamin and Peggy Drake from down in Redding who, when questioned by Eric as to how they knew his mother, Benjamin told him about Hellenia's car breaking down on I-5 and the help they gave her. The least they could do. Saw her obituary notice in the local paper. Only right to pay their respects to a fine lady.

The only other attendees sat in their parked car across the lawn well away from the others but within site of the service. They could not hear the words spoken and could not make out the faces of those in attendance. As the woman sat silently in the passenger seat, her husband reached for her free hand which she allowed him to grasp. In the other, she clutched an obituary carefully cut from the pages of the San Jose Mercury News paper. Her husband detected a silent splash of tear that fell to the print, marring the photo of a beautiful woman whose wisps of curled brown hair framed her young face.

*

A full day passed after Hellenia's internment before Eric brought up the journal again. Pete had not slept well the night before. He dreamt about San Jose, about the night in the parking lot with Hellenia in front of the Bonsai Nursery. He was visited, he was sure, by Kit. He smelled the high sierra pines and the heated earth. He didn't see her but sensed her all around him. He dreamt of his parents, the last time he ever said anything to them. The last time when he did not bother to wave goodbye but headed up to his bedroom to play some stupid video game. He dreamt of his Aunt Emily who tried to be a mother and a father to a fourteen-year-old, never having married or had kids of her own. He dreamt of her coffin sitting in the aisle of the Catholic church, so close to him that he could reach out his hand and touch it, if he had wanted to. He was twenty-one when she got sick and died in a hospital bed seven days later. In his dream, he could smell her sickness but could not see her face. And he dreamt of millions of cardboard puzzle pieces that, when fitted together, did not stay together; instead, just as a clear and almost complete image started to appear, one by one they fell into the darkness from the invisible surface the puzzle was built upon and were impossible to retrieve. And his dreaming was filled with his searching for a word, a name, that, like the puzzle, almost came to be, but was also irretrievable

He was exhausted and longed to go back to bed when he heard Eric call him from the kitchen. Half-dressed and shaved, he let him know that he'd be right out.

Eric had made a big breakfast. It was like he hadn't eaten in days. It occurred to Pete that that might be the case. He hadn't shared a meal with him nor seen him eat anything. The guy was starving. A pile of pancakes, a bowl of scrambled eggs, a plate of bacon and a pan of hash browns sat on the table. Two bananas sat above each breakfast plate. A large pitcher of orange juice and a carafe of what he assumed to be hot coffee waited on the counter next to two glasses and two mugs.

"Good morning!" Eric, upon noting Pete's surprised

countenance, continued. "Figured we deserve a good start today. Get things back on track. Get yourself some liquid and sit down. Food's getting cold and I'm starving." He turned and poured his coffee and juice. Carrying them to the table, he gestured to Pete to do the same.

"Wow, Eric. This looks great. Thanks for doing it."

"Not a problem. I figure we need a good start to the day if we're going to finish our conversation." He filled his mouth with egg and pancake.

Pete struggled to stifle yawns that kept coming in waves. Eric noticed. "Rough night?"

"Yeah, sorry. Lots of dreams. Feel like I've been dragged through the ringer."

"Understood and can empathize. Even more reason for getting our business taken care of. Time to put the puzzle pieces together for good. Don't you think?"

Pete's thoughts, exactly. For a moment, he toyed with the idea that Eric had just confirmed that he could read Pete's mind but dismissed it as another coincidence. He wasn't sure, though, how many more he could take.

*

"Thought we could start with this entry, if you don't mind me reading it to you?" They each sat in a rocker on the porch, coffee mugs in hand, the carafe refilled and strategically placed on the table between them.

"You read whatever you think I should hear, Eric. At least I'm better prepared this time." He wasn't referring to the hot coffee that was finally taking effect on his weary brain.

Eric took a long sip of his coffee, rested it on the arm of the rocker momentarily while he flipped through the pages of the journal. Laying the ribbon in place, he lifted his mug off the wooden arm and, with the other, lifted the journal closer to his face. "So, you know I've skipped plenty. The day to day entries. I'm not purposely leaving anything out. I mean other than those. But what I want to share with you has to do with you and with me. Okay?"

Pete already figured that was the case but found Eric's remark thoughtful. "Of course."

"December 20, 1952

Got a Christmas card from James and Barbara Murphy today. Their baby is two already and sounds like they've got their hands filled. Brings back memories of Eric and Jean. Wonder how I survived it? Anyway, he says in his card that maybe next year when the boy is another year older and easier to travel with that they want to come up here to visit. I can't remember if I've ever had visitors stay at my place. Don't think so. Got time to spruce it up a bit, especially if a little one's going to be running around. Eric and Jean will be good playmates. I'll write him back and tell him it's okay. Something to look forward to, that's for sure. Supposed to be the season of miracles. Read that somewhere."

"*February 25, 1985*

There have been days lately that I just want to give it up. My boy, Eric, is a blessing. Don't know what I'd do without him. But even his presence is beginning to bother me. He's not doing anything different. He's gone most of the time driving his rig for days before I see him again. And when he's here, no matter how tired he is from the job, he takes care of me and he's always got a good humor about him. No, it's not him. It's something with me. I'm feeling it in my bones worse than ever, the cold. It's been snowing now for a whole week and the temperature hasn't gotten above thirty in the day. Night time it's got to be down in the teens. I'm afraid to look. My body is in pain. I won't tell Eric that. I can deal with it because I know why it hurts so much. But something else. I can't put my finger on it. Just a real sadness. I can't shake the feeling that I've lost something. Can't find it if I don't know what it is, now, can I? Maybe it's depression? You'd think I'd be used to the long winters. And if it's the long winter, that will surely be over soon. Spring isn't just around the corner, but the calendar says it is. Don't know why I'm rambling on. Better close this now and get under the warm covers."

"*August 14, 1985*

It's a hot one today. The mercury is up around 101. Supposed to stay like this for the next two days. My god! Hunker down in the shade somewhere. But I can say that my bones are enjoying it even if the rest of me is sweltering. I envy Eric driving south in his air-conditioned rig but not the sitting for hours in there. Almost too hot to walk down to the mailbox today but glad I made the effort. Looks as if a miracle just happened. Well, two miracles. A letter from Jean was sitting on top of the catalogues. Well, not a letter but an announcement like the one I got when she got married. Looks like I'm a grandfather! A baby girl. Sent a picture and everything. Says in the announcement that she weighs seven pounds and fifteen ounces. She's a long one. Twenty-three inches. Born on August 1 of this year. Probably never get to meet her but at least Jean had the decency to inform me of the family lineage continuing. Will need to send a congratulations card from grandpa. Oh, and her name is Catherine Helen Eagan."

"That's Kit's name!" Peter blurted out startling Eric, who almost knocked the mug off the arm of the rocker.

Eric turned to Pete who was visibly shaken by what he had just heard. "Who's Kit, Pete?" Eric's curiosity kicked into high gear. Whoever Kit was to Pete had not crossed his radar. How could it? Kit, he learned, when he read his father's journal on his own months ago was his niece. He had no idea that he had one until then. She would be twenty-nine years old now. About the same age as Pete, he guessed.

Pete wasn't sure how to answer Eric. He desperately tried to unravel the information that Eric seemed to innocently reveal in his father's words. He had listened, out of curtesy to Eric but had not followed. "Okay. Wait a minute. I'm trying to make sense of this. So, your sister, Jean, had a baby and her name was Catherine Helen …. What was the last name?"

Eric ran his finger along the entry stopping when he found it. "Eagan. Last name is Eagan"

"I can't believe it. I really can't. Can there be two Catherine Eagan's in the world?" He wasn't asking, not really. Only avoiding affirming another truth.

"Can't say, Pete." Eric stared straight ahead.

"Okay, let me try again. If this is the Catherine or Kit that I know…knew, then that means that you are her uncle?" He paused before he went on as if waiting for the calculations in his brain to catch up with him. "How can that possibly be? I mean, what are the chances that we have this connection?" He turned to Eric. "Can't be."

"Pete, you want to tell me what the connection is? I'm feeling a bit lost here." But he knew exactly what Pete was experiencing. He had gone through it on his own when his father's words told the untold story for the first time. He was not on solid ground for weeks after.

If he started to explain, he would not be able to stop. Pete knew that much about himself. And he also knew that he would have to tell his friend that his niece was dead. There appeared to be nobody else to tell him based on what he understood about Eric's family dynamics. A really sad situation for everyone, he reflected.

Suddenly, it came to him. He knew why he was here. It became crystal clear why he had contacted Eric, a stranger, really, and then made his way to his home in Shasta. To the volcano, to the gem shop. To the self-healed crystals. He could go no farther with her when Kit was alive, turning back before he should have. He could go no farther with Zeke other than to mend the wounds he had caused and promise his friendship. But he couldn't remember the last time he had spoken to Zeke since then. He could go no farther with Hellenia when she wanted to take him to his doorstep. All he wanted was to escape from her, to be free of her. And he was not allowed to go any farther with his parents when their lives were taken too soon. He knew. He knew, and he was frightened by the knowledge, more frightened than he had ever been. But he knew. Kit, Hellenia, and Benny knew it too. He had no choice but to go as far as he could go. And he knew that he would recognize when he had gone far enough. So he murmured a "Yes" so that Eric thought he had heard him, nodding in confirmation of his young friend's decision.

As Eric listened to Pete's explanation, he struggled to fathom the significance of his words. He didn't want to accept that his only niece, a human being who he did not know existed until recently, who had some of his blood running through her veins, who might have some resemblance to him, was dead. He didn't want to consider what he had lost in never knowing her. And he fought back the simmering hatred he had toward his sister who was the cause of his pain. As Pete continued to reveal to Eric his relationship with Kit, Eric's desire to know everything about her was overwhelming. But he waited, outwardly patient for Pete to finish but inwardly falling apart.

"Did you attend her funeral?" he asked as Pete finished.

"I did, Eric." He hoped that Eric would not pursue it. He had worked hard on coming to grips with that day and every day after.

"So, you saw Jean and her husband?"

"Yes." The less said, the better.

"Did she say anything to you? Did you talk to them?" Eric knew he was delving but he didn't care. His sister was becoming something of a legend to him. A pretend character who caused pretend disasters. But he knew better.

"I think I just paid my respects, Eric. I don't remember much about it." He sensed that Eric would not accept that. And he was right.

"That's it? Weren't you dating their daughter? No, you were living with her, right? You had to be close to them."

"As a matter of fact, I wasn't. Her mother didn't like me and her dad…I don't know. He kept his distance. Maybe because of her mother. I don't know. So, yeah. Said hardly anything other than paying my respects." He knew Eric wanted to go farther but there was no farther to go for Pete.

"Okay. I understand, Pete. Guess that isn't surprising considering my sister's decision to cut my dad and me out of her life. Now I think about it, you were a threat, weren't you? You could have taken her daughter away from her and she would have been left with no family. Well, other than her husband. A real piece of work, my sister." He felt the bile rising in his throat. So angry, so betrayed, so devasted was he.

"Maybe so, Eric. I'm sorry that everything is such a mess."

"Yes. Well, I'd like to say that it's all water under the bridge. But it feels more to me like the flood waters are rising and I'm taking us both under. There's no one in sight to save us." He closed the journal, leaving the ribbon hanging out against the binding. "I'm headed in for a while. You do what you need to do." He slowly pushed himself up from the rocker, his journal in one hand, mug in the other, and shuffled past Pete who was taken aback by how old Eric suddenly appeared.

And even though both harbored the same thought in the back of their minds, neither one found the courage to acknowledge aloud that something much greater than either one of them was at play here and had so much farther to go with them before it left them alone.

1999

When the body wants to give up, sometimes the brain disagrees. And it challenges the body to fight along with it. Sometimes the brain wins. Most of the time it does not. As Benny struggled to breathe, he adjusted the breathing tube that he found uncomfortable and demoralizing. The fresh mountain air was all about him, but he needed a plastic tube to breathe in canned air. And his body had not cooperated with him for days now. His legs, even though not paralyzed, might as well have been, the little he could use them. They had no strength left in them. The rest of him was giving out as well. His back ached continually, even though Eric had bought just about every device and pill out there for his father to help relieve his pain. His appetite was nonexistent. Nothing sounded good to him and he wasn't hungry anyway.

And there was one more thing that plagued him. It had plagued him for years but when in better health, he could ignore it and occupy his time with the present. He had kept busy, going to work every single day. Making enough to survive. Living in a place that he loved. But his past would not rest easy. Even though he had kept his word and done right by his silent promise to Hellenia that her kids would be okay, he had kept secrets from them. Had been a coward and only told his journal. He had decided numerous times that he would tell them everything. But the momentary courage that seemed so strong and demanding of him, quickly subsided until he found comfort, once again, in opening the leather journal and putting his pen to the paper.

And this night was no different. The tray table lay across his lap as he semi reclined in his bed. Three pillows were carefully placed behind his back and Eric also brought the reading lamp closer. He knew what his father needed. The journal was kept on the bed stand in full view. But Eric never touched it until now. His father needed his help in reaching it tonight. And when it lay closed on the tray table in front of Benny, Eric gave him his pen. Then he left the room. It was not his place to be there when his father was writing. A lesson drilled in to him from an early age and now silently understood even as Eric stifled his weeping on the other side of the closed door

"*December 1, 1999*

It's time. I can feel it tonight. Tomorrow? If I'm lucky, I won't be here. I can't say where. I don't know. The one thing that bothers me is leaving my Eric by himself. I know. He's a grown man. Probably, with me gone, it will open a whole new world for him. Maybe finally meet somebody. He shouldn't be alone. That will be my final wish for him. Not to be alone.

In recalling my life, I can say that, for the most part, it's been a good one. I don't need to go back and read my own words to know that. Anyway, I don't think I have the time. I think I've done right by everyone I've met along the way. Well, there's Joe. I didn't do right by him, keeping his children from him. But the circumstances have to be considered. I've got to believe he was not fit to be a father or else he would have done it. When I adopted Eric and Jean, I knew I had done the right thing. The only thing I could do, considering Hellenia's abandonment of her own kids. And of me. But I go to my final resting place still loving that woman and wondering what might have been. I write these words with every good intent: I love you still, Hellenia, and forgive you.

And my Jean. I'll never know what I did wrong with her. Maybe she is just one of those unhappy people in this world. She has kept away from me, from Eric and me. And now she's a mother of a teenager. I figure Catherine to be about fourteen now. Maybe Jean will remember her own teen years when she made life miserable for me and Eric. Maybe. But maybe Catherine is different. Maybe she takes after her father. I can only assume that he's a good man to be husband to Jean. I regret that I never met him. I regret that my granddaughter never knew her grandfather. I regret that my daughter isn't my daughter anymore. Her decision, not mine.

It seems to me that if anyone reads this journal, it will be you, Eric. You've been a good boy and now a good man. I have tried to tell this book everything that happened in my day for the last sixty-five years. I was a good son. So now, you are reading the last entry and still have questions, I know. But I want you to know that I would answer any of those questions now as I wait for death if you asked me tonight. But you won't, and I'll just write not knowing what you want to know. I've been a coward, Eric. I've closed you off and found this haven for my thoughts. I've cheated you from the truth because I am a coward. If I could tell you where your mother is, I would. But I never knew. I'll draw my last breath wishing I knew. And if she is dead, and if there is a place where we all meet up again, I'll find her and let her know what a good son you've been. That I know and that I promise. Eric, my son, I'll wait for you. Don't forget me. I love you, son."

*

Two days had passed since Eric last read aloud to Pete from his father's journal. Pete stayed out of Eric's way as much as possible during this time. There wasn't much to keep him occupied, but the space Eric needed was more important to Pete than his own growing boredom. He contemplated heading back to the valley. Whatever Eric was dealing with, Pete could not help. Besides, other than the freakish coincidence that Eric was Kit's uncle, and that Hellenia was Eric's mother, Pete wasn't sure why he should stay. And each time he convinced himself that he should head out, he could not carry through. Eric's words nagged at him. "…the flood waters are rising and I'm taking us both under." He had no idea what Eric was alluding to and, frankly, he didn't want to know.

Although, the more he thought about it, the more uneasy he became. The whole lore about Shasta City, Mount Shasta, the spiritual and mystical powers she held, had seemed just that when he first arrived and explored the town. That he found himself in a gem shop for the first time in his life and that he actually bought "self-healed crystals" confounded his thinking. If asked, would he deny that maybe there really was something about this place that he didn't fully understand? Before he arrived, his answer would be "yes". A resounding "yes". But not now. Not after what would seem coincidences to others felt so much more than that to Pete. Hellenia, Eric, Kit. And Benny's journal. What had Eric not read to him? What had he purposely left out that could even begin to realistically explain his presence here? And the crystals? The same kind found in Hellenia's boxes for her children. What did they mean in all of this? Another coincidence? He had no idea. The longer he dwelled on the unknowns, the more confused he became.

The only answer to his questions was right here in the house with him. He suspected that Eric had more to tell and Pete needed to know. He would wait no longer for his friend to reengage with him. It was not Eric's choice anymore as to when he'd expect Pete to be his audience. No. Pete knew he had to confront Eric and insist that he had no intention of going under in the rising waters he could not see.

Eric was in his bedroom where he had been since Pete last saw him. The house was eerily quiet and for a moment, Pete considered that his friend might be dead. He lightly tapped on the door. There were no sounds, no movement as Pete strained to hear, his ear against the cool wood. He knocked this time. A low grumble and a bed's frame creaking under its occupant's movements indicated that he had disturbed Eric. Too late to undo his error, he backed from the door and waited.

As old as Eric looked when he shuffled by Pete two days ago, his appearance now was even worse. Pete was shaken by the ashen facial skin almost the color of Eric's grey hair. His eyes drooped into the skin sacks that sat like carelessly applied playdough. His unshaven face was a prickly landscape of black and grey stubble. The little hair he did have left on his head was shooting up in multiple directions as if in rebellion. And the sadness that shrouded his whole body alarmed Pete. Eric said nothing. It appeared to Pete that Eric didn't recognize him.

"I'm sorry, Eric. I didn't mean to wake you up," he lied. He had every intention of confronting Eric.

Eric turned and walked back to his bed as Pete watched in surprise. He didn't crawl back in but sat wearily on the edge of the mattress. "You didn't wake me."

"Oh, well, that's good. Are you okay?"

"If you mean physically, I guess everything is still in working order." He didn't look at Pete when he said this. His eyes were focused on the bedside table.

"So, do you think that we could talk a bit more today? It's been two days, Eric. You kind of left me with not so cheery thoughts." He wondered if Eric even remembered anything from two days ago, judging by his state of being.

"What makes you want to accompany me to Davy Jones' locker?" This time Eric broke his gaze and looked directly at Pete.

If this was Eric's attempt at humor, it fell flat on its face. Pete was in no mood for any more games. "Okay, Eric, I don't have a clue what you're talking about, but I do know one thing. You're not telling me everything and you're playing a stupid game with me. I've been in limbo for two days now while you've been doing whatever it is you've been doing." Pete gestured with both arms towards the landscape of Eric's bedroom. "If you're going to drag this out any longer, I've just got to get out of here. I mean head home."

Eric, still observing his young friend, smiled. "Is that a threat?"

Pete reeled from the question. "Why would you say that? No, it's not a threat. It's just the facts. Why do I need to stay up here with you? You obviously don't care if I stay or go. I could have slipped out of here in the last forty-eight hours and you would never have known it or cared." Now he was becoming emotional. Pete shut it down quickly. "So, you have just got to say the word, Eric. I'll be out of your hair in no time."

Eric pushed himself up from the mattress, picked up an envelope that rested on the bedside table, and held it up. "You can't go just yet. There's one more item I need to share with you. When I've done that, you can do whatever you want." His words were evenly spaced and almost monotone in presentation.

Pete's mind was racing. Maybe Hellenia had not been a troll on I-5. Maybe Eric was! Stupid, stupid thinking, Pete chastised himself. But was Eric serious about keeping him here and did he really mean that he could do whatever he wanted? Solid ground was giving way under Pete's feet. "Okay. Look. I'll give you the rest of today. I mean it, Eric. I'm heading out the door at sunset, if you don't do whatever it is you need to do."

Eric's smile grew larger now and Pete thought that he might laugh out loud. "Sunset, huh? Well, I better get a mosey on now, partner, so we can finish up our business. If I had an OK Corral out back, I'd say meet you there, but I don't." Then he did laugh, and the tension in the room dissipated immediately so that Pete couldn't help but laugh right along with his friend.

*

They sat in their respective rockers. The late afternoon breeze was beginning to pick up, showering the two men with a welcome relief from the early heat of the day. Eric had cleaned himself up and was looking more like the Eric that Peter knew. A calmness joined the men as if a third participant in anticipation of Eric's long-awaited revelations. Two bottles of beer and Benny's journal rested on the little table.

"Nice out here right now." Eric's words thrown out as a prelude picked at Pete. But he played along.

"Yeah. It is." A very short prelude.

"Well, I guess I better give this a try before that sun sets." Pete suspected that Eric was waiting for a laugh, but Pete did not oblige.

"I'm ready." Pete took a long drink and slowly placed the bottle on table.

"Everything that you know so far has to do with my side of the family. With Jean and with Kit. And the little bit that got you involved was when I read your parents' names to you."

"I wouldn't say that was a 'little bit', Eric. But, yeah, still plenty of unknowns here." He wanted Eric to get on with it but was careful not to push.

Eric picked up the journal and opened the cover. He took one of the two envelopes that he had slipped into his journal and held it up. "You remember this?"

Pete had no clue. "One of the envelopes from the shoe box?"

"No. I was about to read this to you when we got sidetracked with the shoe boxes. Never got back to it. As I think about it now, there was a good reason. It wasn't the right time. You weren't ready." Eric paused knowing that he was creating anxiety, but it couldn't be helped. "But whether you're ready or not, sunset is fast approaching, my friend." Now it was Eric's turn to take a long drink. Then, with animated movement, he slowly lifted the bottle from his mouth and firmly placed it next to Pete's. He kept the journal in his lap.

Pete's mood was souring and if this man didn't get to it right now, he feared he might say something he'd regret. The sound of Eric's voice interrupted his thoughts. A relief, finally.

"Pete, this is a letter from my mother, Hellenia, to Jean and me. My guess is that she wrote it shortly before she died, maybe even the night she died. There's no date but judging by the newness of the paper, that's my guess. And the reason I'm reading it to you is because you need answers. So here goes.

"To my children, Eric and Jean.

I'm writing this to you because I want you to know the truth about your mother. I want to be the one to make things right. My name is Hellenia Wade. That was my given name. I was born and raised on a ranch in the Santa Clara Valley. I guess you know it now as the Silicon Valley. A horrible name for what used to be a wonderous place. My childhood was special and, like all of us, I took it for granted. When my parents died, your grandparents, and long before you came along, I was left to take over the ranch. It was hard work, I can tell you that. And there were times when I just wanted to give up. Sell it. Move on. But I couldn't. And then a gentleman came along looking for work and I hired him. His name was Joe Terner. Well, he worked hard and if it hadn't been for him, I don't know what would have happened to the place.

It wasn't long before we fell in love and got married. We were so happy, at first. He took on the ranch as if it was his own from the beginning, and I often prayed to my parents telling them that all was well down here. Things started changing when I had you, Eric. It wasn't your fault, mind you. How could it be? You were a tiny baby. And sickly too. You needed my attention and I gave it to you. But your father got angry about it saying that I wasn't paying enough attention to him. He said things about you that I won't even mention. I know he didn't mean the things he said. But I think that he was just a selfish man. That's a fact. And maybe the truth is that he did mean every word he spoke.

When I found that I was pregnant again with you, Jean, I was scared. I was afraid to tell him, knowing how he was with you, Eric. When I did tell him, he left for three days. I thought I would never see him again.

261

But he came back and for the next nine months made our lives a misery. He was mean and cruel. He didn't love me, and he didn't love either one of you. I am sorry to write this to you, but you need to know the truth.

So, one afternoon, I packed the two of you up. You were just shy of your first birthday, Jean. And Eric, you were my big boy. I told your father that I was going into town. He didn't even look up from his paper. I took the truck with my babies and never went back.

Well, again, I need to tell the truth. I did go back once. But before I tell you why, let me finish this bit. Joe and I had friends in the valley. Ranchers, like us, whose spread was about ten miles down the road. Benjamin and Savannah Hopkins. Poor Benny. He lost his wife too soon. Found her in the yard. A bad heart. So Benny was alone and childless. They'd only been married a short time before she died.

I went to Benny. It was Benny who took us in. His heart was bigger than anything. And he didn't ask for anything in return, if you know what I mean. He just wanted to take care of us. And in the time that I was there with Benny, your father never once looked for us. We were right under his nose. And when Benny asked me if I wanted to go with him to Shasta City, I said yes. It would be a new start for me and for you two. But I wasn't sure about Benny. He told me that when I was ready, I could leave at any time. So, I wasn't sure about his feelings. But I couldn't stay in the valley.

On the night we were to leave, I asked Benny to take me by the ranch. It was in the early morning hours, so I knew your father would be asleep. I wrote him a letter explaining that we were leaving town, but I didn't tell him where we were going. I wished him well. Some part of me still loved him. Benny pulled up to the mailbox and I left the letter in there for your father to find.

I must tell you that Benny tried to reason with me. Tried to convince me to go back to your father. It was not his fault that he took us in. Do not blame him for anything.

I'm going to shorten this. I remember too much, even at this stage of the game. There is one final truth that I need to reveal. It has been my secret for so very long. But it will do me no good to keep it a secret any longer. The last mistake of my life would be to take this to the grave with me. I have betrayed enough people in my life. I will not betray another. It explains the rest of the story and may give peace to those involved.

We made our home in Shasta City. I never married Benny. But everyone assumed it and we didn't tell them any different. He was so good to you both, to me.

But I didn't love him. Not like I had loved your father. But one thing led to another and both of us, longing for the comfort of someone's arms, laid together only once. When I realized that I was pregnant, I panicked. I was afraid to tell Benny. I was afraid to ruin what we had. And I didn't want him to love me because of a baby.

So, I said goodbye to you both in the middle of the night. I kissed you on your cheeks. I knew that you would be taken care of. And I was right, wasn't I?

And the baby? I returned to the Santa Clara Valley to have it. A boy. I named him Benjamin Wade. I didn't hold him. I didn't want to see him. I told them that I didn't know who the father was. He was put up for adoption. I gave up all rights to him and, if he was adopted, to any information about his new parents.

The news came of your father's death, a suicide, when I was working in Oakland. I saw it in the newspaper. I will always carry that weight with me, knowing that it was me that killed him.

I know. I can hear you. You are angry. You never knew. I am sorry. I had no choice. My job was to be your mother, to keep you safe from harm, and to love you like nothing else. I don't ask for your forgiveness. I don't need it. But I ask you to be good to yourselves and know that you never did anything wrong.

If you are still reading this, thank you. But you have every right to burn this. You have every right to speak unspeakable words about me. It is all right.

I have no right to ask this of you, but it is the only way I can reach out to my past. Maybe there is someone still alive who remembers me. It would give me comfort if you would do this. I've included a small obituary that I want in the San Jose Mercury News. Would one of you do that for me? Don't know the cost but the sixty dollars I've included should be enough for however many days that will cover. If you can't, I understand.

My dear Eric. My dear Jean. My life has been a long one, longer than I deserved. Maybe my old age is my punishment for all that I did wrong in my life. Please know that there hasn't been a day that I have not longed to see you, to talk with you, to love you. It was never my intention to leave you, but it is what I did. Whether you understand or not, whether you forgive me or not, does not matter to me now. But know that I will be with you every day for the rest of your lives. When you feel a gentle cool breeze next to you, know I'm there. When you travel the highways, Eric, know I am sitting right beside you. And Jean, my dear Jean. I did not have enough time to know you, but I am with you now. I will always love you, my dear children."

Hellenia Wade Terner

Eric kept the letter open on his lap. Neither man spoke immediately, each digesting Hellenia's words. Having the advantage of reading the letter beforehand, Eric was painfully aware of the impact it might have on Pete, just as it had on him. It was obvious that Pete was related to Hellenia. The unread letter, the second in the envelope would confirm it.

"You doing okay?" The concern in Eric's voice was evident.

"The name…Wade… keeps coming up, Eric. But I'm still not making any connection. Was I supposed to?"

Eric thought carefully before answering. "I think the other letter will help you understand." He carefully folded Hellenia's letter, placed it in the envelope and slipped it back in Benny's journal. Sliding the second envelope out, he debated whether to let Pete read it on his own. But he thought better of it. Better to let him hear it all the way through. He could read it as many times as he wanted to later.

"Eric? Is this about to change my life?" Pete pointed to the folded paper in Eric's hand.

"It will change what you thought you knew. Seems like neither one of us is going to escape that fact." Eric took a deep breath. "You're still young, Pete, with your whole life ahead of you. You have time to make sense of it all, maybe even learn from it and find a way to forgive. You're going to be just fine. Me? Not so sure. The one thing I don't have is time." He had said too much and when he looked at Pete, he knew he had confused and alarmed his young friend unnecessarily. "Let me read this, okay?"

Pete was alarmed more so than confused. Was Eric dying too? Whatever the Wade connection was seemed to diminish in importance as he thought about losing Eric. The weight of the world, an expression he had heard somewhere, suddenly felt very real and it rested on his shoulders.

"Eric, are you sick?" A simple question but whose affirmation would wreak havoc on Pete's fragile grasp on reality.

"No, of course not. Tired, and getting on in years, yes. But not sick." As he spoke, he understood why Pete would ask the question. "No, you misunderstood me. I meant that I don't have time because I'm closing in on the end of my life. Not like you. You see?"

Pete was embarrassed. "Oh, sure. I get it. I get it now." His embarrassment was brief as he sighed deeply, relieved that Eric was going nowhere. "Sorry."

"Don't be. My poor communication skills. Anyway, speaking of that, are you ready?" Eric unfolded the letter and held it up.

"Yes. Let's do this." Pete was unaware of both of his clenched fists pushing down on his thighs. He was unaware of how tense his whole body had become.

"I'll tell you who it's from before I start. That way it will make better sense."

Pete nodded. "Okay. Sure."

"This is from James Murphy. Remember him? He married Barbara Murphy and they adopted my mother's baby boy." Pete nodded. "It appears that that communication was the beginning of many, all by letter. My father never mentioned the man's name to me. But it appears that I met him when I was just about five. He kept his promise and came to visit us. Brought his three-year-old boy with him. He would be my step-brother, right? Anyway, this letter I found tucked way back in one of his dresser drawers.

"November 4, 1981

Dear Benny,

 I write this with great news. But first of all, how are you? Imagine Eric is still on the road most of the time. Hope you do okay without him there. You raised a good boy. Staying with you all these years and helping you out. Have you heard anything from Jean? Such a sorry situation. You know how I feel about that.

 This household is in the throes of wedding planning. Never thought it could be so complicated and crazy! Forget the expense. I won't even tell you. But Benjamin and Marty are so excited and going full speed ahead. I believe I told you the date but just in case, it's April 1, 1982. (of course) Invitations go in the mail next week. You need to be looking for yours. Sure do hope you can make it.

Write back soon,

James"

 Eric stopped reading but did not put the letter away. "There's more than one letter here. I'll go on."

 Pete saw no reason to respond.

"November 8, 1981

Dear Benny,

 It's been a confusing and stressful time in this household. Benjamin came to us with a question the same day I wrote the Nov. 4 letter. We thought the day would come but we still are not prepared. So, I never got around to sending this letter. Just adding to it now.

 He wanted to know if he was adopted. I can tell you that Barbara and I were in shock. We were expecting the question years ago. The boy, man is thirty! Not his fault. But he explained that because he was getting married, he wanted to know the truth, especially if they were going to have kids of their own. Makes good sense. We told him the truth, of course. A visible relief on all our parts. I guess he suspected it for some time. Ever since he started comparing his adult looks to the two of us. Caught him going through photo albums of me and Barbara when were even younger than he is now. Even going through our own baby albums. Didn't think much of it at the time. Probably should have put two and two together but we didn't. And I have to tell you, he doesn't resemble either one of us in even the smallest way. I know what you are thinking. Of course not! He's adopted. But we've got friends that adopted and by god, if I didn't know better I would swear that those kids were their biological offspring. But no such luck with us.

We told him that the adoption was closed, meaning the biological parents want everything kept secret. And, as I told you long ago in one of my letters to you, that was fine with Barbara and me. But Benjamin isn't resting until he knows who his real parents are. He says that there's a way. He's already looked into it. As hard as it's going to be, Barbara and I have come to peace with it. It is his right, after all, to know his roots. So, say a prayer for us, if you're so inclined.

I was going to close but I think I'll keep this letter going for a bit. If the search goes on too long, I'll come back here and tell you. But according to him, he can find out pretty darn quick. So, I'll tell the outcome soon."

"November 19, 1981

Dear Benny,

Benjamin found what he was looking for. Just yesterday. And you're not going to believe it. Barbara and I have a strong disagreement about me sharing the information with you. She thinks if anyone should do it, it should be our son. But I disagree and that's why I'm writing to you today.

Benjamin's mother's name is Helen Wade. She gave birth to him in Santa Clara County, San Jose, California on March 10, 1950 and he was adopted by us on March 20, 1950. Father was listed as unknown.

If my memory serves me, wasn't there a ranching family in the valley when we were growing up whose name was Wade? Did your family know them? I remember my father talking about them, the Wades. They were good people, according to my father. I think that there were only three big ranching families in the area at the time: The Hopkins, your family; the Wades: and us, the Murphys. It's a bit of a reach but it's got me wondering. Did we adopt a baby from that Wade family? And the name, Helen Wade, doesn't sound right to me. Didn't she go by a longer name? Something about the Greeks? Seem to remember the teacher giving us a lecture about the meaning of her name? I can't remember it. Do you?

So that's what we know. Benjamin is trying to locate her but is having no luck. Wants to invite her to the wedding, if you can imagine that. Barbara and I want what's best for him but between you and me and the lamp post, we won't cry if he never finds her.

Closing this up now. Left you with some things to think about. Let me know in your next letter if you remember her name. It's going to drive me crazy until I know.

Write soon,

James"

Eric folded the letter and slipped it into the journal. He left the envelope in his lap. "If you don't mind, I'd like to continue before you say anything, Pete. My father's journal entry dated November 23, 1981 needs to be read first. Okay?"

Pete's head was reeling but he managed a barely audible "Okay."

Eric had already marked the entry with the ribbon and quickly flipped to the page.

"November 23, 1981

I don't know how to start tonight. How to write down what happened in my day. My pen feels like an iron rod, so heavy and unwilling. If I could take today back, if I could wipe it from my history, I would in a heartbeat. But that is not possible and would be wrong. So, I will force myself to follow my father's directive as I have done every night since. It might be important, after all, somewhere down the line.

James' letter arrived this morning. I expected to hear more wedding news what with Benjamin's marriage imminent. It began that way. Seems that he was interrupted, and days later just added another letter and another. I was not prepared.

James' son, Benjamin, asked James and Barbara if he was adopted. Seems that Benjamin took it in to his own hands to find his real parents when they confirmed it. My god! If I could only go back in time. If only things had been different. From what James tells me, it is my Hellenia who is Benjamin's mother. I have thought of nothing else today since opening James' letter. It makes sense now. Why Hellenia left me and her children. But how could it be? We laid together only once. Could she have gotten pregnant then? And why didn't she tell me? Why leave when I was the father? Why didn't she know that I would love her even more and our child? I am heartbroken tonight. I cannot think clearly. But I know. I know the truth now. I don't need to be convinced. My darling Hellenia left me before I could ask her to marry me. She left with my baby. My child who is now my good friend's adopted child? Yes. That would be right. How can that be? How can life be that cruel? Have I taken care of her own children all this time never knowing that I had a son of my own? That his life could have been in jeopardy? That there was nothing I could do about it? I will say "thank you", Hellenia, for keeping our child, but I cannot forgive you for what you have taken from me. I will never tell Eric and Jean any of this. It is too shameful. I can write no more."

Pete remained perfectly still and silent. His eyes focused on something in the distance.

"Pete, there is more. I need to finish what I have begun." He gently turned the journal's pages until he stopped and placed the ribbon, once again, along the binding.

"March 30, 1986

James is a good friend. His letters continue to arrive telling me of our son's life as a married man. I have never told him that I am Benjamin's real father. I would never do that to James. Instead, I have found peace in knowing about him through James' letters. I'm not sure if he has ever forgiven me for not attending the wedding, but I just could not. They said that they understood my weak and false excuse of illness, but I believe they knew I was lying. In any case, they have not brought it up since. Bless them.

Benjamin and Marty delivered a baby boy on March 20. James' letter was full of joy. And I celebrated my son's and wife's wonderful news quietly and happily. To love from afar continues to be difficult. I will never learn how to do it. Never. The baby's name is Peter Wade-Murphy. And now I am a grandfather again. Catherine was born last year, Jean's little girl.

There are times that I want to yell it out from the roof tops, to have the church bells in town ring loudly, to tell everyone I see. But I cannot. I will not. That is not the Benny of Shasta City that everyone knows. That is not information that I will ever be able to share. For now, then, I will wait on James' letters and I will tell him of my life, such as it is. And to you, my dear pages, I will always reveal my secrets, my truths."

Eric did not wait. He did not prepare Pete for what was to come. He could not.

"December 28, 2000

Dear Benny,

I can barely stand to write this letter to you, so sadden are we by recent events. But you have been my best friend for so long. I must share this news.

Benjamin and Marty were killed five days ago in an automobile accident. Peter was not with them, thank God. He was staying with us while his parents went to a Christmas party with their neighbors. Not far from their home. You remember Bollinger Road? Happened along there. The police have determined that they were hit head-on by a drunk driver who survived for two days and died in the hospital. The report indicates that

Benjamin and Marty died instantly. For that, we thank god. Barbara is devastated as am I, but I am sick with worry about her. She cries all day and all night. She will not be consoled. I am struggling with the loss but in my own way, Benny. But I need to be here for her too.

And Peter? I believe he is in shock. He hasn't said a word to me since he learned about his parents' deaths. He's staying with us right now, but he stays in his room, the door locked, and won't respond to me. I just don't know what to do. I think that I might be going crazy, Benny. I feel completely alone, and my heart is broken, so broken. My tears have not come yet. I know they will but not now. I really could use a friend right now. I am sorry that we are not closer. Is there any way you could come down for a while? I know I'm asking a lot, but would you consider it? Don't worry yourself if you can't. I will understand.

Marty's sister, Emily, has been a great help what with all the funeral arrangements and letting folks know. She's just as concerned about Peter as I am. She and Peter have always had a good relationship. Never married, no children of her own but she has a way with kids. Been a school teacher for years. Maybe she'll be the one to break through with him. Someone has to.

I'll write soon. Not much more to say now. Think about coming down, if you can.

Your heart broken friend,

James"

"And this is the last entry from Benny's journal that I'll read to you, Pete."

"December 28, 2000

How can you be so cruel? So heartless? Dear God, you ask for my faith and trust in you but all you do is bring me anguish and loss. I am through with you. All my prayers have been wasted on you. I am done.

James' letter came today, and I wish to god it hadn't. My son, my only child, is dead. His wife is dead. A senseless tragedy. A heartless act on your part, god. Because of you, they leave behind a child who no longer has a father and a mother to guide him and to love him. And because of your "divine plan", his own grandfather cannot reach out and console him.

I have tried to understand what I did wrong in my life to offend you. Everything I have done was done with good intentions. How can you punish me this way? How much longer am I to suffer? You took my Savannah. You took my Hellenia. You turned my Jean against me. And now you have taken my son, Benjamin? And I fear that you are not done. My Eric. What part does he play in your plan? He will not leave me. I forbid it of you. You will take me before you take my Eric. Do you understand? You will take me first. I will have no more of this.

I am tired. Too tired to carry my anger any longer. Too tired to carry my losses any longer. But, unlike you, Joe. I cannot find the will or courage to end my own life. I am leaving it in His hands because I must. Not because I want to.

I am too sick and tired to be by my friend's side. No longer an excuse but a fact. I will write to him explaining my absence from his, my son's funeral. But I will be there in my heart. I can do that much for you, my son. And for your son? My grandson Peter? Maybe someday, after I am gone, he will find his way to the truth. If there are such things as angels, he will never lose his way. We will be with him as far as he wants to go.

There is nothing more to say."

"And finally, this. This letter is dated just six days before my father, your grandfather, died." Again, Eric did not pause. He could not look at Pete.

272

"*January 20, 2001*

Dear Benny,

I am sorry not to have written sooner. So much has happened since the funeral. I understand why you couldn't come. I felt you there, even so.

Barbara is doing a little better but we both have horrible days. We miss them so much, Benny. I only pray that you are spared such tragedy in your life.

The big news is that Marty's sister, Emily Aimes, has adopted Peter. Benjamin and Marty had named her legal guardian when the baby was born. It was in all the legal papers found in Benjamin's file cabinet. She knew, of course, but we did not. Probably not necessary anyway. Now in our late seventies, no need to tell you that, we are no match for Aunt Emily. I believe she's only forty-eight. She can handle a fourteen-year-old teenager. So that is a blessing and a relief for everyone. Peter loves his aunt and seems to have accepted the outcome. He is still struggling, of course, as we all are. Emily is getting him counseling to help him through it. Never believed in that stuff myself, but if it helps my grandson, wonderful. And she is holding up considering she has lost her only sibling. I have to remind myself that she is suffering, not just us.

So, we will get through this. God has a plan. That I am sure of. Got to keep the faith, right? Someone said to me the other day that no parent should have to bury their child. It's not the natural path. And I said to him, "Who's to say what the natural path is?" In my opinion, Benny, there are no set paths. You start on one and finish on another. And no telling how many you travel in between. No one is controlling how far you're going to go on any one of them. Just my opinion.

When you can, write. Take good care of yourself.

Your friend,

James"

Dropping the letter on to the open journal in his lap, Eric leaned his head against the back of the rocker and closed his eyes. Hardly perceptible to Pete, Eric slowly rocked. He felt drained. Physically and mentally unable to do anything more than rock in the darkness. If Pete had said anything, he did not hear him. He continued to rock.

Pete did speak but only two words. "The crystals." He rose from his rocker, silently as if an ethereal presence and left Eric who still rocked, rightfully elsewhere.

This time he knew where he had put the crystal. He carried it carefully, along with the explanation sheet, to the living room. The two shoe boxes, now on a table by the window, seemed neglected and tossed aside as Pete approached them. He set his crystal on the table. Lifting the lid on the box containing the baby clothes, he didn't see the small bag at first. Eric had removed nothing from the box. Just two days ago, Pete would have felt like he was trespassing as he gently moved the clothing. But now, he had no concerns. These were not only Eric's shoeboxes but also his. His grandmother's boxes. Lifting the small velvet bag from under the tiny garments, he placed it next to the larger crystal. The lid was missing on the second box, its contents of opened envelopes in disarray. Again, he searched for the second velvet bag. Lifting it from its hiding place, he placed it next to the other bag.

His heart was racing as he sat down on the couch and reread the description of the crystal. His eyes had difficulty focusing, at first, on the print and he kept wiping the moisture from them. A sense of urgency swelled in him. An unrelenting need to confirm what his brain could not yet do. Not until he knew for sure. If Eric was resting, Pete was on the opposite end of the spectrum of consciousness. He had never felt so alive. So very awake.

He skimmed the print, his eyes seeking out the profound message to him, the one that he did not comprehend upon first reading. That meant little to him until this very moment.

Your purchase of this quartz crystal is for a reason. Yes, your eye was drawn to it, but why? ... Perhaps you are in need of healing? Is the universe giving you a little prodding? ... the possibility of moving forward positively in your life, if you choose to do so.

Examine your crystal. ...one end looks different than the other? ... appears unscathed. But at the other end, it looks quite different. This part of the crystal was the broken end, injured end... see what looks like stone upon stone. ... called Self-Healed is because this disturbed end has been overgrown with Quartz crystal; the crystal's attempt to heal its wound.

... more explanation ... can help you examine your life. We all have past experiences, some good, some bad, and some quite terrible. You are who you are because of them. ... we work at submerging the uncomfortable experiences in favor of gliding through life, tentatively relying on the strength of the happier moments.

... to help you heal from the uncomfortable experiences, you must find a way to accept them and to understand how you have grown because of them.

Pete stared at the crystal and its two hidden companions as they waited for him on the table. He went over to them. One by one, he released the smaller versions of his own from their velvet darkness and placed them on either side of his crystal.

It was uncanny how similar they were to each other in structure. Almost as if they had, at one time in their histories, been one formation. The three crystals caught the rays of the late afternoon sun coming through the window. It was as if they had come to life for him at that very moment. To accept what lay in front of him would be difficult. To understand it was not possible. He had no other path to take, so he knew that he had to try. He lifted the large crystal first and then its companions. He brought them to the screen door with the intention of sharing with Eric their significance. The shadowed figure standing on the other side of the screen brought Pete to a sudden halt, almost causing him to drop the precious gems to the floor.

Eric opened the door and waited to enter as Pete stepped back into the room. He made no mention of the crystals in Pete's hands. He said nothing as he passed by Pete on his way to his bedroom. Pete turned in time to see the bedroom door close behind his uncle.

This time, he would not wait. He had just as much to digest as Eric; more for that matter. And he knew that he needed Eric to help him, to reassure him, to help him stay on the path. The puzzle pieces were now in place, thanks to Eric, but he had no idea whether Eric accepted everything that had happened in both of their lives to bring them to this moment. He wasn't even sure that he did.

"Eric, would you please open the door? We need to talk." Pete consciously controlled his tone. A simple request, that was all. With no response, he tried again. "Eric, please. I don't want to be alone right now." He realized this to be true as soon as he said it. "I don't think you want to be alone either." He had said too much and wished he could take the words back. He had no right assuming anything about Eric.

"Give me a minute."

Pete, in an audible sigh, released his pent-up breath and moved away from the door. He wasn't sure where he should be when Eric came out. Suddenly, he felt anxious and out of place. He moved to the couch and sat down on one end. Still holding the crystals, he strained to listen for the door to open. A million thoughts collided in his brain, none settling down as a place to start the conversation with his uncle. Now he wished that he hadn't been so impatient, had thought things through before bothering Eric.

"Pete. Sorry about that back there." Eric was standing in front of him startling Pete.

"No, no. It's okay."

Eric moved to the other end of the couch. "You mind?"

"Of course not." Why was he feeling so uncomfortable with Eric? He forced himself to calm down.

Eric sat heavily into the couch, but he didn't relax. Instead, he sat erectly, his hands folded and placed between his legs as if ready to go at any minute. "How are you doing?"

"About as good as you, I expect." The room suddenly felt too hot and stuffy. Pete felt his nervousness drip from his forehead while a film of sweat sat on his upper lip. He thought to reach up and wipe his face but remembered the crystals in his hands.

"Well, I guess we need to say what we're both thinking. Try to make sense of it. I guess I could start by saying thank you."

"What for?" Pete was taken aback.

"For coming into my life. I'm beginning to understand that some things are meant to be. You happen to be one of those things."

"For some time now, I've felt stuff that I can't explain. Can't begin to understand. Eric, you're going to think I'm crazy, but going back as far as Kit, me leaving her on the trail up to just a few minutes ago with these crystals," he lifted them up to show Eric, "something has been trying to get me straight. It's a feeling, sometimes a thought that I can't make out but that is just there, unreachable. There were times that I thought I was going crazy. When I was in the car with Hellenia…"

"Not Hellenia. Your grandmother, Pete," Eric corrected.

"Yes, thanks. With my grandmother. When I was with her, something told me to pay attention to her. That she was there for a reason. That she just happened to be at that rest stop when I needed her. I knew, Eric, somewhere deep inside, that there was more to the ride than just a lift. But all I wanted to do was get out of that car. To see her drive off and to get back to my house. I had no idea, Eric." Pete slumped under the weight of his regret.

"I understand, Pete. Believe me. Like I told you before. That car, her car parked there so close to me all this time. I felt something inside too. But, like you, I didn't pay attention to it. I didn't act on it. Whatever the 'it' was."

"These crystals, Eric. You know what I think?"

"No, but they are beautiful, aren't they? Where did the big one come from?"

Pete realized that he had never shown Eric his purchase from the gem shop. Never even brought it up. "I bought this here in town. At the gem shop you took me to. One of the days while you were on the road. I forgot all about telling you. Then I remembered the little velvet bags in the shoe boxes." He held them up again.

"Do you see what I see?" Eric's question preceded Pete's as if he read his mind once again.

"I do, Eric. And I'm glad you see it too." Pete hoped that they were referring to the same thing.

"How can that be?" Eric moved closer to his nephew and to the crystals.

"Of all the crystals in that shop, Eric. Of all the hundreds to choose from, I bought this one."

Eric finished his thought for him. "And my mother, your grandmother, bought the other two, one for me and one for Jean, your aunt. And who knows how long ago she bought them, how long ago she tucked them among the baby clothes, the birthday cards?"

Both men sat for a long time in silence, focusing on the crystals, in Pete's hands.

"Eric, she knew that we would find one another. I'm sure of it. I want you to read this." Pete gave him the folded sheet from the gem shop. He waited for Eric to finish before he spoke. "You see? She knew that when we found each other, it would only be the beginning of all that needs to happen for each one of us. The healing, Eric. We need the healing. This was her way of making sure that we were taken care of. I'm sure of it. Sure of it."

"I don't know what to think. I just don't understand anything. How any of this has taken place the way it has. And these crystals? So long separated and now back together?

Pete laughed loudly, too loudly, surprising them both. "Yes, that's exactly right. Exactly!" He placed the crystals on the coffee table and turned to Eric. "So, where do we go from here, uncle?"

"This is a good place to start." He stood up and indicated to Pete to do the same. "We are blood, Pete, and nothing can separate us from that fact. Not like the crystals. We are stronger, aren't we?" He didn't wait for Pete to respond but reached for him, encircling Pete in his arms and Pete held on for dear life.

After supper, Pete remembered the photos in the house.

"Eric, would you tell me about the photos you've got, the ones in there?" he pointed to the living room while remembering the fragile frames shifting in his hand.

"Sure. They would make sense to you now, wouldn't they?" Eric went into the living room and Pete followed. "This one is of my sister and me, Jean, your Aunt Jean, when we were little kids. I guess Benny took them." Eric focused on the fading images. "The only picture I have of my sister. Wouldn't know her if she walked right up to me now."

"That's too bad," was all Pete could manage to produce. It dawned on him that he was looking at Kit's mother as a little girl. And that was too much to absorb even though it was the truth. He suddenly felt Kit's strong presence in the room with her uncle and cousin. He wanted to escape.

"And this one," Eric picked up the frame which instantly fell apart as it had done when Pete did the same, "Oops. There we go." He managed to grasp it, as Pete had done. "This is my mother, Hellenia. A beauty, wasn't she?" He smiled. "As much as I try, I don't remember her looking like that. I guess the truth is that I don't remember her face at all. So, this is special, this photo. Deserves a new frame, though." Eric removed his mother's photo and carried the empty frame to the kitchen counter placing it on his grocery list. "I'll get one the next time I'm in town."

"What about that one up there?" Pete pointed to the photo on one of the high shelves of the bookcase.

"Yes. That one is Benny," Eric said as he reached for it. He stared at it before continuing. "This was taken by me when he was beginning to fail. Needed that cane to keep him upright until his legs just wouldn't cooperate any longer. Hated to have his picture taken. Must have been my lucky day to get it."

"Do you have others, like family albums?" He was sure Eric would allow him to go through them.

"Not in this household, Pete. Maybe because nothing seemed permanent to them. I guess I could say that was how I felt most of the time. You got to remember that your grandmother left your real grandfather and left behind everything that they had together except Jean and me. Anyway, people in those days didn't take pictures like you kids do today."

"So, these are the only photos you have of your family?" Pete didn't mean to sound incredulous, but he was.

"That's right. You're looking at them." Eric placed Benny's photo back on a shelf, but this time a lower one right at eye level. Then he moved Hellenia's and then Eric's and Jean's photos on either side of Benny's. The three together now resembled a family. But the four images, now so close together, disturbed Pete. Their combined sadness and distress could now be explained and, briefly, Pete wished he hadn't asked Eric about them. Long after leaving Eric's home, these images would fill his dreams and his wakening hours. That he knew for sure. And he longed for his parents more than he ever had before.

He understood what transformation was, and Pete realized that Eric was in the process of doing so. He watched as a gentle, loving son appeared; he watched as a brother's regret for the loss of his sister appeared; he watched as a son's ongoing grief for his father appeared; and he watched as a grown man's struggle to recognize his own mother's face appeared.

It was late in the evening before they decided to end the day. Too exhausted to keep their eyes open while trying to absorb how quickly their lives had changed in a matter of days, they agreed to sleep on everything. The morning would bring a fresh start to their lives, a start they both understood they must accept.

*

     The mail came early but Eric put off bringing it in from the box at the end of the drive. Never anything worthwhile in it except bills for the month. Nothing that couldn't wait. As the morning progressed, both men busied themselves without getting in each other's way. Pete had made up his mind that it was time to head home. He couldn't see any reason to stay. How much more could there be left to reveal? And even if there was something, he didn't really want to know. He had enough to work through as it was. He felt good about Eric and his relationship with him. He had living relatives and that meant the world to him. This was not going to be the last time he would see his uncle. He now understood why he needed to come north, and he promised himself that he would get up here as much as he could, that is, if Eric was okay with it. And he planned on inviting Eric to visit him, maybe on the return trip from a job?

     "You getting hungry?" Eric asked Pete as he passed him in the kitchen.

     "Yeah. You?"

     "I am. Got a thought. How about walking to town to Elsie's and grabbing a bite. Could do with getting some fresh air and exercise. You up for it?" To Pete, Eric sounded relaxed and happy.

     "That sound's great. I need the same."

     The café was filled with mostly regulars. A few visitors, who stood out like sore thumbs, sat in booths while the regulars hunched over their meals at the counter. The counter folks were deep into conversations that crisscrossed one another as if the long line of seated customers had super human powers in listening and carry on multiple conversations at once. Two stools sat empty at the far end of the counter and Eric made a beeline to them. Once seated, he told Pete to hold his stool for him. He'd be right back. Pete watched Eric slowly walk down the line, stopping here and there to say hello to some of the counter folks. Pete was surprised how many people Eric seemed to know.

     "Okay," Eric said as he took his seat again. "Anything

look good?"

"You know all those people, Eric?"

"Well, it's a matter of how you define "know" I guess. None of them well, but they live in the same town as me. We see each other on the street and in here, and they all knew Benny." He turned his head as far as he could to the right and used it as a pointer to indicate the counter customers.

"That's nice, I mean to know folks enough to be recognized. And even better, to stay out of each other's business, I guess." He thought about the craziness of the valley and the number of people he knew among all those people, he could count on one hand.

"That's right. So, have you decided? This one's on me. The least I can do for family." He turned to Pete, a genuinely warm smile taking over his countenance.

*

Eric stopped and picked up his mail as the two men started to head up the drive. As he walked, he shuffled through the few unsolicited pieces of junk mail. He stopped suddenly, and Pete did the same. Turning to his uncle, he watched as Eric held up an envelope from the rest. Pete could see the handwritten address indicating that maybe it was a personal letter or card. His mind began to wander, wondering when Eric's birthday was.

"I'll be damned!" Eric looked at Pete while he held the envelope up to the sun as if he trying to make out the contents before opening it.

"What?" Pete's curiosity was peeked.

"According to the return address, this is from your neck of the woods. As a matter of fact, I expect that you know this address."

Pete was not in the mood for more surprises. "What do you mean? Come on, Eric."

"Let's head inside. Need to use the head." He almost chuckled at his own words but was not in the mood. "Then we got two empty rockers waiting for us, my young man. Thought we were through with all this, but not according to this." Eric waved the envelope, his frustration evident.

In her letter to her brother, Jean explained how she got his address by asking a local when she and David had come up for the funeral. Yes, she had been there but did not have the courage to face him. But now, all that consumed her was to make things right between them. She wanted to see him, if he would allow that. She let him know that, even before their mother's death, she had suffered continuously with "an indescribably unsettling feeling" that would not let go of her. She touched on Catherine's death without going into detail and on the depths of depression that almost destroyed her marriage. She gave him all her contact information and told him he could contact her any time, night or day, when he felt ready. She would wait to hear from him.

As had happened so many times in recent days, the two men sat in silence for a long time before speaking. The only sounds were creaking wood against creaking wood as they rocked back and forth, back and forth.

If each had spoken, their thoughts would have become one. Both, sorting through their own relationships with this woman, the one clarity that persisted was that she was so remote in all that had transpired. Pete had not given her a thought, not until Eric identified her in the photo. And Eric? Of course, he had thought about her briefly, but she had been lost to him for so many years that she wasn't a part of the family formation anymore.

Eric broke the silence. "Well, this is a hard one." That was all he could manage to say.

Pete thought carefully, this time, before responding. "I've decided to head back home, Eric. I've been gone for a while now. Need to take care of some business. Not to mention work." What he meant was finding a new job.

Neither man looked at the other when he spoke but kept his eyes on the distance in front of him.

"Sure, Pete. That I understand. But one thing that gives me comfort is that I know you're not going to vanish from my life. Are you?" Eric tried to make light of his question as he fought off the unthinkable; never seeing Pete again.

Pete was touched and turned to his uncle. "No need to worry about that, Unc. I know where you live now," and he reached his hand out to Eric who grabbed on tightly.

"So, do you think I should respond to her?"

Again, Pete knew better than to speak too quickly. He rocked for a bit more then stopped. "I can't tell you what you need to do when it comes to your sister, Eric. But if you decide that you want to see her, I just had a thought." His building excitement took him by surprise.

"What's that?" Now both men were facing each other.

"Why not come down to the Bay Area with me? I owe you a stay. And you could see Jean. If you want, I could go with you. She doesn't like me, but what the hell? I don't think she has a choice anymore."

Eric's half-cocked smile broke into a loud burst of laughter. When he controlled himself, he stood up and walked to the porch rail, leaned against it facing Pete, and shot both arms into the air above his head. The letter waved in his hand, reminding Pete of a white flag of surrender.

"What the hell! You have a point there, nephew. You've got a point."

"So, is that a yes? You'll come back with me?" The tension that he had felt moments ago was gone. The air seemed crystal clear and easier to breathe.

"I'll have to call in and see about my scheduled runs. Pretty sure I got one coming up real soon. Maybe I could cancel that one, make up for it by doing double shift later." Eric was working it through as if Pete weren't there. "Yeah. Dip into savings a bit to do it but make it up later. Okay. Okay."

"I can help you out, if you'd let me. You've got a place to stay and meals. Don't worry about that. And would you let me pay airfare for your return trip? I can do that for you, Eric…Uncle Eric." Pete already knew the answer. A resounding no.

"Well, okay. I'll take you up on that offer, Pete. Thank you."

Pete managed to hide his surprise and slight panic at the thought of adding to his credit card line with no salary. "Great! That's really great." And he meant it, he realized.

*

They drove straight through. Eric had packed two small bags. Pete noticed that he had tucked the two wooden horses in between his clothing. He had asked Pete to take pictures on his phone of Hellenia's horse collection. In the other bag, he placed the two newly sealed shoe boxes and Benny's journal. Hellenia's letter to her children lay snugly between the journal's pages. It appeared to Pete that this visit was going to be difficult for Eric, a repeat of everything he had just gone through, with the added anxiety of facing his sister after so many years apart. Pete's heart was breaking for his uncle but there was little he could do for him. He had to travel this path by himself.

When they passed the rest stop where all of this began, Pete suddenly remembered. He had left his crystal at Eric's, right on the shelf with the others, just as Eric had arranged them! He considered mentioning this to his uncle, to maybe even turning around. But he let it go. Perhaps they were meant to be there. Like everything else recently, he had no understanding of why things were the way they were. They just were. Whatever happened from this point on in his life, was out of his control, he concluded. What was meant to be was meant to be.

The arrangement was made within a day after arriving in San Jose. Eric, not ready to hear her voice and speak to her over the phone, asked Pete to text her about meeting. Pete reminded him that it might not be the best of ideas, messaging her from his phone. They weren't exactly texting buddies. He talked Eric into leaving a voicemail using his own phone, taking the chance that she wouldn't answer if he called in the early hours of the morning. And he was right. Eric managed to leave a short message with a place and time. Pete had written it out for him so all he had to do was read it. Both felt relieved after Eric completed his task. And both felt a bit ridiculous, like nervous teenagers egging each other on.

She called back, waking Eric up. It was nearly six in the morning. He did not pick up but let it go to voicemail. If he hadn't been ready to talk to her earlier, he was certainly not ready to talk to her before he even got out of bed. If she agreed, she would say so.

Pete had been the one to suggest that they meet in Central Park, in Santa Clara. Just a short distance from his home in San Jose. A public place would be best. He had seen enough movies to know that. Eric had gone along with his nephew's suggestions, almost robotically at times. Pete assured Eric that he would go with him but hold back somewhere so that she didn't see him. And they both wondered if she should. He was, after all, a part of whatever this was, wasn't he? Forget the bad blood between everyone and get on with it? They both agreed to see where the inevitable would take them. In any case, Pete did not want to sour this sibling meeting right off the bat. He would be there but out of sight. Just give me the high sign, Eric, and I'll be there for you, he had told his uncle.

Eric debated about leaving the boxes and journal behind. On one hand, if everything went well, he wanted to share them with his sister. But if, what he felt was more likely to happen took place, the last thing he would do is hand over his mother's belongings to an ungrateful daughter. He shared his dilemma with Pete. Once again, Pete felt in the middle and wished he could just tell Eric to grow up and face it. But he couldn't because he had his own issues and empathized with his uncle.

"Just bring them. Leave them in the car. If things go south, no loss. If things go well, then you've got an option," he advised Eric.

"Who made you so smart? Must take after someone in the family. Certainly not me." Eric's self-deprecation rubbed Pete the wrong way.

"Quit that, Eric. You don't give yourself enough credit. You're more of a man than I'll ever be." He was nervous, for Eric and for himself. To be this close to Kit again was too soon.

*

It was a one of those beautiful fall mornings, closing in on the end of the season when the last hold-ons of hot summer days started to be fewer. The golden light that bathed the valley unmistakably belonged to the season of falling leaves and crisp mornings and nights. It was Pete's favorite time of year. As he sat on a park bench, he could see Eric doing the same across the wide lawn. Although the distance between them was enough not to draw attention to either one of them, Pete had a visual vantage point. If Eric needed him, he could see well enough the agreed upon signal; Eric would put on the ball cap that he held in his hand. It had been Pete's idea, not original, but something he saw in a movie. He only hoped Eric would remember. But, once again, let things fall where they will. He had no choice.

A distance separated the two men, but Pete was sure that he could sense everything that his uncle was sensing. He imagined that if the shoe was on the other foot, he couldn't do what his uncle was about to do. Never having had a sibling to lose, he knew he had no right to assume anything about his uncle, no matter what happened next. If it all fell apart for good or if he watched the estranged siblings fall into an embrace, he would support Eric in every way he could. He knew Eric would do the same for him.

As she approached, a chill ran through Pete's body. He shook it off as he strained to see her face. He couldn't make out her features, but he was taken aback by her stride. For a moment, he was convinced that he was watching Kit move towards her uncle. Her body sent a strong, determined, and unforgiving swagger toward Eric, and Pete wondered if she was purposely on the offensive. A defensive tactic. Poor Eric, Pete thought. The ice queen approaches.

He watched as Eric stood up but didn't move. When she finally stood in front of him, Pete was surprised by her height, almost as tall as Eric who was well over six feet, Pete guessed. She turned from him and sat on the bench first. Eric joined her keeping a body's width between them.

Neither made any gestures that Pete could interpret. He had no clue as to what passed between them. They were like statues who were hardened in place. But something had transpired between them. Pete had no idea how much time had passed when he saw her stand up first. Eric remained on the bench. She was walking away when Eric stood up and called to her loudly enough for Pete to hear her name spoken. In mid-stride, she stopped but did not turn immediately. As she slowly walked back to him, Eric placed the ball cap on his head and waited.

He knew Jean recognized him even before he was half way across the lawn. She did not greet him, did not move. Pete could see that she was visibly shaking. He glanced at Eric for a clue as to how to proceed. Nothing.

"Jean, I want to introduce you to your nephew, Peter Wade-Murphy." It was only then that he looked directly at Pete as if to say, "you're up."

"Hello, Mrs. Eagan." He could not call her Aunt Jean. Before he realized what was happening, Eric reached out to steady his sister.

"Let me drive you home, Jean. Pete, follow us in your car, would you?" There was no discussion as Eric took control and led his sister to her car.

*

David waited anxiously for his wife to come home. He had supported her decision to write to her brother and, now, to meet him. All he could do was be here when she came back. When he heard her car pull into the driveway, he did not wait but went to the front door and opened it. He stepped onto the porch. He had not considered what was to happen next. If anything, he assumed that the initial meeting would be just that if all went well.

He watched as a stranger helped her out of the passenger side of her car. The second car pulled up in front of the house. As he watched Peter walk up the drive, he could make no sense of anything. Eric gave his arm to Jean that she gratefully accepted while Pete walked just behind them.

"David? I'm Eric, Jean's brother." He reached his hand out to the stunned husband who, for a moment, forgot all about his wife standing there. "And this," he angled his body toward Pete who stayed behind them, "is Peter, who I believe you already know."

Jean released her arm from Eric's, went to her husband and kissed him gently on the cheek. "Please, come in," she said over her shoulder.

David could not find his voice at first. He watched as Jean's brother made himself comfortable on the couch, keeping his canvas bag close to him by his feet. He watched as his daughter's boyfriend sat next to Eric, obviously nervous and cautious. But he couldn't say anything to assuage Peter, and he was still in shock to see his brother-in-law. Jean offered coffee and other drinks. The men all said yes to the coffee.

"You've got a nice place here, David." Eric broke the silence much to Pete's relief.

David smiled cautiously. He wished that he had had a heads-up from his wife as to the status of their meeting. He would know how to support her right now.

"Thank you."

Guarded small talk continued until Jean brought out the

coffee.

Jean did not hesitate but looked at Eric and Pete. "You said that you had much more to tell me, to share with me, Eric." She looked at David who she knew was completely lost. "David, I want you here. I know you're confused but I think that Eric is going to help with that. Right?" She turned to her brother.

"Yes. If you are willing. Don't forget your nephew here. We've been through a lot in the last few weeks and he's the reason I'm here now."

Jean's smile reassured Pete that he was on solid ground with her. He relaxed slightly.

"What? Your nephew? Pete is your nephew?" David could not have looked more surprised if Kit had walked in the door to join them.

"Yes, David. Peter is my nephew. There's so much we don't know. Please, go ahead, Eric." She sat back, nestled close to her stunned husband. Pete noticed her hand reach for the neckline of her blouse and then her fingers delicately resting just above her heart.

"Of course." Eric reached his hand into the canvas bag. Pete watched as Benny's journal surfaced first, then one after the other, the shoe boxes. Finally, he lifted two small wrapped objects and placed them next to the journal and boxes on the coffee table that separated the siblings.

As the afternoon wore on, Eric managed to reveal everything that had been revealed to him and Pete was in awe of his uncle. As he listened to Eric, it reminded him of sitting in a history class listening to an engaging professor whose passion for his subject was mesmerizing. Pete realized that he had no idea how many times Eric had visited the journal before he landed on Eric's doorstep. The familiar was not so threatening. But even with the content of the boxes, he remained steady and in control. It dawned on Pete that Eric was letting his sister experience all of this without his emotional interference. He was allowing her to mourn without mourning with her. Pete knew that he was in the presence of a remarkable man as his love for his uncle overwhelmed him.

Jean, still holding her wooden horse, stood and took in the evidence of her step-father's and mother's lives now strewn across the coffee table and onto the floor. She placed her horse on the mantel piece. Turning back to the men in her life, she knew what they needed to do.

"David and I visit Kit every day. We haven't gone yet today. Would you come with us?"

Neither Eric nor Pete answered immediately. But when Eric looked at Pete, Pete knew his decision.

"Of course."

Pete would have said the same thing.

"Can you give me some time to get ready? Probably should gather this up too." She indicated with a sweep of her hand the coffee table and floor.

Eric nodded and began to gather the precious items. As he reached for Benny's journal, he stopped. "You know, I have had enough time with dad, for now. Why don't you hold onto this? You and he need the time together. He's your dad too." He lifted the leather-bound book and held it out to his sister.

She took it from him. "Thank you, Eric. I will send it back to you when Dad and I are ready." She carried the journal up the stairs with her. "Be back down in a bit."

During the afternoon, David had managed to keep quiet, except for a question or two for the sake of clarity which Eric graciously supplied the answers. But now, he wanted to talk. And he wanted Pete to listen.

"Do you mind, Eric, if Pete and I have a word?"

Pete, taken by surprise, watched Eric's expression change from the man in charge to the sudden outcast. Before Eric could answer, Pete spoke up.

"David, considering our current situation, that we are family now, I, for one, have no desire to keep anything from anyone ever again. Whatever you need to say to me, my uncle, your brother-in-law, should hear." He did not flinch as he spoke.

"Okay. Well said, Peter. I need to listen a bit better, don't I? Would you both mind coming to the backyard with me, for just a minute? Just before we go see Kit."

David had started toward the back of the house and Eric, gesturing for his nephew to go first, grinned at Pete.

"Well done," he murmured to his nephew. "Well done."

David was standing in the middle of a wide expanse of freshly mowed lawn. As Pete and Eric came towards him, David held his arms out from his sides, palms facing up, and tilted ever so slightly side to side. "This was my little girl's playground."

Both Pete and Eric were regretting their decision to follow him.

"Kit was one for adventure, even as a very little girl. This tree?" He walked to the edge of the lawn and placed his hand on a mature camphor that towered over the yard and the roof of the house. "She used to climb this thing like a monkey. Wouldn't come down until I threatened her with never getting to play out here again if she didn't obey. That always got her down in a flash. Over there," he pointed to the opposite side of the yard where a freshly planted garden bed lay, "that's where she made her campfires. All in her head, mind you, but I knew by the sticks she collected and put in a small pile. She'd bring her tea set out here and try to balance the tea pot on the top of her pile." David stopped. They knew he was elsewhere. "And her tent? She took her mother's best throw and brought it out here. Can't quite remember how she rigged it up but when Jean saw her throw in the dirt, well, let's just say that an old sheet became the tent from then on."

"Quite an imagination," Eric commented.

Pete was struggling with the Kit he never knew. He wished he had.

"The best thing that she ever did was ask me to build her a mountain right here in the backyard. She wanted to learn to climb." David focused on the lawn in front of him. "Couldn't do that for her but promised when she got a bit older that I'd take her mountain climbing. And we did, many times while she was growing up."

Pete found his voice. "She loved the mountains."

"She did indeed, Pete. You would know that, wouldn't you?"

"Not like you. We only hiked together a few times before the PCT."

Not waiting any longer, David got to the point. "I want to apologize to you, Pete, for allowing the situation between Kit and her mother to continue. And for our cold shoulder towards you. We had no reason to act that way. I had no reason. But I was a coward. And I regret the time wasted, the time I could have had with my daughter, we could have had as a family. I hope that you can forgive me."

Pete, once again, was taken aback. He was not expecting this. "Sure, David. Of course." He didn't know what more he could say at this point.

David reached his hand out and Pete grasped it in a firm handshake.

"Maybe, some time, you could tell us about your time with Kit, the year you were together?"

Pete proceeded cautiously. "Yeah, sometime. Sure." He wasn't ready. And at that moment, he wasn't sure he ever would be.

"Good. That's good, Pete. Thanks. Well, we better get going. Jean's bound to be ready by now."

As Eric and Pete followed David into the house, Eric drew Pete to his side. "I'm proud of you, son," he whispered in Pete's ear.

*

As Pete crouched next to Kit's headstone, he ran his hand over the unfinished granite ledge. Sensing Kit's strong presence, he left his hand in place, unwilling to let go. Eric stood behind him while David and Jean stood across from the grave, serene and at peace. No words passed. The silence was deafening but welcoming, allowing individual thoughts to unfold in the privacy of each of the four souls attending Kit.

He felt his movement before he saw it. Eric was reaching into what Pete thought was the empty canvas bag, its contents left on the coffee table. Eric tapped Pete on his shoulder. Remaining crouched, hand firmly grasping the jagged granite, Pete looked up at his uncle. In one of his hands he held Pete's crystal and in the other hand, both Jean's and Eric's crystals. Pete did not hesitate but let go of the stone and took the crystals from his uncle's hands. Placing each one carefully on the smoothest surface of the granite edge, the formation of separate crystals became one, as if balanced just right to do so.

Jean leaned forward as if to get a better look. She unlatched the necklace that was tucked inside her blouse and slowly lifted it out. Holding the chain vertically, she let the small crystal slip from the chain and fall into her open palm. The crystal that she had found in her daughter's possessions. The crystal that she had worn close to her heart ever since.

Pete and Eric looked on, neither able to comprehend completely what was taking place. But when Jean placed the small crystal next to the other three on her daughter's headstone, Jack London's words appeared to Pete, forceful and crystal clear.

> "...It was his ancestors, dead and dust, pointing nose to star and howling down through the centuries and through him. And his cadences were their cadences, the cadences which voiced his woe and what to them was the meaning of the stillness, and the cold and dark."

*

On his birthday, Pete received a package from Shasta City. The card from his Uncle Eric was a photo of a stallion on the wide-open plains, head lifted, mane flowing, nostrils flaring, and legs rearing his magnificent body toward the sky. He had written several lines to his nephew on the blank interior pages.

> "I would rather be ashes than dust! I would rather my spark should burn out in a brilliant blaze than it should be stifled by dryrot. I would rather be a superb meteor, every atom of me in magnificent glow, than a sleepy and permanent planet. The proper function of man is to live, not to exist. I shall not waste my days in trying to prolong them. I shall use my time."
>
> Jack London 1876-1916

From the package, he lifted books. The first was a biography of Jack London. The seven books that followed included, *The Call of the Wild* and *White Fang* as well as the short story, *To Build a Fire*. These were not new books, but the ones he had read from his uncle's library.

Pete collapsed on his couch, his beloved books surrounding him. He understood clearly now, the path he had been on. He understood with blinding clarity that where he was this very moment was where he was meant to be. That all the twists and turns, the deviations from the path were leading him to this place. He never had a choice. Not once. And he had never been alone.

He remembered Kit's question to him. "How far do you want to go?" If he could do it all again, he would respond to her the same way. "As far as you want to go, I guess," for it didn't matter how far either of them went or in what different directions. And the paths of the three adults now so present in his life, and of poor Joe, of his Savannah, of Benny, of Pete's own parents and Aunt Emily, and of Hellenia…all their paths had been created long before they took their first breaths. Again, London's words broke through his thoughts.

> "Thus, as a token of what a puppet thing life is, the ancient song surged through him and he came into his own again…"

His path did not stop here. He knew that now. And how far did he want to go? Until he could go no more.

Bibliography

Teacher, Lawrence, Editor & Nicholls, Richard E. Editor, The Unabridged Jack London, Running Press, Philadelphia, Pennsylvania, 1981.

Acknowledgements

In the creation of this story, I called upon four generations of my family. Their presence I felt deeply with every sentence written. Other than Mr. London, all my characters are creations whose reason for being is because of the living and dead whom I love and still love.

Thank you to my mother and father, no longer living but who are only a thought away at any moment. In 1957, their sense of adventure and fearless curiosity brought our young family from Massachusetts to the Santa Clara Valley. And the adventures never ceased as our family spent every free moment exploring the beautiful valley and the country beyond.

Thank you to Kathy who shared the backseat of the '54 Chevy station wagon with me, our modern Conestoga Wagon, that carried us three thousand miles from all that we had ever known. And who is the only one whose childhood memories congealed with mine in helping me remember.

Thank you to Jason who will never know the Santa Clara Valley as his mother, his aunt, and his grandparents knew it but who has a deep appreciation for the past that has helped generate the young father he is today. And for his wisdom and experience in guiding me along my imaginary trek on the PCT.

Thank you to Oscar, Louella, Raymond, and Finley, the grandchildren, who have no concept of what this book is about or that it even exists. One day they will and, perhaps, the legacy of their great-grandparents will help to shape who they will become.

A final thanks to Mr. Jack London. He has been my companion ever since I tread on his land in Glen Ellen when very young and then discovered his books. His spirit is present in this story. I felt him next to me each time I composed.

The cadences of our separate lives on this earth go unnoticed, not comprehended, not until they must be. Generations, one after another, continue their cadences, some never knowing how similar their own cadences are to the other's. Some, a very few, comprehend and are in awe. Thank you, Jack.

About the Author

Born in Massachusetts but raised in California, Linda M. Mutty knew the Santa Clara Valley before it was Silicon Valley. In *Cadences*, her debut novel, as in her second novel, *A Stone's Throw Away* (August 2018), she draws on her memories and experiences while exploring the power of the unknown and its inevitable impact on human interaction. Her stories create a playground where fact, fiction, and the unknown collide.

Linda M. Mutty lives in Carmel, California with her wise and loving husband.

www.ingramcontent.com/pod-product-compliance
Lightning Source LLC
Chambersburg PA
CBHW020412260626
47156CB00007B/2343